**"I found your** stranger.

She watched the man stride up the incline. Dani's focus caught on the length of this guy's legs, the way his gray camo pants wrapped around muscular thighs.

He tapped his thigh with a soft come-here whistle. The dog ignored him. "Huh. Valor doesn't usually behave like this."

"Oh!" Dani pushed Valor away. "I didn't mean to interfere with your work." She stood.

The guy extended his hand. "Tripwire Williams with Cerberus Tactical K-9."

Cerberus K-9 was a working group within Iniquus, a private security company. Highly regarded in the industry. Golden reputations.

Dani stretched out a hand to meet his. "Dani Addams."

But after the shake, they didn't release the grip. They stood there, hand in hand, eyes locked. A tingle went up Dani's arm. He was "up on her tiptoes, tilt her head back for a kiss" tall. She blushed. That thought was all kinds of poorly timed and inappropriate.

She wondered if he was reading her mind because a slow smile slid across his face, warming his eyes.

A grin replaced his gentle smile, and Dani snatched her hand back.

**Fiona Quinn** is a six-time *USA TODAY* bestselling author, a Kindle Scout winner and an Amazon All-Star.

Quinn writes suspense in her Iniquus world of books, including the Lynx, Strike Force, Uncommon Enemies, Kate Hamilton Mysteries, FBI Joint Task Force, Cerberus Tactical K-9 Team Alpha and Delta Force Echo series, with more to come.

She writes urban fantasy as Fiona Angelica Quinn for her Elemental Witches Series.

And, just for fun, she writes the Badge Bunny Booze Mystery Collection of raucous, bawdy humor with her dear friend Tina Glasneck as Quinn Glasneck.

Quinn is rooted in the Old Dominion, where she lives with her husband. There, she pops chocolates, devours books and taps continuously on her laptop.

Facebook, Twitter, Pinterest: Fiona Quinn Books.

# SURVIVAL INSTINCT

## FIONA QUINN

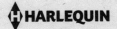

 **HARLEQUIN**®

Recycling programs
for this product may
not exist in your area.

ISBN-13: 978-1-335-74490-6

Survival Instinct

First published in 2020.
This edition published in 2022.

Copyright © 2020 by Fiona Quinn

For questions and comments about the quality of this book,
please contact us at CustomerService@Harlequin.com.

Harlequin Enterprises ULC
22 Adelaide St. West, 41st Floor
Toronto, Ontario M5H 4E3, Canada
www.Harlequin.com

**Printed in U.S.A.**

# ACKNOWLEDGMENTS

**My great appreciation—**

To Dr. Carlon for helping me find this story and for her help throughout.

To my cover artist Melody Simmons.

To my editor Kathleen Payne.

To my publicist Margaret Daly.

To my Beta Force, who are always honest and kind at the same time: E. Hordon, R. Tarantini, M. Carlon.

To the S. Bishop for her generous help.

To my Street Force, who support me and my writing with such enthusiasm.

To the real-world K-9 professionals who serve and protect us.

To all the wonderful professionals whom I called on to get the details right—

A. Fraguada for his skydiving expertise and for the excellent time I had in Florida with the indoor skydiving experience.

Veterinary Tactical Group for their excellent K-9 tactical first-aid training program. There, I got to rappel down an incline to rescue an "injured" dog. The whole experience was amazing.

Dr. K. Connor for her guidance on several veterinary questions and her consistent K-9 inspiration, both through her stories and her amazing photographs.

Virginia K-9 search and rescue teams for their work in our community, their dedication and professionalism. Every time I search and train with you, I'm inspired.

Please note: This is a work of fiction, and while I always try my best to get all the details correct, there are times when it serves the story to go slightly to the left or right of perfection. Please understand that any mistakes or discrepancies are my authorial decision-making alone and sit squarely on my shoulders.

Thank you to my family.

I send my love to my husband, and my great appreciation. T, you are my solace. You are my encouragement and my adventure. Thank you for giving me both space and support as I grieve.

And of course, thank *you* for reading my stories. I'm smiling joyfully as I type this. I so appreciate you!

# Chapter 1

*Trip*

Harrison "Tripwire" Williams reached for the Kong, covered in slobber. "Release." He ducked his chin and lifted his brow as the word whispered from his lips.

His German shepherd partner, Valor, complied instantly. She wasn't really a toy kind of gal, anyway.

Tripwire thought she probably chewed the Kong to please him. Play drive wasn't Valor's thing. That was the reason Lackland's Military Working Dog program released her for adoption. In the military, play drive was an absolute requirement in dogs deploying to foreign soil.

Food worked to get Valor's attention, especially bits of dehydrated duck or salmon. But there were few dog jobs where food rewards were a good idea.

Luckily, Trip had discovered that Valor was driven by love and attention. If she got a high-pitched "Good girl!" and a vigorous fur scrub, she was motivated to work whatever job he gave her.

The biting needed for takedowns, though?

Yeah, that might be a stretch.

When Valor was released from the military training program, Trip flew out to Lackland Air Force Base to see if she might make a good addition to Iniquus's Cerberus Tactical K9 team. In the demonstration, Valor would race out and bite the guy wearing the thick protective gear that saved him from the worst of the onslaught. Valor was an amazing, powerful athlete as she sailed through the air to make the tackle. She did as her handler asked, one hundred percent. But when Valor got her release command, she'd whine and rub her body up against the "bad guy" as if she were trying to apologize and offer comfort.

It was pretty funny.

And it was how she got her nickname, "Little Mama". Valor was willing to mete out a necessary punishment even if it hurt her heart to do it, like mothers do.

No, Valor wasn't meant to go to war. She was way too much of a love bug. Valor was born to do the job that they were here training for, tactical search and rescue. Together, Trip and Valor were honing their skills, so they'd be ready for the calls that would certainly go out.

Inevitably, they'd be jumping into the fray, heading out into the storms, and saving those in desperate straits.

"Hello, beautiful." Trip laughed, as Valor pushed

her wet nose up under his chin and gave him a string of tongue licks. He scrubbed his fingers into the caramel and black fur at her neck, down to her haunches, and back up to her ears where he pressed and rotated his fingers until she made deep moaning sounds at the base of her throat and pedaled her back paw. This was what Trip called her "expensive reward". She wanted ear massages more than anything else. Dried duck on the ground or the chance of an ear rub? The massage won out every time. He offered this up when Valor did the hard stuff.

Staying calm and centered while they got ready for their skydive *was* the hard stuff. Trip wanted her to feel relaxed, rewarded, and safe. If he could do that for Valor, then this training mission would be golden.

When Trip rested his hand on Valor's scruff, to let her know the massage was over, Valor thanked him with another lap of her wet tongue up the side of his cheek.

Trip reached for her goggles. "Ready to go to work?" He raised his brows, and Valor comically raised hers, too. Yeah, she was ready. She was always ready. Bred for strength and tenacity, she was a proud descendent of a Czech line of war dogs. There was nothing she liked better than to hunt for a missing person, and she didn't mind at all the tactical side of things—fast roping down cliffs and what have you.

For the last week, Valor and Tripwire had been up here in West Virginia, training with international search teams that got called up and deployed in natural disasters worldwide. They'd been working the search dogs on and off helicopters, fast roping into ravines, getting them ready to deploy in hard to reach areas should a disaster strike.

Today, they'd be jumping out of planes.

"You ready to show them how it's done?"

Valor stood still while Trip adjusted the straps of her mirrored dog goggles into place. "Looking mighty badass, Miss Valorie." He reached down and scooped up the new CAPS—Canine Auditory Protection System—developed by the Army to protect military working dogs' sensitive ears. It fit like a hoodie over her head to form a seal against the noise. It was Valor's least favorite piece of equipment, so Trip stopped to reward her with a kiss and a full body hug once he'd adjusted it into place.

He knew she was ready for the next step when her tongue reached out and gave him a swipe.

Trip held out her muzzle. Valor would never bite him, not in a thousand years. But the training organizer required muzzles on transports with other dogs. Sometimes, in cramped quarters, dogs could spook. On the plane, they'd be packed in tight with all those sharp teeth and crazy strong jaw muscles. No good reason to take chances.

"Ready, girl?"

She stuck her nose into her muzzle, and Trip tightened the straps into place.

As the other handlers prepped their dogs, the K9s whined and paced, their heads down and slobbery or yawning widely, shaking their coats, trying to relieve stress. The K9s were picking up on their handlers' anxiety.

Most of the rescue workers were jumping out of a plane for the first time. Stressful enough without a dog. But the first timers would be in good hands when they jumped, strapped tandem to a professional sky-diving trainer.

"Let's go, Little Mama." Trip gathered up Valor's lead, and they walked side by side out of the hangar to the jump plane.

When the other dogs in the group saw Little Mama's confidence, they calmed a bit and seemed to follow alongside their handlers without shying away from the plane's high-pitched engine noise.

Their plane had ten rescuers with their K9s on this jump run. Six trainers joined them to assist the newbies. Each plane was a mix of nationalities. The exercise leaders were trying to develop connections and trust between the teams.

On assignment, the Iniquus Search and Rescue Team was typically employed by a private corporation or government institution to go into a disaster zone to find and extract their people. Get them to safety. Or at least help them survive until next steps could be taken. The last disaster Trip worked had the Iniquus team tasked with pulling a group of university students out of the rubble heap when their dormitory collapsed in a South American earthquake. All the missing students in that building were accounted for. Injured, but alive.

Little Mama had made three of those finds.

Lives saved. Job accomplished.

If their search and rescue team wasn't hired to find specific faces in dust-covered crowds of survivors, then Iniquus often sent the teams in as part of their charitable outreach. On those occasions, Trip went where he was directed.

A K9 team—a handler and a dog—was usually divvied up one dog to each search grid. Iniquus's K9s almost never worked side by side on searches. That was why training events like the one they'd been participating in this week were a good idea.

Trip signaled for Valor to jump onto the plane then followed her in to find space on the bench next to the two other Iniquus handlers on this same jump run—the Cerberus team leader, Ridge with his K9 Zeus, and oldtimer Bob, who handled mission tactical support, and his K9 Evo. The rest of the Iniquus team were loading onto the next two planes on the runway.

After settling Valor under the bench, making sure her paws and tail were safely tucked, Trip glanced out the window.

A man, with clipboard in hand, ran toward the pilot. Lots of wide-armed gesticulating. Trip followed the line of the finger point to see an airport flag flapping wildly in a gust of wind. It looked okay to Trip. A little wind was good to train in. You didn't usually get your pick of weather conditions, especially when you were jumping into a disaster zone caused by Mother Nature.

The pilot checked her watch then jogged to the plane.

Tripwire glanced between his knees where Valor lay. Her head held high, she was alert and interested, her paws crossed ladylike in front of her. "That's right, Mama, we've got this."

The pilot took her seat, pulled on her belt, and soon they were gliding up through the clouds.

This would be Valor's first jump from a plane. Though, the Cerberus Tactical K9s had spent some time down in Florida at an indoor wind tunnel that simulated the feel of skydiving without the risk. Before Iniquus made the trek to West Virginia for this training, Command wanted to make sure the handlers, as well as their dogs, were comfortable in the rigging, and the rescuers could maneuver with the added seventy or so pounds of K9 bulk.

Trip had had his fair share of jumping out of planes when he was still with the SEALs.

For some of the rescuers from other countries, it was their first time jumping. It was these first timers who were freaking out. Even Trip could smell the adrenaline sweat wafting through the cabin. No wonder the dogs, with their sensitive snouts, were showing signs of anxiety.

Valor swung her head, assessing each one. Calm. Even if she was the youngest one here. She'd just had her second birthday, the time when most military working dogs had left their foster families and were finishing up their first stages of training.

"Get ready. Ten minutes," the pilot's voice boomed over the speaker.

Trip pulled Valor's jump bag over and laid it out. He put his hand in front of Valor's face and signaled "in."

Valor stepped to the center of the bag, adjusted, and lay down.

Trip checked her leg positions before zipping the neoprene-lined bag together, leaving Valor's head sticking out. Trip preferred this rigging to the ones that left the K9s' legs dangling free. He thought there were too many ways the dog could get hurt if the jumper came in for a hard landing.

Trip and the Iniquus team had practiced this until their dogs had it down pat. Valor, Zeus, and Evo were packaged up just fine.

"There's a cold front moving in fast," the pilot said. "Don't mess around out there. On signal, get out, get down, get your parachute gathered and get ready for the truck to pick you up. This isn't the time to be floating around sightseeing. Got it? Out. Down. Ready to exfil."

The search professionals each gave her a thumbs-up.

The plane dropped and lifted. Swayed and then balanced.

"See that?" the pilot asked into her mic. "We're cutting this tight."

Trip ran his hands over his equipment doing a mental check, imaging the steps he'd take once they were out the door. In his mind's eye, he ran through his emergency sequences.

"We're over the mark in five mikes."

The men all held up five fingers to show that they understood that the door would open in that many minutes.

Trip stood. He balanced Valor's weight that hung from him at various attachment points. He jostled around until everything felt correct, then made his way toward the door. They'd be the third in line.

Another buffet of wind caught the wings.

Trip stretched his arm out to the sides and pushed against the frame to keep his balance and stay upright. No matter what, he couldn't face plant, or Valor would take the full impact of his weight crushing down on top of her.

No way would he let that happen.

"I've got you, girl." He gave her a rub under the chin with his gloved hand. He worked to let any of his own stress about the new weather information roll off him. Fear was contagious for humans and the cabin was already thick with that. For dogs? Yeah, they picked up on the prevailing mood and magnified it back.

Especially with Valor's first jump, fun was the name of the game. He rubbed under Valor's chin. "You've got this."

This first imprint was the important one.

The Iniquus dogs needed this tool in their toolbox in case they ever needed to jump into remote areas cut off by natural disasters to pull people to safety.

This was imperative. Without this skill, Valor couldn't stay on the team. Trip would be assigned a different K9.

His fellow Iniquus teammate, Ridge—now retired from Delta Force—double-checked Trip's gear: all the straps, the altimeter, the pins in the back, and finally Valor.

Ridge turned and Trip did the same for him.

Three experienced jump teams out first. Ridge and his K9 Zeus had the most experience. They'd be the first team out, then Pierre from the Swiss team and his dog Hugo, then Trip and Valor.

Pierre was getting a once-over now by the jump master.

Since their fellow Iniquus teammate Bob, with K9 Evo, were the ones with the second most jumps under their belt, they'd be last in line so someone with experience would be above the rest, keeping an eye out for problems.

The door slid open, and the dogs' anxiety levels escalated as the wind battered the interior of the plane.

"You're okay, girl." Trip wriggled his fingers into her scruff.

Her tight muscles relaxed.

Ridge moved into the doorway, waiting for his signal from the jump master.

Trip made a mental picture of wrestling around with Valor and giving her a belly rub. He projected that picture toward Valor just as he moved up behind Pierre. Trip would swear Valor turned her head and sent him a smile.

Ridge was out.

Trip loved that first step out of the plane into nothingness. Free floating on a cushion of air. He grabbed the door frame as Pierre hugged Hugo and turned his back to the opening ready to let himself fall away.

In that nanosecond, the plane lurched in a stomach-dropping fall, then a gust tipped the plane hard, tossing first Pierre, then Trip and Valor out the door.

Trip flipped to his back to look up, resting Valor on his stomach and taking the brunt of the air speed. He watched the tip of the plane's wing scoop back upward and tag Pierre as the pilot righted the plane.

Pierre went limp. His mask broken. Pierre's face was covered in blood. He hung like a rag doll, his limbs riding the current.

Hugo pedaled his paws furiously trying to gain control.

Pierre and Hugo spun toward Earth at terminal velocity.

On his back, looking up, Trip saw that the pilot had leveled out. The door was closing.

No other jumper was detaching his dog and going after Pierre.

It was up to Valor and Trip to save them.

# *Chapter 2*

## *Trip*

A gust of wind flipped Pierre onto his back. He was passing below Trip about twenty or so meters down.

Trip had trained to give an assist to fellow SEALs when jumps went bad. He'd never witnessed a guy impact with the plane before. If he hadn't seen it with his own eyes, Trip wouldn't have believed that was possible.

From what he could tell from this distance, K9 Hugo looked physically okay, but he was frantic. His gear with the open leg holes meant he was raking Pierre with sharp claws as the K9 scrabbled for safety.

Earth was getting closer. They needed their chutes opened stat.

There was no immediate remedy other than for Trip

to get to the other team and see where he could go from there.

Trip angled himself head down, legs extended with pointed toes, torpedoing through the air toward Pierre.

This was going to freak Valor but good. They were moving about a hundred and eighty miles an hour.

Trip's helmet sliced into the air.

His streamlined body powered forward.

Valor tucked her head up against Trip's chest, her snout following the curve of his neck. Her wet nose tucked under Trip's chin; Valor's warm breath displaced the cold wind.

One of the things going for Trip was the Iniquus choice of putting the dogs in neoprene lined bags. They hugged the dogs tightly like a thunder vest to help keep their nervous systems calm.

Valor wasn't flailing like Hugo.

*Count your blessings where you find them.*

Pierre and Hugo disappeared into a cloud.

Trip pulled up, rounding his body like a cat jumping from a roof. This slowed his descent enough that he could search for the lost team.

The ground was ever closer.

The window of time to pull his chute and save himself was narrowing.

There! Pierre had been pulled to their left by a gust.

Trip prayed Pierre was unconscious and not out and out killed by the blunt force trauma.

Hugo clawed at his handler, but it didn't rouse Pierre.

As he flew closer, Trip was grateful for the muzzle on the Malinois.

Little Mama was hanging in there.

She was getting a steak for dinner tonight for sure.

"I've got you, Valor. I'll get you down soon. I swear," he hollered, hoping she could hear him past the wind and her ear protection.

Trip checked his altimeter, 2500. It was the decision altitude, now or never. Anything below this could kill them.

5.5 seconds equals a thousand feet of descent. That comes up quick.

Extending out, Trip swung his arm wide, snagging his gloved fingers into Hugo's straps. Gripping tightly, Trip pulled the two teams together.

Trip maneuvered Pierre so he was facedown. He grabbed at the green ball on Pierre's rigging, and deployed their chute.

Pierre's red canopy filled with wind. It tugged him higher into the sky.

Now, Pierre was descending toward the ground feet first.

He had a chance to survive.

Trip pointedly pushed the image of their imminent impact out of his imagination. He didn't want to conjure the picture of what could happen if Pierre didn't rouse by the time they hit down.

Trip hoped the ground crew had binoculars on them, had seen the emergency in progress, and would be ready. Whatever *that* looked like.

Trip pulled his own chute open. As he hung there, feet dangling, he rubbed at Valor's ears. "Sorry about that, Little Mama."

They jerked up and to the left by a gust of wind that blew him way too close to Pierre for comfort. The last thing he needed was for them to get their lines twisted together. Normally, you'd cut away and pull the emergency chute. But if it came to that, only Trip and Valor would survive.

Cutting away from Pierre would sign his death warrant.

Trip pulled at the bright yellow toggles that moved his steering lines, trying to buy them some space. The move put him into another current that lifted him and threw him even closer to the other team.

Trip's mouth went dry. Prickles raced across his scalp. He licked at his lips, tasting the salt of his fear sweat.

The wind played with Hugo and Pierre, tossing them about like a wild-dancing marionette on strings.

Somewhere below him, Ridge was fighting the gusts, too.

Trip tilted to see over Valor's back. The ground raced toward them.

The bright orange canopy of Ridge's gear skated along the ground, dragged by the wind, Ridge and Zeus still attached. Trip needed to keep as far from Ridge as possible, as Ridge and Zeus got lifted and dropped again and again.

Trip scanned for the ground team. No trucks or men running, just sloping farmland and lots of trees. The three jumpers must have blown way off course, far from their targeted landing zone.

Working his toggles in micro movements, Trip eased them away from the tree line. Getting tangled into the limbs with Valor attached would only make this day that much more dangerous.

Touching his breakaway pillow, Trip reminded himself of its exact location so the moment he touched the ground he could grab it and cut away from his canopy.

He needed to jump into action for Ridge, Pierre, and their K9s.

This is what the SEALs would rightly label a clusterfuck.

# Chapter 3
### Dani

"This is it?" Tiana leaned into her seatbelt to stare out the windshield of Dani's rental car.

Glimpses of the iconic Wild Mountain Lodge peeked between massive hardwood trunks.

As their car rounded the drive, the expanse of the rambling lodge came into view. Somehow it was a marriage of bucolic peace and conspicuous luxury. As if the backwoods had married royalty and the two had harmoniously blended their tastes. It was the kind of place where senators and post-term presidents had come to hunt. Where their wives walked the paths for bird watching and quiet contemplation. Where turn of the 20th century families of urban financiers had retreated from the city's heat in the summers before air conditioning was available. So said their webpage.

Dani hadn't known any of these details until she'd made their reservations for the lodge two days ago. In her mind's eye, this had been more like a summer camp. She'd imagined rustic cabins dotting the woods. The paint, curled by humidity, exposing splintered wood beneath, and smelling of rot. This place wasn't anything like the picture Lei Ming had painted for them in those long, anxiety-filled nights when the bombs fell outside their base in Afghanistan.

But it *was* the right place.

In the "History of Wild Mountain Lodge" section of their website, Lei Ming's grandfather had his own tab. Jordan Peter Carmichael (1918-2007). He'd been a Yale professor—that was a new detail, Lei Ming had just said, "he'd taught." During summer breaks, Lei Ming and her mom had joined him here in the Appalachian Mountains.

Dr. Carmichael had been the resident poet at Wild Mountain Lodge from the time he returned from the front lines of WWII until his death. His poems brought a different kind of fame to the lodge. He lent an air of erudition to its aristocratic history—that was Dani's takeaway after reading his bio.

Many of Dr. Carmichael's poems were included on his web page. They were lovely. They conjured warm days and the sweetness of discovery in nature. Written like a southern Thoreau, his works lauded the respite found beneath the boughs of ancient trees.

Lei Ming had inherited her grandfather's gift with words. Though she typically preferred the four-word rhyming verses that spoke of her father's Chinese roots. Lei Ming had a way of writing that evoked deep emotion.

Had.

Past tense. Never again would she style vowels and syllables into visceral responses.

Unlike her grandfather, Lei Ming didn't get to return home victoriously from the war to sit in flower-dappled meadows.

Maybe that was why Lei Ming's poems were so... woebegone.

Yeah. There wasn't a better adjective to describe her writing.

Lei Ming's boyfriend, Amir, had teasingly called her Woebegone Kenobi. Poor Amir. He was heartbroken.

They all were.

Lei Ming was special. It was an honor to have been part of her life.

Thirty years old. Just like Dani was.

Tiana was only two years their junior.

Thirty was young to die.

"It's not the same primitive picture Lei Ming painted in my imagination," Dani said as she rounded the drive toward the parking area.

"Not at all." Tiana spun toward Dani. "I thought we'd be splitting a thirty-dollar camping fee. I can't afford this."

"I've got it," Dani said, spotting a place by the walkway and steering in that direction.

"I'm embarrassed." Tiana rubbed her hands on her thighs with a frown. "I'm sorry." Tiana sent her paycheck back to her husband, who was out of work while recovering from a fall.

"I told you no worries. Seriously." Tiana had been abnormally silent the whole ride. She had leaned her chair back and thrown her arm over her eyes. Dani interpreted that as her way of dealing with the grief of today's trip. Dani understood and was grateful that she could be alone with her thoughts as they drove through the mountains.

Tiana swallowed audibly as she took in the lodge. "Maybe it won't be too bad. I mean, beginning of March... Not even a bud on the trees. Has to be off-season prices."

*Even those are pretty steep.* Dani swiveled in her seat to back into the parking spot. She was surprised there were as many cars as were taking up spaces. Dani had assumed few would venture out into the woods when the paths were sure to be muddy and the nights cold. "You're right though, there's not much welcoming about nature right now, except perhaps for the lodge bonfires that they light every night." She shifted into park.

"That sounds nice," Tiana said with a forced smile.

"Complimentary hot cider or toddies." She bobbled her brows.

"Where'd you get that from?"

"Off the website when I made our reservations." Dani scanned the woods ahead of them. "It might be nice to sit under the naked branches, watching the fire crackle." Dani imagined the cold air on her face, the flames heating her knees.

"It seems rightfully melancholy."

This was a melancholy journey.

"We promised." Dani reached over and squeezed

Tiana's hand. "We'll feel better after we do our duty, don't you think?"

Tiana rolled her lips in and pressed them together as she focused straight ahead at the tree line and nodded her agreement.

# Chapter 4

*Trip*

"**O**kay, Mama, here we go." Dangling from the parachute lines, Trip raised his legs at the hips. The wind gusts wrestled with his canopy. Every time Trip thought he'd get his heels down, their parachute would sweep upward again. It was like being a rag doll in a toddler's hand.

Trip grabbed his cutaway handle.

The next time Trip was close enough to tap the ground, he sliced away the lines, dropping flat on his back with Valor on top of him, pressing the air from his lungs.

Ridge, with Zeus at his heels, raced toward him.

Trip cupped his hands around his mouth so his voice would carry in the wind. "Get Pierre! He was knocked unconscious." Trip still had hope that was the case, that Pierre had survived the impact.

Ridge scanned the open field, then focused on Zeus.

With an arm command, Zeus put his nose in the air then took off running. Ridge sprinted behind his partner.

Trip worked to release his rigging then freed Valor from her bag. "You good?"

While he took a moment to check her over, Valor's body was held rigid with concentration. She stared off in the direction that Zeus had vaulted. She wanted to be in on the hunt.

"Track," Trip commanded, as he scrambled to his feet and shucked his equipment.

Valor chased forward, her nose to the ground. Her fast-paced snuffling told Trip that she was glued to Zeus's scent. Up over the undulating hill they bee-lined toward their teammates. Tripwire pressed his comms button that was functioning now that he was on the ground. "Tripwire. Clear the net. Clear the net. Clear the net." It was the call that was put out in an emergency to get everyone over that radio frequency to stop the chatter and focus on the situation.

"Go for Command."

Trip slowed his pace to check the GPS coordinates on his watch and read them to the ground crew working their comms. "Life-threatening injuries sustained by Swiss team Pierre and Hugo. Paramedic and life-support equipment requested by quickest means possible. Emergency extraction required. Over."

"Roger. Paramedic and extraction teams are deploying to your GPS coordinates. Sitrep." The comms guy was asking for the situation report, and Trip still didn't have the team in sight. There wasn't much detail that Trip could offer. The truth was, Trip wasn't even sure if Pierre had survived the impacts with either the wing or the ground.

"Three teams jumped from Plane One. Team Ridge-Zeus are on the ground. From a voice distance, they appear functional, though they may be in need of medical assistance. The gusting winds slammed them into the ground. Team Tripwire-Valor are uninjured. The plane tossed Team Pierre-Hugo out the door in air turbulence. The wing smacked Pierre in the head as the plane leveled. From what I could see, he sustained blunt force trauma to his helmet. His visor was smashed and fell away. His face was bloody. He was unconscious when I pulled his parachute at 2500 feet. Team Pierre-Hugo are on the ground now. Ridge is closest team member. K9s Zeus and Valor are searching for the Swiss team."

"Good copy," came the response. Emotionless, though surely the emotions were there. It was reflexive for the teams to push their feelings off to the side so that their brains could fire on all cylinders.

Trip raced behind Valor. She'd run forward then pause to look back, making sure Trip had her in view. "That's right, Mama, keep going," he panted out, pushing hard to get on the scene and offer what assistance he could.

During this exercise, they hadn't jumped with their rescue packs. None of them had a first aid kit.

Until help arrived, they were limited in what help they could offer.

"Command. Tripwire, be advised a rescue helicopter is en route with paramedic support. Call in precise

coordinates as soon as possible. ETA your last location fifteen minutes."

"Tripwire. Wilco."

Trip did the mental math. The accident happened
in the air about twenty minutes ago. Fifteen minutes
to get the paramedic on site. Another, say, ten minutes
to get Pierre packaged and loaded. Fifteen minutes to
a trauma hospital, maybe… Trip didn't know where
the helicopter had taken off from or which hospital
was receiving trauma patients. But, say, fifteen to the
hospital roof. Ten minutes to get Pierre unloaded and
into a surgery or under a specialist's care. That meant
Pierre would have blown through his golden hour, the
hour when a victim had the best shot at survival following a traumatic injury.

Getting beaten in the head by the wing of a plane
certainly qualified as traumatic.

As Trip ran, the high winds whipped against his
jumpsuit, pushing and dragging him backward.

Valor wagged her tail furiously as she ran. She must
have the other team in sight.

They pelted down the hill.

Zeus was in a down stay, and Ridge was fighting
a frantic Hugo, trying to get the K9 detached from
Pierre's rigging.

The Iniquus team had gathered in the locker room.
Ridge and Tripwire were the only members of the team
that jumped. The pilots deemed it too risky and called
the training mission after alpha plane lost control.

The Cerberus Tactical K9 Team was waiting for
word on Pierre from Ridge.

They quieted as their commander made his way to the front of the room.

"Gentlemen." Ridge stood six foot three and built like an NBA player. His muscles were developed for elastic movement and the strength to get the job done. Like the rest of the team, he wore the Iniquus uniform of gray camouflage tactical pants and a long-sleeved compression shirt. Beyond being designed for pragmatism, Iniquus wanted their teams to exemplify their fitness motto "strong bodies house strong minds". The uniforms wouldn't hide any slacking off.

Iniquus hired their tactical teams almost exclusively from retired special forces operators, so as a mindset, slacking wasn't part of their team's DNA.

Hands moved down to signal their dogs to quiet. The team was hard focused on what Ridge was about to say.

"We had prepared today to deal with some winds associated with a low-pressure system. The international managers had hoped for a jump that was challenging enough to develop our inclement weather skills without experiencing any serious events. Parachuting, even in the best of conditions, has its inherent risks. We trained for today, and some of you will feel disappointed about the change in plans, but we all know what it's like to gear up, stack up, and have a mission called. This, too, is an important component of our training, and I want you to feel assured that I'll be arranging for us to participate in another jump exercise in the near future."

Ridge crossed his arms over his chest and sent an assessing eye across the team. "An update on Jean Pierre Roujean from the Swiss team. He arrived at the hospital and is listed in critical condition. His team will keep us apprised. Captain Baptiste sends his gratitude to Iniquus for our efforts on Pierre's behalf." He stopped and nodded toward Tripwire. "Kudos for a job well done."

Trip lifted a hand to acknowledge the praise but indicate it was line of duty—no commendation was needed.

"The K9?" Bob asked.

"Hugo was taken to an emergency veterinarian clinic where he is undergoing surgery for his broken leg. The local tactical veterinarian who was providing this evolution's K9 support says she expects Hugo will make a full recovery."

"He won't be jumping out of planes no more," Bob said.

"Quite possibly true." Ridge bladed his hands on his hips and studied the floor for a long moment. "It'll take some serious training to come back from that event psychologically if not physically." He looked up at the crew. "I was deployed to an avalanche search in Italy with Hugo and his last handler. With Hugo's experience, it'd be a darned shame to lose him from the international rescue team. At least we know that he pulled through the fall. That should help Pierre in his recovery."

Trip wrapped a hand under Valor's neck and gave her a rub. If the lineup had been different, if they had been number two out the door, that could have been him and Valor getting crisis care.

This was where Tripwire had led his adult life, a hair's breadth from disaster.

"We still have two days of training exercises." Didit slid to the front of her seat, tapping her dog on the nose, so he'd stop chewing on the bench in front of them.

"How is this impacting us going forward? Is the Swiss team pulling out to go support Pierre?"

Ridge held up two fingers. "That's my second item. There's been a change of plans, not due to the accident, but due to weather. There's a dangerous cold front moving into our area. It's already hit the mid-Atlantic coast. The National Weather Service expects the storm to last three more days. This sudden change is bringing high winds and high snow accumulation. We should start feeling the effects today by afternoon. Noah's been monitoring the situation and was in contact with Headquarters while we were jumping. Headquarters has decided our current lodgings are inadequate for the duration of the storm and heading home is impractical and dangerous with the dogs. We'd be driving into the storm instead of away from it. Washington, DC, is tangled in traffic and accidents made worse by already icy conditions with wind gusts that are toppling semis. Roads are clogged all the way out to Winchester, Virginia."

Noah walked over and handed Ridge a note. He looked to the back and raised his hand to Bob, who waved in reply and left with Evo at his side.

Ridge refocused on the team. "Headquarters pulled a few strings and got us into a place called 'Wild Mountain Lodge' an hour down the highway. Besides being the only place with rooms available for our whole team, they accommodate pets and have enough food on hand to assure everyone at their facility has three meals and a snack buffet available until the roads are clear to drive again. We're looking at possibly a week, maybe more."

The team shuffled around on the benches.

"Dog chow?" Ryder asked.

"That's where Bob is heading. He already called a pet shop between here and the lodge and bought two weeks' worth of kibble and supplies just to be on the safe side. He'll beat us to the lodge and get logistics handled as well." He scanned the team. "Other questions?"

"I'm assuming laundry facilities and products?" Ryder asked. "I'm wearing my last uniform change and unless this lodge is on the extreme edge of rustic, after a week I'll be ripe…"

Ridge stepped toward the table, his finger running down a sheet of paper lying there. "That's listed under amenities, yes. Laundry on premises. I'll text Bob about laundry products. Any of you delicate flowers allergic to anything that's going to break you out in hives?"

There was a general shake of their heads.

"Bar with whiskey?" Didit tipped her head.

"Check. But you're representing Iniquus, so mind your manners." Ridge pointed his finger her way then let it drift around to encompass the whole group. "This isn't a paid vacation. While we're holed up, we'll be doing tabletop exercises to practice simulated emergency and rapid response situations. Once the immediate high-risk weather blows out, we can work the dogs in the woods surrounding the lodge. My understanding is that they have hundreds of acres with some pretty good cliff action for practicing rope skills. I'm hoping we can do some semi-tech rescue practice for humans and K9. We don't want you all to get cabin fever or strain yourselves from twiddling your thumbs."

"The dogs are going to love this." Tripwire grinned.

"All right, let's get crated up. Contact your loved

ones, tell them the change in plans, and that you're there in spirit. Your Iniquus support operator is also reaching out to your significant other list. The ISOs will provide them with anything they need to be safe and comfortable, snow removal and so forth is already planned for them. Rest assured, your families will be safe and well cared for while you're on mission."

Iniquus made sure the operatives were fully mission-focused by stepping in with the kinds of support that families needed while the teams were off grid. From car repair to yard and house maintenance, emergency childcare to food delivered in or nursing support during illness. It wasn't just a perk of the job; it was a cog that kept the machine running smoothly.

Tripwire didn't require this Iniquus service. He didn't have anyone waiting for him at home. Never did. Dating was one thing; a relationship was another. He'd never met a woman that made him feel like he wanted to hitch on for the long haul. Sometimes he thought he might be missing the gene that could make that leap from the enjoyment of a woman's company to dedication.

That sounded callous in his ears. A lot more callous than he felt.

Trip had assumed the right person would come along, the one that he wanted to love and cherish in sickness and in health. And when she came into his life, he'd know it. A wife, a few kids...

It always seemed to him that one day he'd turn the corner and there she'd be—someone that he *needed* to be with like he needed his next breath. Someone that, when he couldn't get home to them in a winter storm, he'd get that look in his eyes, the one his teammates had, the one that said they knew the situation was handled, but they'd still prefer it was them doing the supporting.

His teammates with families all had that same look on their faces as they thought of home and their loved ones alone in a storm dangerous enough to reroute them for days if not an entire week. Trip watched them weighing the sacrifice of being away. The tug of war between their duty to the job and their duty to their hearts and home lives.

Here he was, thirty years old and as single as they come.

Maybe his opportunity had passed him by while he was out on his missions with the Navy.

In moments like these, Trip felt the void in his life more acutely than at other times.

He just wasn't one of the lucky ones.

Trip leaned over to scratch along Valor's neck. "It's you and me for now, Little Mama."

# Chapter 5

*Dani*

Dani turned her attention to the clock on her dash. "We made good time." She tapped the button to kill the engine. "I'm going to go in and get our room key if you want to wait here for a minute." Dani reached her arm over the seat to snag her purse from the back. "I think if we can get unpacked and changed, we can take the Eagle's Nest trail today and do Hermit's Cave tomorrow." She ducked her head to see the sky out the windshield. "Looks like a warm front is moving in. It'll probably rain in the next few days."

Tiana rubbed at her temples. "Good we got here when we did. We can be on the road to Ohio and Lei Ming's mom's house by Wednesday."

"Here's hoping the weather holds." Dani popped her door open.

Tiana swiped her phone. "While you get us registered, I'll check the local weather hour by hour. Hey—"

Dani climbed out then ducked down to catch Tiana's eye.

Tiana was holding her phone at an odd angle. "Ask them about cell phone coverage in the area. I barely have a bar."

"Gotcha."

Dani shut the door and headed toward the front of the lodge. The morning sun glared at her through spaces in the wispy clouds. If they could dump their bags in the room, they could easily make their first hike to Eagle's Nest and get back in time for the lodge dinner.

Like the room, the restaurant was going to be pricey. Dani wasn't going to sweat it; the menu had looked amazing, and this was a celebration of Lei Ming's life. It seemed like the right thing to do, walk the paths of her childhood memories, eat in the dining room where she ate her meals during her childhood summers, enjoy the mountains as Lei Ming had described them in her journals.

They had promised Lei Ming they'd take this pilgrimage if she died in Afghanistan.

Dani was duty bound to be here.

She was glad to be here. To have a ritual she could perform. To know that ritual was exactly the thing Lei Ming wanted.

Dani stopped just shy of the lodge's front door, not quite willing to go in and get her key card.

She had made this promise lightly, almost sarcastically. Dani never thought in a million years that she'd need to see it through.

Sure, they were in the Army and that had some inherent risks.

Not so much for her, Tiana, and Lei Ming. They all worked in the veterinary clinic.

Dani had run out of fingers on which to count her deployments to Afghanistan, some short, some much longer. She was a veterinary surgeon, there in theater to support the military working dogs who in turn supported the troops.

From bomb sniffing dogs to patrol dogs who did the bite work, the K9s, like Cairo the dog who helped take down Osama bin Laden, were a force multiplier.

Once listed as "surplus equipment" at the end of the Vietnam War, when they were euthanized or simply left behind, things had changed drastically in the ensuing time frame. It would have to have, or Dani wouldn't have considered signing up for the job.

Though the dogs were tattooed inside of their ears once they had their job designations, that was for keeping track of them much like a soldier wearing a dog tag. These dogs were worth their weight in gold. Each one cost about fifty thousand dollars in training alone. And of course, the training was provided for dogs that were specially bred for the work. The pups came at a high cost to begin with.

It was Dani's job to protect and heal the dogs. For the military, it was an investment she was saving, not just the money that went into having the dog, but the impact each dog had on the troops who braved the trips outside of the wire.

Dani loved her job as a K9 surgeon, as physically and mentally challenging as it was.

Lei Ming had been a vet tech. When asked what she did in the Army, she'd say she stuck thermometers in K9 butts and then laugh.

She had been safe within the walls of the base. Dani had believed that and had tried unsuccessfully to convince Lei Ming of that.

And it turned out that Dani had been wrong.

Lei Ming died.

Lei Ming *died*.

Dani threw her shoulders back and lifted her chin. Yup, it was taking a little more bravery than Dani had anticipated to pull the handle and walk into the lodge. The first step in what was sure to be an emotionally difficult week.

The front door to the lodge popped open, startling her.

A young woman shot a glance around the parking lot, then turned to the man behind her. "That wasn't them." She turned back and caught Dani's gaze. "Oh, sorry." She laughed nervously as she pushed the door wide and stood holding it open for Dani to pass through.

The man in the vestibule that the woman had spoken to was military.

Not now military, but at some point military, and from the way he held himself, Dani would say he had been a special operator. With the shift in mission in Afghanistan, Dani worked almost exclusively with the K9s that deployed with the Green Berets, the Deltas, and the SEALs. She'd learned to spot operators at a distance.

The man stepped crisply back with a nod. "Ma'am."

From the way he looked at her, he knew she was military, too, an officer. A "ma'am" was required by habit, even here at Wild Mountain Lodge.

He was dressed in charcoal gray camo tactical pants and a gray long-sleeved compression shirt. From the way his fleece-lined black jacket lay, Dani could see there was a logo with a growling, blue dog's head but couldn't tell what it said.

This was a pretty out of the way spot, and he looked like he was working.

She moved by him with a sense of curiosity, heading to the registration desk to get her key.

The luggage porter trailed behind Dani as she moved to the room door and swiped it unlocked.

When she went in to hold the door wide, she heard the water running in the bathroom sink.

Dani stood to the side while the man brought in their things, tucking the luggage into the closet area at Dani's request. She held out a five-dollar bill as he bowed himself out.

She was embarrassed. She thought that was the right amount to tip. Two bags and a couple of duffels. She didn't know for sure. And handing money to another human felt ugly to her. She'd prefer that her room price go to paying the workers a full and robust wage.

Yeah, five dollars thrust into another human's hand and the bow—Dani didn't like that.

She wondered, vaguely, as she jostled her bag around and opened it, why she had no problem giving or receiving a salute, but a tip and a bow rubbed her like this. "I'm not used to being in the United States," she muttered as she pulled out her day pack.

"What's that?" The water stopped.

"I just gave the luggage guy a tip, and I was muttering about how I'm not used to being in the United States. We don't tip in Afghanistan."

"No. And we also don't have baths. And we don't wear high heels."

"Are you putting on high heels for our hike?"

The door popped open. "Psh," Tiana said. Her face was red, her eyes glassy.

"You okay?"

Tiana stepped over where Dani sat on the floor with her legs spread wide, digging in her suitcase.

"Did you see trees out front?" She slogged to the bed and lay down with a moan, her hands plastered to the sides of her head. "The pines? They were turning their leaves over."

"What?" Dani shot her a glance before returning to her task. "Pines have needles not leaves, and trees can't turn the needles over. They're round. What *are* you talking about?"

Tiana crossed one ankle over the other and pulled the pillow out from behind her head. "It's a sign that a storm's moving into the area."

"Nah-ah. Where did you learn such a thing?" Dani scooped up her various layers of clothes that would help her stay comfortable through a wide range of temperatures. "I'm going to change into my hiking gear." She moved through the bathroom door, leaving it open so she could hear Tiana. "Speaking of weather," Dani called. "What did you find when you looked up the forecast?"

"There's a storm moving in. But not until Wednesday like you thought. They're expecting temperatures to drop this evening. The bonfire will feel good."

"Yeah, I think so." Dani leaned her head out the door to look at Tiana. "Are you okay?"

"Why?" Tiana asked. She lay with her arm across her eyes.

"You're lying there like that," Dani called through the open bathroom door as she yanked her fleece lined hiking pants up her thighs and over her hips. "Your voice sounds weird." She looked down as she did up the button and pulled the zipper. "Are you okay?" she asked a second time.

"To tell you the truth, I'm seeing halos. I have a migraine coming on like a steam engine."

Dani reached behind her and picked up her merino wool base layer and pulled it over her head.

"It must be this weather system," Tiana said. "I think I left my medication on the bathroom sink at my house. The bottle's not in my purse."

"Okay." Dani moved into the room and perched on the corner of the other double bed. "I can drive to a pharmacy and get some more if you can reach your doctor's office and have them call it in for you."

"Too late. Once I get to this stage, all I can do is ride it out."

"How is it that I didn't know you got migraines?" Dani pulled on her liner sock.

"Brand new arrival to the shit show."

Dani lowered her voice to a whisper not to aggravate her friend's pain. "From the car accident?" She pulled an elastic band from her hair and made a fresh ponytail.

"Must be. I didn't have migraines before then."

"I'm sorry. Is there anything I can do?"

Tiana twitched her head. "Mm mn."

Dani looked around the room, then reached for her boots. "I'll just take my Kindle and go hang out in one of the sitting rooms and read. Give you some quiet." It might add another day to their travels, but that would have to work. "Okay—food? Something to drink? What helps?"

"A cold rag on my head. A dark room. No movement or noise."

"There's no guarantee of that in a hotel."

"Top floor. Last room on the hall. It should be okay. Listen." She reached her arm out and waggled her fingers toward Dani. "Can you do one of the trails alone, pretty please? The Hermit's Cave one? I should be well enough tomorrow to go to Eagle's Nest. Then we can get to Ohio on time for Lei Ming's memorial service. I really don't think I can do both tomorrow."

"We'll just do this over more days. You promised Lei Ming."

"We can't postpone. The memorial service is set." Her words were barely audible. "I know I promised Lei Ming. And I will follow through. Just not this trip. Please just do what I'm asking. I haven't got it in me to argue with you."

Dani stalled. She looked at her watch. She pulled the map over and stared at the trek. No reason not to...

When she was signing in, the manager had given her a topo map of the area with the trails clearly marked. The times for an average hiker were listed along with the difficulty of the trail. Lei Ming had asked them to take the two hardest ones on there. Lei Ming had liked solitude when she was in the woods, so that had made sense to Dani. Their friend would have wanted to go where few would be willing or able to follow her.

"Can you do it yourself?" Tiana came up on one elbow and reached for the map. Her eyes squinted to almost shut. "Or do you think it's too dangerous?"

"I live on a base in Afghanistan, and you're wondering if a walk in the mountains along a cleared trail is dangerous?" Dani moved to squat in front of her suitcase and tugged her day pack out.

"Take everything. Take food and water. Survival ten—but you know. Alone. Plan for if something horrible happened."

"Well, that's cheery." Dani wasn't going to argue about it. "Fine, if it makes you feel better."

"It makes me feel better." Tiana lay back down. "Tell me what you're packing."

"A first aid kit. A headlamp. You're acting *really* weird."

Tiana had had a lot thrown at her lately. She'd become a little hyper about safety and preparedness. *A lot* hyper about safety and preparedness. Dani's safety and preparedness. Tiana didn't seem to pay much attention to her own, like leaving her medicine behind.

"My brain misfires when these headaches are getting a kick start," she whispered. "I've got enough adrenaline running through my system that if they could figure out a way to hook me up to their electrical grid, I could light this place up with excess energy alone."

Dani looked over to her with a frown. "That sounds bad."

"It's not a lot of fun. Can you help me out? Take a worry off my plate? Pack so you're extra safe?"

"Fine." Dani stood with her water bladder in hand. "I'm filling my reservoir."

"All the way up."

"This isn't the desert. If I end up sheltering under a ledge somewhere away from the rain—then Mother Nature will provide me with drinking water."

"Okay," she whispered. "Do it anyway."

"I'm doing it, anyway." Dani filled the bladder in the bathroom and screwed the top on tight. She tested the drinking hose, then held it up for Tiana's inspection.

"And food."

"I have a big bag of gorp, and some Luna bars. Good?"

Tiana sent her a thumbs-up.

"Okay, the ten—I have an emergency blanket, a whistle."

Tiana flicked her hand toward her bag. "Take my whistle too."

"In case mine doesn't work?"

"I had a friend—are you going to make me tell survival stories right now?"

Dani picked through Tiana's things, packing the extras into her bag to relieve Tiana's worries, though it added extra weight that would probably do her more harm than good. "I'm not making you do anything right now."

"Okay, so a friend had her whistle on her right shoulder."

"Uh-huh."

"And she fell, and she got her shoulder wedged under her."

"Okay." The zippers strained as Dani tugged them shut over the new bulk.

"And she couldn't reach the whistle. If *only* she'd had one on each shoulder."

Dani had Tiana's hurricane whistle in her hand. "You're making this up."

"Yeah, I am. And take my Mylar bivouac sack."

"I have my own."

"You have an emergency blanket." Tiana sounded like she was trying not to cry, and Dani wanted to get out of there to let her rest. "Take my tube tent. Please?"

"Are you being serious right now? How bad is the weather going to get?" Dani reached for her cell phone. "No bars. They said that the only place with cell phone connection was in the parking lot. It's supposed to be a feature not a bug. It lets the wealthy and well-placed escape from the burdens of the rabble."

"No bars is my point. What if you turned your ankle, and you were stuck out there until they could send someone? What if while you were waiting the temperatures dropped? What if I fall asleep with this headache and didn't tell anyone you're not back the way you're supposed to be? You shouldn't hike alone... Maybe this is a bad idea."

"It's you're not supposed to swim alone. I hike alone all the time."

Tiana frowned hard.

"Fine, I'll pack like I'm a Sherpa going up the Himalayas on my own. Feel better?"

"No, actually. I feel really bad."

# Chapter 6

*Trip*

Ridge drove lead on the convoy of five Iniquus vans down the backroads with Tripwire sitting shotgun, and Noah on the bench seat behind them.

It was an easy drive toward the mountains. A beautiful day. Trip tipped his head to take in the sunny sky with a few high, wispy cirrus clouds. The kind that normally meant the weather was at the beginning of a warm front. He'd spent enough days and nights in this part of the country that, had no one told him that a disaster of a weather front was moving in, he would probably expect rain in the area in a few days. With the bright blue expanse, and warm-for-March temperatures, it was hard to believe that Mother Nature was about to rage across their pathway.

Tripwire had learned through hard-won lessons to always respect the capacity of Mother Nature to change her moods.

Unexpected cold fronts could be life-threateningly violent.

A sudden cold front had been the defining moment that led Trip down this career path.

Back in his high school days as an Adventure Scout, his troop had decided to take a paddle across the lake to camp for the night. They waited for the sun to set when the air would still. Then, the teens set out across glossy waters that mirrored a full harvest moon.

It was a moment of perfection.

Trip had internalized every sensory-dazzling moment of that experience. It settled vividly into his psyche because in that moment, he had, for the first time, experienced being one with the universe. There was no beginning or end. No demarcations or delineations separating him as an individual in a space.

He *was* nature.

The warm air on his skin, the loons calling from the shoreline, a velvet sky shimmering with starlight.

Fully saturated in the grandeur, he had dipped his paddle into the water and pulled against the resistance, heading his canoe toward one of the islands where he and his buddies had decided to camp. With their headlamps strapped in place ready to signal any passing motorboats, they moved through the night in silence.

Not a single teen broke the spell.

About halfway into the stretch of open waters, two miles away from the relative protection of the shoreline, out of nowhere, a gust of wind hit them.

Danger banged against the hull of his canoe.

The black, winter-cold waters had swelled into waves, threatening to flip them over.

Trip had dropped out of his seat, kneeling in a wide legged position on the bottom of his boat, searching for stability against the growing waves. He dug in and paddled hard for the island. He could hear his fellow scouts shouting toward each other, but the wind whipped their words away.

Looking over his shoulder, he counted silhouettes. They were all plowing ahead. Even if one of them got into trouble, Trip wasn't sure he could do anything to help.

What should have been an easy hour of gentle paddling became a life-or-death fight for the shore.

And once they had each dragged their boats high on the rocks, they realized that their battle had just begun.

The storm raged.

A cold front that had been a black line on the distant horizon, seen and discounted as the sun set.

Wet. Cold. Hungry. Battered and bruised.

On their second morning on the island, a rescue boat arrived.

That moment—stepping onto the water patrol boat and heading toward shore—was *the* pivotal experience of Tripwire's life.

Trip wanted to be the one who did the rescuing. He wanted to be the one who took people from despair and gave them relief. He wanted to battle against whatever forces were at play that put an ordinary person into extraordinary circumstances. And he wanted to learn how to survive against the mightiest force in the world, nature.

He decided to follow in his father's footsteps and join the Navy.

Trip wanted to become a SEAL, no matter what it took.

And he followed through.

It had been a great job for him for over a decade. Now, he'd moved on to this new role on the Cerberus Tactical K9 Team. Every experience he had tucked under his belt improved his skills and helped him save endangered lives, and that, in the end, was his calling.

"I wonder why they're tucking us away at a lodge." Trip turned to Ridge. "It seems the distance we're heading southwest, we could have been heading southeast and getting home even if it was a circuitous route maybe coming up 95 from Richmond."

"They called it right," Noah said from the back seat with his Newfoundland, Hairyman, sprawled across him.

Hairyman was the only K9 not crated in any of the vans. Dual trained as Noah's stability dog and water rescue, he got to sit where Noah sat, with a towel laid out beneath his big, slobbery jaw.

Hairyman sat up and gave a full body shake.

Warm wet dripped down the back of Trip's neck. "Hairyman!" he yelled, as he spun in his seat. Noah reached out a hand towel that Hairyman wore under his collar for just this problem. He was a drool machine, a prize-winning spittle flinger.

Trip wiped at the goop. "Sloberus maximus," he muttered under his breath, handing the towel back. He nodded toward Noah's computer. "What are you seeing there?"

"It's not looking good. When we get to the lodge, I'd say we need to prepare to hunker in."

"Why's that?" Ridge asked. They were in vehicles that should be able to power them through almost anything Mother Nature could throw their way. "How long is this going to last?"

"The coast is taking the brunt of this already. You know that from your initial report to the team. Central state, the barometric pressure started dropping like a stone. It's looking like a setup for a bomb cyclone. Pretty darned unprecedented in this area. We don't want to battle that. Heading southwest, Command has us routed for safety. We'll have plenty of time to get to the lodge and get settled in before it hits."

"How long?"

"Educated guess... I'd say things will explode around seventeen hundred hours, give or take."

"We can unload, work the dogs, wear them out a bit," Trip said, "and get cleaned up for dinner before it hits."

"That's about right." Noah shifted around in his seat, snapping his shoulder belt. "The lodge will probably be running on generators tonight. I'm betting it'll take out power. We'll need to set up our systems, bring in our backup batteries for electronics."

"All right. I'll have Bob interface with local emergency management to let them know we're around in case they need help with welfare checks in their community or for rescue backup."

"Bomb cyclone," Trip said. "I wouldn't mind seeing that up close." He turned toward Ridge. "I think it'll set us up for some good training even if it's observational and done on a tabletop."

"I would never have thought of Shenandoah Valley and bomb cyclone as going together," Noah said. "You might just get your wish."

While Noah told folks he got his call sign because he was so good with animals, the truth was he got his moniker because he had an undergrad degree in meteorology and had done some work with the National Oceanic and Atmospheric Administration, NOAA.

In the early days, that was the way his Air Force buddies had spelled it, NOAA. But that confused folks, so to clarify, it was modified to Noah.

Noah had joined the Air Force with the hopes of being assigned to the Air Force's 53rd Weather Reconnaissance Squadron—the hurricane hunters that fly into tropical cyclones to get the data needed to feed to the computers and develop warnings. It was his dream job.

It hadn't worked out for him. Though, it had come close. Noah was assigned to the Air Force Special Warfare Tactical Air Control Party (TACP). They were special imbeds with the Army and Marines on the front lines, tasked with calling in air strikes on the right target at the right time.

Noah had survived enough bombings that his ear drums had been damaged. With the help of hearing aids, he could hear fine, but his balance could be tenuous. Better that he had a hand resting on Hairyman's stability harness.

Noah was a game changer for their team. They were lucky he'd signed on with Iniquus after he left the military. His expertise allowed the Cerberus Team to drop into some extreme areas with the dogs and come out again in one piece.

Ridge reached for his bottle of water. "I'm starving. Command said this place would have three squares and a snack buffet going. I wonder if Iniquus told them how much Cerberus can eat when we've come in from the field."

Noah laughed. "I can't imagine they'd believe Command even if they did. No one's prepared for that." His cell phone pinged. "Didit is pulling off to hit the head and check on a low tire pressure."

"Copy." Ridge budged up their speed a bit. "All right. In terms of training exercises, how much snow are we expecting for the mountains?"

Noah tapped at the computer. "Upward of forty-two inches."

Trip tipped his head and looked at the sky. He had been comfortably dressed in a fleece jacket with a windbreaker over top. To think that a snowstorm would be raging through here in short order. "That's crazy for this area."

"It's going to set some records, for sure."

"You gave us a weather readout this morning before our jump, man. NOAA wasn't sounding the alarms then?" Ridge clicked on his blinker and slowed to turn off the highway onto a country road.

"There was a nor'easter expected up north of us. We saw the wind gusts. They were about an hour behind on projections, or we wouldn't have put the teams in the air. Pierre wouldn't have been beaten to hell by a plane's wing." Noah looked up from his computer screen. "So let me explain this monster." Noah leaned forward, holding up his finger and circled it in the air where Ridge and Trip could see it in their peripheral vision. "A high-pressure goes clockwise." He spun his finger in the opposite direction. "A low-pressure system circulates counter-clockwise. You churn the air like that over the ocean before it reaches the coast and it's called 'fetch'."

Hairyman sat up when he heard that word and offered an excited bark.

"Shhh." Noah petted a hand over Hairyman's coat. "That fetch is going to make some epic wave action along the coasts, but it's also going to mean that we're facing a long fierce storm."

"Crazy." Trip called toward the back, "Hear that, Mama? We're going to be playing in the ice and snow. Even though we're here at the lodge and not headed home, I'm still gonna try to finagle you a steak. You deserve it."

"Yeah she does." Noah turned to look over the seat at Valor as Ridge's phone rang. "You done good on that jump. Saved your buddy, Hugo, didn't you? Steak's the least you should get. You should tell Tripwire you need you a doggy massage. A good one, too."

"Ridge here. You're on speaker phone. Tripwire and Noah are in the van with me."

"Bob. Is your ETA still accurate?"

"Roger," Ridge said. "The GPS puts us twenty minutes out. Where are you?"

"I'm at the lodge, and it's some kind of swanky swank setup. I was looking forward to a lovely evening with billiards, darts, and scotch. But that just changed, we have a contract in place."

"Okay." Ridge cast a glance at Trip, who pulled out a pad and pen ready to take coordinates. "Where are we headed?"

"The lodge. There's a lady here who saw my uniform and snagged me. A Harper Katz, personal assistant to Berlin Tracy."

Noah let out a low whistle.

"Hollywood Berlin Tracy?" Ridge asked.

"Affirmative," Bob replied. "I let Harper talk to Command, and they got the paperwork signed. I'm setting up command in Ballroom A."

"For personal protection?" Trip asked.

"Nothing that easy, brother," Bob said. "This is search and rescue."

# Chapter 7

## Dani

Dani exited the door on the east side of the lodge, map in hand.

She scanned the parking lot until she found the break in the stone wall that led to the hiking trails.

The weather was too nice to wear her winter jacket, but a stiff breeze made the bulk seem comfortable. She'd leave it on for now. She'd adjust when she got warmed up on the trail. Dani didn't want to sweat into her clothes. If temperatures were to drop toward evening, when she was finishing up her hike, dampness could put Dani in danger.

As she maneuvered between the cars toward the trees, she slid her map into the silicone bag she had hooked to the retractable strap of her pack. The bright

orange hurricane whistles bobbled from their ties on
each shoulder as required by the now sleeping Tiana.

There was a canister of bear spray on her left strap.

The desk guy had warned of black bears in the area
when he'd handed her the map and told her to be careful
of boulders since the soil was saturated from a warm
winter and heavy rains. Dani instantly conjured images
of the guy out in Utah who was solo-hiking and was
trapped by a falling rock for five days. She'd be extra
careful of where she sat, avoiding rocks as back rests.

Or trees, for that matter.

The desk guy said that one of their guests had leaned
against a sizable tree, and it had uprooted. Just fell
straight over. No injuries. Startling though.

Yup, she'd keep her hands to herself and keep her
eyes peeled for anything tumbling around.

Including playful bear cubs.

She reached across her chest and slid the pepper
spray canister up and down the elastic loop, making
sure it wouldn't snag if she needed it.

Mamas tended to be overly protective.

Dani left the paved lot and stepped under the
wrought iron arch onto the pebble strewn path, nicely
cleared and easily traversed. The post up ahead pointed
out which direction to start for the various routes
ranked "disability accessible" to "advanced." None of
the trails required equipment. Which was good, since
Dani hadn't hiked in mountain terrains in years, and
her skillset didn't include using technical equipment.

She adjusted toward the far-right pathway and took
a deep breath. *Here I go, Lei Ming.*

Dani had met Lei Ming while sitting next to her on
the military transport to Afghanistan. It had been Lei

Ming's first and only deployment. She'd looked shell-shocked. "I just said good-bye to my family," she'd said. "I'll never hug them again."

Dani remembered how hard her first trip over to work in theater had been on her nervous system. Dani had smiled at Lei Ming, trying to offer her a stabilizing presence. When that didn't work, Dani took Daisey out of her dog crate so Lei Ming could love on her.

Dani had named the stray she'd found and fell in love with 'Daisey' because after her bath to remove the street filth, her coat was the color of Daisey's Irish Cream, and like the liqueur, she was warm and sweet and had a way of relaxing both human and doggos who were in distress.

Daisey had been able to absorb anxiety and shake it off. She had been magical that way.

"I'll never see home again," Lei Ming had whispered into Daisey's ear as she ran her fingers through Daisey's soft fur.

Poor Lei Ming, Dani had thought, the first trip over was the scariest.

"We're on the veterinary team. It's not like we have the really high-risk jobs," Dani had said lightly.

Well…okay, there was always some risk. But it wasn't like they were SEALs, grabbing a ruck, grabbing a leash, hopping on a plane, just to jump right out the door into the clear blue sky and float into enemy territory. That kind of bravery was unfathomable to Dani. That kind of risk?

Serving in the veterinarian hospital was relative safety.

"It'll be new and strange, Lei Ming. You'll start to

get used to things, and then before you know it, you'll be headed home."

Lei Ming had never changed her mind. Some part of her knew that she'd never go home again, and those themes showed up in the poetry Lei Ming wrote while deployed.

Dani had thought of Lei Ming's woebegone poetry as a phase like Picasso's blue period. Yeah, that was the right feel. They lacked the warmth of sun and twittering birds from the poems Lei Ming had shared from the time she was writing back in the states. The deployment poems were more like Picasso's *Blue Nude*.

Dani fully expected Lei Ming to rebound somewhere along the way, especially after Lei Ming got her papers—she was heading home.

Instead of celebrating, Lei Ming drooped down into a great antipathy that no one could drag her out of. She functioned on her job, and then lay on her cot staring up at nothing. When she spoke to Tiana or Dani, it was to remind them of their promise: To be *here*. *To do this*. Then to take her journals to her mother. To tell Lei Ming's mom that she'd known this was coming and was at peace.

It hadn't looked like peace to Dani.

It had looked like despair.

One more day. Just *one* more day, and Lei Ming would have been on the transport flying home, and the spell would have been broken.

Dani stopped to pull off her pack, her jacket, then her fleece sweater. Her emotions made her hot and prickly. She tied the arms through the handle at the top of the pack so the extra clothes would drape down the back out of her way, then she pulled the weight back on her shoulders. It was twice what she would have wanted to carry. It would probably be fine for the hike out. By end of day, though, she might be cussing Tiana.

"Forward," Dani said, popping the handles of her pack and making them settle more comfortably on her shoulders as she moved up the trail.

Dani meant to begin her hike by intoning one of Lei Ming's poems. But the notebook was in the pack, and she didn't want to pull it off again.

The only poem Dani could bring to mind was—

*Write it on your heart*
*that every day is the best day in the year.*
*He is rich who owns the day, and no one owns the day*
*who allows it to be invaded with fret and anxiety.*

*Finish every day and be done with it.*
*You have done what you could.*
*Some blunders and absurdities, no doubt crept in.*
*Forget them as soon as you can, tomorrow is a new day;*
*begin it well and serenely, with too high a spirit*
*to be cumbered with your old nonsense.*
*This new day is too dear,*
*with its hopes and invitations,*
*to waste a moment on the yesterdays.*

"Well, Mr. Ralph Waldo Emerson, today is actually designated for remembering," Dani said aloud. "Yup, today, I intend to focus on yesterdays. All day today, all week, even."

This week was the gift that she had promised herself. "Hold it together while on duty and then this week." Dani swore that she could dive deep into grief, paddle around in it. Lie on her back and let the tide of pain pull her where she needed to go.

Ralph Waldo Emerson.

Did people call him that? "Hey, Ralph Waldo, can you pass me the salt?" Was he "Ralphie" as a kid? "Wally?"

"Waldo, my dude, you're looking wild with those leaves in your hair. Very Earth child."

Didn't matter.

Nope.

Didn't matter.

He signed his poems Ralph Waldo Emerson and no matter who he had been as a person, whatever roles and names were applied, whenever he was talked about it was with the three names.

Was it good to be talked about, remembered, studied after death?

Dani thought that people should be able to read Lei Ming's poems. They were pure and true.

Sometimes.

They weren't all good poems. Some were word salad. Or had the ingredients laid out, but they hadn't been crafted yet into a final sustaining meal.

Lei Ming took a page from Eminem's playbook and pored over the dictionary looking for new words to feed her poetry. They had debated words late into the night with the cacophony of the military's doings keeping them awake. "The word might sound beautiful but if no one knew the meaning then what was the point of writing it?" Dani had argued.

Just then, a gust of wind came up and bent the branches low.

"Yes, thank you. Exactly like that," she said conversationally to the trees. Lei Ming had once insisted on using the word "aeolian" which Dani then learned meant, "caused by the wind to blow." Not knowing the word beforehand, Dani had missed the whole point of the poem. Lei Ming said she knew what the word meant. It was the right word. And that the poems were for her. She wasn't her grandfather, seeking praise and notoriety.

Dani thought that surely there were people who loved poetry enough that they would bestow praise. Notoriety? Had the world moved past the time when poets could gain notoriety? Maya Angelou was the only contemporary poet that Dani could easily name.

Maybe the lack of contemporary poets Dani could recall was a function of her hanging out too much with dogs.

Maybe there were segments of society that fangirled over a good stanza.

"Augean," Dani said as she glimpsed another sign and a fork in the paths around the bend.

"Augean" was another one of Lei Ming's poetry words that Dani had never learned at school. Dani had argued that it robbed Lei Ming's poem of meaning. "Augean" meant something that was difficult and unpleasant, apparently.

As she approached the marker, Dani focused on the neat corrugated aluminum box filled with carved wood walking sticks one could borrow. She fingered their silky-smooth lengths, admiring the whimsically carved animals' heads at the top of some. Dani imagined someone sitting around the evening fire at the lodge, enjoying the flames, and whittling away at a stick they'd found that day.

There was something grandfatherly and kind about this box of walking sticks.

Dani chose two that were a good length for her.

Leaning her weight onto them, she studied the signpost. Tomorrow, she'd be choosing the trail to the left and heading up to Eagle's Nest, a four-hour loop. Today, she was heading to the right.

The post said that, from this point, Hermit's Cave was a seven-hour loop. Dani checked her watch. It was right at ten. If she got to the end of the trail in the average time frame, she could give herself a half-hour, forty-five minutes of time sitting there, maybe eat a late lunch, and then loop back, she should make it to the lodge just before she lost daylight.

Dani certainly didn't want to be alone in a strange wood after dark.

And too, Tiana had been acting weird. Dani could totally see her calling 9-1-1 and getting a search party organized if Dani wasn't back in time for dinner.

She started off, developing a rhythm for using the sticks.

Seven hours hiking. "Lei Ming, I'm sure there's a reason you asked me to make this vow."

Seven hours…

"I need to think about this hike as a day of *shinrin-yoku*, Japanese for 'forest bathing.'" Dani had read about it in a magazine she'd found on a table at the airport.

The benefits had something to do with breathing in the "natural aromatherapy of phytoncides." It said two hours would have remarkable effects on her health and well-being.

So, eight hours out here, well that should be a quadruple dose of feel good.

Hopefully, that would be enough.

Dani had been stuffing her grief for months now. Stuffing it deeper and deeper, hiding it away, and it needed to come out.

Now, it circulated in her system like a poison.

She wanted to make great horrible wails and let hot tears run with snot down her face with only the squirrels and birds to witness.

A crackle off to her left had Dani stopping and staring into the negative space between the trees. A moment of déjà vu. For a nanosecond, she'd expected to see Daisey peeking over to make sure she could see Dani.

*What if I hadn't reached for you during the crash? What if I hadn't grabbed your collar? Would you have been thrown free and lived?*

Dani dropped the walking sticks, bending at the waist, her hands on her knees, she gasped for breath as the enormity of her loss stopped her lungs.

It took her long moments of panting to get herself together enough to pick up the sticks and keep on.

"Today sucks."

# *Chapter 8*

*Trip*

Ridge, Tripwire, and Noah climbed out of the van.

Hairyman stopped to give a full body stretch. Trip and Ridge took a habituated sidestep to miss the arc of drool that went with the inevitable shake that followed.

They sauntered into the lodge where a uniformed hotel worker pointed them down the hall and a sign hung with "Ballroom A" in golden script.

"Teams here." Bob stood, his focus was on a young woman who tugged her shirt away from her abdomen and stared at them with a silent frown.

Anxiety wafted off her. This must be their customer.

She wasn't at all what he'd expected. Hollywood in Trip's mind was high maintenance illusion, and this woman looked down-to-earth in her blue jeans and thick wool sweater. The pencil sticking out of her bun gave her the air of a graduate student preparing for finals.

She'd bitten most of the lipstick off her lips.

"Harper Katz," Bob said. "Meet our team leader, Ridge Decker, and our second in command, Tripwire Williams."

She held out her hand and raced over to them. "Harper Katz," she said, pumping Ridge's hand. Then turning to Trip to pump his hand next. "Harper Katz." Her hand was cold, her voice tight. She blinked in the staccato mechanical way people did when they were out of their comfort zones.

Way out.

"I'm Trip. This is Ridge," he repeated their names. Sometimes it took a few repetitions for stressed people to get names into their brains, and it was important that she had the faces and names lined up so she was more comfortable with the process. "Why don't we go over to the maps? Bob can get us caught up on the situation."

She bobbled her head and twisted her fingers as she moved to the side of the table, looking like she wasn't sure if her input would be helpful or if she were getting in the way.

Bob had a series of screens up; a stack of tasks was already being created.

"We have a missing person?" Ridge asked.

"More like fourteen," Harper said.

"How long have they been missing?" Ridge planted his knuckles on the table, bending himself so he was eye to eye with Harper.

"Just since this morning," she whispered. "They

took off around six. It's Berlin and her photography crew."

Bob pointed toward his cell phone. "Phones are a no-go except in the parking lot. They have no way to communicate. They took off when the weather systems still looked good."

"When were you expecting them back?" Ridge asked.

"Late. They were hoping to get some good night photos around a campfire. But...the...uhm. When? I expected them back around midnight or so." She stopped and scratched the back of her neck and rolled her lips in waiting for the next question.

"And no radios?" Ridge asked. "Proper clothing?"

"No. None of that. Cute clothes for the shoot. I had looked it up for them, and there was...there was supposed to be a full moon." She frowned at Ridge. "That's actually why we came now—bare limbs to make things look cold and a full moon because it's pretty. Photogenic. It's all about the illusion on social media."

"Do you know what trails they planned to follow?" Trip asked. He modulated his voice to be warm and encouraging. Harper's stress might make her brain forget an important detail that would help them get the crew back safely before the bomb cyclone blew up the mountainside.

"No." She said it so quietly the men all leaned forward to hear. She cleared her throat. "No. I know that's a thing. You should leave your plans. But they weren't sure what they'd find in the way of scenery. They were going to stay on the lodge trails. Speaking to the manager, I understand they're easy to follow. There aren't a lot of ways to get off them by accident."

"I hear a 'but' in there," Trip said.

Harper sighed. "The goal isn't safety. The goal is excellent social media pictures. Berlin wants a role in an upcoming movie. The female protagonist in that film is comfortable in the outdoors, and that's not really the reputation Berlin has right now. So she wants to do a series of posts of her being comfortable in nature. They won't stick to trails if they see something that they think will capture the right mood." She did air quotes for that last bit. "They could be anywhere."

"Not anywhere," Trip said. "They're going to be on lodge property because the lodge is surrounded by cliffs. They're also only going to be as far as their weakest team member's ability to walk and pack their equipment in. What have they got with them in terms of equipment?"

"Camera equipment. Video equipment. Wardrobe changes. Makeup. Props. And they had fake food. You know, fabricated, perfect-looking foods to put in the shoots. They aren't edible, uhm, obviously." She swiped her palms down her thighs, then played with her ring, twisting it back and forth.

"I'm sorry, I should have been clearer. What have they brought with them in terms of emergency equipment?" Trip asked.

Harper's gaze landed on the toe of her boot. "Okay, let me think. The wardrobe changes would mean some layers of clothing. They had fake food, but they also had real food put together by the chef. They had some water but not a lot because it was heavy. There's a first aid kit in Berlin's makeup bag, but that's just a few Band-Aids and an alcohol wipe. The only light they had was from their headlamps." She looked up with a moment of victory in her eyes. "They have things to start a fire. They were planning a campfire."

"Some of the crew have outdoor skills then? They know how to start a campfire. Would they know how to make a shelter? How to tell weather patterns and call it to a close if they saw that the wind was building and the temperature dropping?"

She shook her head. "I... I don't know. This is a crew she picked up in New York City. She came down here because someone suggested the lodge was a perfect place to work. I guess they'd been here before. Berlin only stays at five stars and there aren't a lot of five stars that have the bucolic look she was aiming for."

Bob rubbed a hand down his face. "What's Noah saying about the timing of the weather system?"

"Back of the napkin calculation, he's thinking seventeen hundred hours," Ridge said. "It'll take some time before we can get everyone coordinated and get them out of base."

"I'll put the timeframe into the management program," Bob said. "Where's Noah? I need him here."

"He took Hairyman to potty," Ridge looked over to the door. "He's right behind us. He'll want to get in to the nitty gritty of the weather data to get a better timeframe."

Harper lurched forward. "I mean, I want them found. It's important to find them. But I don't want your team to put your lives at risk. Your team needs to be back before they're endangered. I'm not hiring you for that." She gripped the top of her sweater. "I'm not paying to put people's lives in danger." Her eyes were held wide and unblinking.

Ridge gave her a nod and turned his focus to Bob. "Local officials have been looped in?"

"They've got their hands full with the locals. They want to be apprised, but they're not sending anyone over. We're on our own with this mission."

Cerberus would be pushing hard for the next six hours, unless by some miracle they landed on the group out of the gate.

The dogs would definitely be force multipliers. That a fully equipped K9 tactical team had rolled up might just be the serendipity that the Berlin Tracy crew needed to survive.

Given what Harper was saying about their comfort level in the wilderness, one of two things would happen. They'd stick close to the paths—maybe leave someone with the heavy equipment on the path within shouting distance—that would be good. Or, they could underestimate the dangers and just move as a unit, making life-threatening mistakes without even realizing it.

Trip hoped that the equipment was cumbersome and heavy. It would mean the first scenario was more likely and that they might not have gotten too far up the trails.

Hard to say really.

Cerberus was good at this, though. Like the SEALs, they executed missions for twenty-five percent of their work hours, and they trained the other seventy-five percent of the time. When they got the callout, things went like clockwork. They had the strength of body and mind to get the mission accomplished.

What they didn't have was superpowers. And this was a damned bomb cyclone.

The team put on alert, they had been out at the vans prepping their gear and K9s.

The management team—Bob, Noah, Ridge, and Tripwire—drew up their plans based on the statistics— the science of finding the lost subjects—and not on gut instinct.

Trip was first up when the task sheets were assigned. Trip signed off on his task, pulled the white sheet from the top of his assignment, handed it to Bob, and moved out of the way to let the next in line grab their assignments.

He'd take the easternmost trail along the cliff's edge, where the panorama would be photo worthy.

Trip tucked the assignment and maps into his plastic map carrier and strode toward the van to get Valor out of her crate.

Given these circumstances, they had divided the trails between each K9/handler team. The Cerberus team members would jog the trails in a method called a "hasty". Just a quick look to the left and right as they moved through the most likely places to find Berlin and her crew. They'd be able to keep their pace fairly quick, which meant they might catch up to the crew if they had stopped frequently to arrange their shots.

The K9's noses would be in the air tracking any human being that was in the area.

Ridge and Zeus would try a different tactic. Harper was going to give Ridge Berlin's pajamas as a scent to trail. That was their task. Hopefully, Zeus would put his nose to the ground and follow the scent right to her, and they could call it a day, tuck everyone in at the lodge safe and sound before the storm erupted.

Ridge and Zeus would need to move fast. The winds

were picking up, and that meant a wider scent cone, which meant a diminishing chance that Zeus would be able to track Berlin and her crew.

Trip popped open the back door. "Hey, Little Mama."

Valor's whole demeanor changed when he snapped on her orange tactical vest with the reflective tape.

Out on a mission, Valor had to be forced to stop. To eat and drink. To rest.

To let Trip rest.

After completing their search task, if Valor didn't make a find, she'd mope in the corner of the room, becoming depressed.

That was bad.

This job had to be fun for the dogs to keep them working successfully.

If Trip and Valor weren't on the find team, locating the missing person, a volunteer would hide behind a log or under a pile of leaves. Once Valor's wet nose uncovered them, a cheer went up, congratulatory whoops filled the air, and Valor vibrated with joy.

From his crate, Zeus was watching Valor get suited up. He was ticked that he was being left behind. He barked angrily, stomping his paws.

Trip stuck his fingers into Zeus's crate to wiggle into Zeus's fur. "Ridge is getting you a scent. You'll be out in a minute." That did nothing to settle him.

Didit jogged out and popped open her van. Now, all the dogs knew a mission was spooling up. The cacophony of the dogs raring to go filled the air.

"You ready to go to work?" Trip asked.

Valor could air scent or follow a trail.

Her nose and tenacity were already getting a reputation in the search and rescue world.

Trip scratched his fingers through her coat, transmitting his pride in her through his touch.

He grinned, remembering Valor's first mission. An eighteen-month-old had toddled away from his grandmother in the woods. The grandmother had turned her head to answer her granddaughter, turned back, and the baby, Billy, was gone. Blink of the eye.

Trip and Valor were in the area doing their daily training. When he saw the sheriff's lights, Trip had wandered over to ask if they could be of any help.

Seeing Valor's search vest, the sheriff asked them if they could do a quick sweep while they rounded up their resources.

Out Valor went on voice command.

She came back with the toddler dangling from his snow suit. Valor was holding him by the seat of his pants. He wasn't hurt. But he was none too happy.

Trip assumed Little Mama didn't follow the normal protocol of making the find and coming to get him because she was too maternal to leave a baby alone in the woods.

Still, Trip spent some time retraining Valor to leave the lost person where she found them and not try to drag them home like a wayward puppy.

Trip would keep Valor's lead on her until he was up the trail a bit. That would make things less confusing for Valor. Their first waypoint was Hermit's Cave. Once they got there and checked out that photo opportunity spot, they'd jump off the marked trail to reach a set of stairs built into the rock cliff wall where a cabin was tucked halfway down the cliff on an apron of land.

A log cabin against the rugged terrain? Picturesque. A high likelihood that Berlin would be found there.

It was one of the places that the lodge manager had suggested to the group.

If Trip found them there, depending on height of the descent and ropes he had with him, Trip would try to rappel down to the roadway and check cell phone service.

If none, they'd have to drop the superfluous gear and hightail it up the road to the lodge.

After checking the cabin, if the group wasn't there, Valor and he would climb the stairs back to the top of the cliff then trek to a lookout called Eagle's Nest to the west from that point. At Eagle's Nest he'd find a trail back to the lodge. And once he cleared the Eagle's Nest trail, he'd be done with his task sheet.

Tripwire and Valor were up to the first of the posts directing the various paths. There was another trail in between the outer trail to Hermit's Cave and Eagle's Nest. This inner trail formed part of the Hermit's Cave loop. According to the lodge manager, the trail went through the woods without much in the way of photo opportunities. Tripwire would see if Valor had interest in heading that way.

Based on the timing data developed by the lodge management to help keep their guests safe from overdoing, Trip's tasks would take an average hiker eight hours.

They had six hours at best, according to Noah's updates.

Taking this at a fast jog, he'd be hard pressed to make those distances before the storm became life threatening when he'd need to be back at base, per their client's requirements.

Valor was going to love this.

Tripwire released Valor from her lead. "Hey, Little Mama. You ready to save some lives?"

# Chapter 9

## *Dani*

According to the pace count app on her watch, Dani should be coming to the end of the trail soon. That was good. She was physically tired, emotionally wrung out, and hungry. She looked forward to taking a break.

Three and a half hours wasn't a long hike, but it had been all uphill.

Dani planted her walking sticks, using them to hoist herself up and over a rock outcropping. She appreciated the sticks with the flowers and vines intricately carved into their lengths. They had felt silently companionable as she made her way.

She was glad for the solitude of this morning's lonely mission. Dani didn't have to support anyone else's emotions. She didn't have to make small talk or compromise on anything. She wasn't self-conscious of her tears. Or that time when she threw her head back to howl.

The pain of it felt good. *Necessary.*

Dani stopped and took a deep breath of air. She was rethinking the possibilities of that Japanese forest bathing. Those good-for-the-brain chemicals were probably produced by the leaves, and here she was in the winter woods with bare limbs except for a scattering of evergreens, pine, and holly. Disappointing, Dani thought.

Still, the wet earth had a fertile smell, like it was hiding spring behind its back ready to sweep it forward in a surprise romantic bouquet.

Daisey would have loved this hike. She loved to snuffle the greenery and run after critters. Inevitably, Daisey would roll around in something dead until she stank so badly that Dani didn't want to put her back in the car. Dani remembered how Daisey would bound out of the tree line with her mouth clamped around a forest find, treasures that she'd sniffed out and lugged back—deer antlers and the odd hoof or deer femur. Her body would waggle with pride, and Dani would praise her and give her gratitude kisses even if she was going to leave the items behind.

The last time she was with Daisey, riding through the streets back on base, Dani had promised Daisey a long walk.

Daisey didn't survive that drive. Dani would never be able to fulfill her promise.

And with that thought, Dani was fully back at the site of the car accident in Afghanistan, pinned by the crush of the frame around her.

The hot metal scalded her leg and back, but she couldn't move away from it. Pinned.

Dani tried to call out to Lei Ming and Tiana, but she couldn't muster the breath. Couldn't get her lips to round into words. Her brain had stuttered trying to figure out why she was stuck like that. Her leg burning like that.

The three friends had been making plans for their last night together before Lei Ming's departure. Lei Ming wanted it to be a low-key good-bye. "How about we lay out and watch the stars? Maybe drink a beer or two?" Lei Ming suggested.

Tiana had been listing all the foods she missed that Lei Ming could eat in a matter of hours. Sushi. Tiramisu. Fresh fruit salad...

There had been a scream of tires and then flailing. Crushing. Pain.

In that moment, Dani's hand had shot out to grip tight around Daisey's collar to protect her.

It was reflexive.

Dani lay there not understanding. Her brain battling for comprehension. The shouting voices, yelling "accident" and "medic," helped Dani realize her situation.

Roaring motors brought new terror. What if another vehicle would come up, the driver not paying attention, and they'd run her over where she lay in the street?

Trapped, the only thing Dani could move was her head. Her gaze followed up her arm to where it was stuck under a portion of the seat, her fingers wrapping around Daisey's collar.

Dani couldn't tell if her dog had survived.

She had crooned to Daisey. Begged her to hang on.

Told her that as soon as Dani could get free, she'd take Daisey to the hospital and fix her. *Please hang on.*

But Daisey had died on impact.

Lei Ming died just as fast.

And Tiana, who had been driving the vehicle, was broken.

Dani had walked away with second degree burns and a gash easily sewn up with a few stitches.

If Dani hadn't grabbed at Daisey's collar, would Daisey have been thrown free?

Would she be alive?

Did Dani kill her sweet dog with her reflexive action?

She gasped at the pain of her guilt.

Dani started her survival mantra, the seven words she pulled up and chanted when her anguished thoughts suffocated her. "Nothing I can do to change it." It helped. Sometimes.

"Nothing I can do to change it." It formed a bridge until new thoughts could gather. And it was true. No matter how many times she thought *if only*…there was nothing she could do to change reality. There was no way to bring Lei Ming or Daisey back to life.

They were there riding under the hot sun then gone.

Just gone.

All of her thoughts today were going to be daggers. Today was designed for that, she reminded herself, forcing her feet up the path. If she didn't keep moving, if every memory stopped her momentum, she'd never make it through this pilgrimage.

*Oh, wow. This is stunning.* Dani leaned a hand on the post carved with "Hermit's Cave" and looked out at the expanse in front of her.

There was a broad terrace of land that jutted out over a valley far below.

Dani moved toward the split log rail that protected the edge and looked down at the ribbon of road that ran below. That was probably the road they'd driven to get to the lodge, she thought.

Dani stepped back and turned to find a two person-sized recess in the cliff that ranged above her for another twenty or so meters. Shaped like a Gothic cathedral window, Dani thought it did have a chapel-like feel. A religiosity. A sacredness.

She exhaled. "I'm here, Lei Ming."

Dani gratefully shrugged her backpack off her shoulders and laid it inside the lip of the opening. Crawling into the dark recess out of the sun, bright despite the cloud cover, Dani scooped off her baseball cap. She swiped her hand over her brown hair, its shoulder length was held back in an elastic, the edges of her hairline curled with the humidity of her exertion.

Dani rubbed her hands up and down her arms. Now that she'd stopped and was out of the warmth of the sun's rays, it seemed to Dani that the temperatures had seriously dropped since she'd left out just a few hours ago. Since it was early afternoon, she'd have thought things would be warming up.

Untying the sleeves from the backpack handle, Dani pulled her fleece sweater over her head and sat with that for a few minutes. She decided to add her jacket on top. Maybe it was the wind wicking her perspiration off her skin that was chilling her.

Dani unzipped the jacket's pocket to grab her phone and check the weather, then remembered she'd left it back at the lodge since she was out of cell range.

Tucking her heels closer to her bottom, Dani wrapped her bent knees with her arms, lacing her fingers to hold them in place.

It was a beautiful site. Dani could well imagine Lei Ming here, a blanket spread on the floor of the indentation, too shallow to *really* be counted as a cave, but enough space to sit up against the back wall, stretch out her legs and write or daydream in the relative cool of the shade.

On Dani's right were two large rocks with a slab of slate across them. A handful of colorful gemstones were arranged there. In the center sat a small aluminum bowl where a tea candle had burned through its wax.

Dani reached out and fingered the stones, cool and smooth. She brought the rose quartz up to her lips and wondered who had made this little altar-like addition. Why were these particular rocks chosen? Had they done their magical duties or was she disturbing some kind of meditation or spell work? Dani put the quartz back where she'd found it. "Sorry," she said.

Dani was tired from the almost four-hour climb. She'd decided to take it slow on the way up, allowing time for the emotions to sweat out of her system and slough off her skin. She'd make up the time on the downward trail.

Tugging her day pack closer, Dani lifted the water hose into her mouth, turned the spigot, and drank long and deep. Water from her hydration system always tasted of plastic and that was probably the reason Dani never felt sated by drinking it.

She unclipped the backpack cover and dug out her lunch, deformed by all the jostling. She'd picked up some grab-and-go food while she and Tiana filled up at the gas station down the road from the lodge.

Eating mechanically, Dani didn't register the tastes—a sub with humid cheese and wilted lettuce. A plastic cup of carrots and another of grapes.

Dani lifted a pack of cookies, then chucked them back in the pack. She wasn't hungry. They'd be good as a pick-me-up on the way back when a shot of sugar might help her get down the trail faster.

Shoving her garbage into one of the cups and sliding it into her bag to dispose of back at the lodge, Dani rubbed her hands on her hiking pants to clean them off before pulling out the little black notebook with Lei Ming's poems that Tiana and Dani had chosen to leave here.

As she lifted the front cover and leafed through the pages, Dani's thoughts were suddenly intruded upon by three sharp barks.

Someone else must be climbing the trail.

Dani had assumed she'd be alone. She was in no mood to be friendly. It was irritating that her solitude would be interrupted, especially in *this* moment. This *sacred* moment. She put the notebook on the little altar. She didn't want anyone to ask, "Hey, what have you got there?"

Maybe they'd just come up, take a couple pictures of the scenery, and leave again. Dani would make sure to give them a good head start so they didn't pass each other on the path going back.

Three more sharp barks from just outside of the cave sounded like a signal.

Dani scooted forward on her bottom until she'd emerged into the sunlight.

There stood a magnificent German shepherd, pink tongue lolling out.

The dog put her nose in the air and sniffed before giving a happy bark and coming up to Dani, head down, whole body wagging.

"Hello there, beautiful." Dani held out the back of her hand for the dog to sniff. "You're a working dog," Dani said. "You have your search and rescue vest on."

The K9 sniffed around her neck, in her hair.

Dani giggled and pushed the shepherd away when she stuck her wet nose into Dani's ear.

Around and around, wiggle, wiggle. It was the body language that Dani usually saw when a handler was re-united with their K9 after injuries had kept them apart. Same sounds. Same joyful energy. "Hey there, pupper." Dani laughed and leaned back as the dog tried to give her face a tongue bath. "Do I know you?"

The K9 responded by climbing into the space created by Dani's crisscrossed legs, sitting her butt down on Dani's ankles, and draping her head over Dani's shoulder. The dog let out a deep sigh followed by a strange noise deep in her throat that was somewhere between joy to see Dani and a chastisement that Dani had gone away in the first place.

Dani leaned back to see the K9's face, but the dog was having none of that. Her left paw came up and wrapped Dani into a hug.

Reaching across, Dani pulled the dog's collar around so she could read the name plate. "Valor." There was a contact phone number and a URL.

"Valor." Dani scrunched her fingers into the dog's thick scruff. "A noble name for a noble dog. You sure are acting like we know each other. Do we know each other? Have I treated you before?" She once again tried to lean back so she could look at Valor's face.

Dani wasn't much with humans, remembering names or faces, but a dog? Dani remembered every single dog she'd ever met. This dog didn't seem familiar, though. She checked Valor's right ear for an MWD—military working dog—tattoo. None there.

"Maybe you're in the contractor working dog program." She lifted up onto her hip so she could check Valor's left ear for a tattoo. "Nope. So you haven't been sent to a conflict zone. It's doubtful we met." Dani pressed her fingers into Valor's skull at the base of her ears and rubbed until Valor let out a low moan. "You seem young. Can I see your mouth?"

When Dani stopped rubbing Valor's ears, Valor pouted.

"Just for a second. Mouth," she commanded, and Valor dropped her lower jaw. Dani pulled back Valor's lips to inspect her teeth and gumline. "Well, whoever your handler is, they're doing a good job with your dental hygiene. I'd say you're around two years old. Were you out here training? Are you looking for someone? Should you be working?"

Valor answered by draping her head back over Dani's right shoulder and resting her paw on Dani's other side, giving Dani the K9 version of a full body hug.

"Oh you're just a big baby, aren't you? A sweet lovebug." She rubbed her hands through Valor's fur and closed her eyes to absorb the goodness of it.

*Did you send Valor to come check on me, Daisey? If you did, thank you. This helps.* Dani's breath caught. Her lashes were heavy with tears.

Dani was exhausted from the emotions of her trek.

She took respite in this moment as she hugged Valor, skating her hand through her soft fur, breathing in the doggy scents.

After a few minutes of indulgence, Dani started to feel guilty. "Are you looking for someone? I'm out here all by myself. If you're air scent searching, then you might just be looking for human beings." She ran her hand down Valor's side and patted her haunches. "I fit the bill all right. I don't want to take you off task. Where's your handler?" She looked past Valor, who seemed to have no desire to move on. "Is there a way you signal them? Were you trained to stay with the found person like a St. Bernard? Were those three sharp barks your signal?"

She pushed Valor's head back so Dani could look to see if there was a camera and a radio collar on her, the kind SEALs used to direct their K9s from a distance. Valor had a tracking device, but that was it. "You know, if you were going to play St. Bernard keeping me warm this way, it would have been nice if you had a little cask of rum. Is it rum they keep there?"

Valor lifted one brow then the other. It was so comical that Dani burst out laughing, then buried her head in the scruff of Valor's neck and sobbed. "That's what you call whiplash emotions, Valor. You found me having a moment. Sorry about that."

Valor spun around, delicately placing her paws on the ground in the little opening made by Dani's crisscrossed legs. Then Valor managed to curl her whole body into the nest made by Dani's thighs. Valor's tail thumped against the hard ground while she settled her muzzle onto Dani's knee.

"Here to stay?" Dani asked as she moved practiced

hands over Valor. Valor was clean and well-muscled. Hydrated. Her coat was brushed, and her vest looked fresh enough. Just a few stick-tights and some forest debris clinging to the weave. The smell of Dani's half-eaten cheese sandwich would be easy for Valor to smell, but Valor had ignored Dani's backpack completely. It didn't seem like Valor was lost, not for very long anyway.

Thoughts of Tiana's weird behavior flitted into Dani's mind, but she let them go again. Even if Tiana was paranoid, it was way too early for her to have rounded up a search team to put on Dani's trail.

"It's unusual to train you to stay with your found person and not go alert anyone. You don't seem to be hurt." Dani was at a loss for what to do here. She couldn't continue on with her planned ritual for Lei Ming. She couldn't leave with or without the dog.

She was kind of stuck.

Though, Dani couldn't let herself be stuck for long. Dani wasn't willing to be on the trail after the sun went down. She'd allocated a half hour to her lunch, then she was going to read the poem Lei Ming had designated.

And say good-bye.

The second half of the ritual would be tomorrow at Eagle's Nest, hopefully with Tiana.

But Valor's being here changed things up.

Valor lifted her head and sent out three sharp barks.

"Is your handler able to locate you that way? Seems odd, especially on a windy day like today." Dani strained to hear a voice calling from a distance.

Valor pushed her front paws into Dani's thigh.

"Ow," Dani complained, pushing to get Valor off.

Now, Dani could hear a come-here whistle.

Three more sharp barks, then Valor stood, turned, and settled into a seat on her thigh, draping her head over Dani's shoulder, hugging Dani once again, which Dani selfishly loved. "I wouldn't mind you keeping me company on the hike down."

With that thought, a man jogged into sight.

"I bet that's your guy heading in. I hope you're not in trouble."

Valor's tail swept back and forth across the smooth rock, perfectly content.

They must have just come into the guy's view. He stopped on a dime. His hands came to his hips as he assessed the scene.

"Yeah. I think you're in trouble, Valor," Dani whispered.

# Chapter 10

### Dani

"I found your dog," Dani called over. "Or she found me. Hard to tell. Chicken or the egg scenario."

That got the guy moving again with a cadenced gait. He had broad shoulders. A beanie pulled down to his brow. Clean shaven.

She watched him stride up the incline.

Valor hadn't moved from full-body hugging Dani. Though from the hot breath on her neck, Dani could tell Valor had turned her head to watch the guy.

"Hey, Little Mama." His deep rich voice was bemused.

Dani lifted a single eyebrow.

"Sorry, I wasn't saying that to you, ma'am." His face pinked as their gaze met. Held. "My dog, Valor," he gestured over, "isn't usually that, uhm, friendly on a first meeting. Or any meeting." He was standing in front of them now.

Dani's focus caught on the length of this guy's legs; the way his gray camo pants wrapped around muscular thighs. Where she sat, her gaze was right at his crotch height. As she thought that, Dani self-consciously tried to figure out where to rest her focus. She decided to look at Valor.

The guy tapped his thigh with a soft come-here whistle.

Valor ignored him.

"Huh," he said, obviously perplexed. "Valor doesn't usually behave like this. I hope she didn't frighten you. Or smoosh you."

Valor brought her head around to keep her eye on the guy, who had shifted to put a foot on one of the rocks.

And there was that whole crotch issue, again.

"I don't get too nervous around dogs, as a rule." Dani petted a hand down Valor's coat, looking the dog in the eye. "We've bonded."

"You two look pretty cozy. Do you always have this effect on stranger dogs?"

"Yeah, I do. It's a gift." She moved her fingers to the base of Valor's ears and made circles until Valor moaned.

"Oh, well if you're going to do that—" the guy hitched his thumbs into the straps on his backpack "—I understand why Valor's taken to you. That's her high-dollar reward."

A high-dollar reward in K9 speak was the positive

reinforcement that a dog got when they performed their most difficult command.

"Oh!" Dani pushed Valor away. "I didn't mean to interfere with your work." With one hand on Valor's collar to give herself space and the other pressing onto a rock, Dani stood.

"Now that you're up. Let me introduce myself." The guy extended his hand for a shake. "Tripwire Williams with Cerberus Tactical K9."

Dani swiped her hands across her hips to get the dirt off.

Cerberus K9 was a working group within Iniquus, a private security company. Highly regarded in the industry. Golden reputations. Dani had interacted with one of their task forces once when they were providing security to a government oversight group on her base.

A senator had wanted to go outside the wire for a photo op that had gone bad, as he'd been warned was almost a hundred percent guaranteed to happen.

The Iniquus K9 took down the bad guy but had sustained multiple stab wounds in the fray.

Dani had performed surgery—it must be about three years ago now—a Malinois named Wolverine. Sadly, there hadn't been much that their surgical team could do. Wolverine had to be put down. His handler had been devastated. Dani wondered if this guy was on the same team with... What was that handler's name? All Dani could recall was that he was a retired Green Beret.

Iniquus liked to hire out of the very select pool of retiring special operators.

This guy had that same strange young and old at the same time look to his face. Dani was sure that he'd been plucked from some specialized operative unit.

Dani stretched out a hand to meet his. "Dani Addams." After the shake, they didn't release the grip.

They stood there, hand in hand, eyes locked.

A tingle went up Dani's arm and her jaw dropped as a sigh escaped.

He was "up on her tiptoes, tilt her head back for a kiss" tall. He wasn't like some of the other special operators she'd gone out with who were so tall it was like climbing a tree to get a kiss. This guy was the perfect height for her. She blushed as she realized she was thinking about him as a date.

That was all kinds of poorly timed and inappropriate.

She wondered if he was reading her mind because a slow smile slid across his face, warming his eyes.

Her tongue slicked slowly across her bottom lip as the guy's focus dropped to her mouth.

A grin replaced his gentle smile, and Dani snatched her hand back.

"Are you with the film crew, Ms. Addams?"

"Major Addams. Call me Dani, please. I'm not with any crew. It's just me on a solo hike. Are you...missing a film crew?"

"They went out this morning before the weather changed. We were hired in to make sure they get home safe. I'm assuming you're not aware of the danger or you wouldn't be sitting here."

"No, I know about it. But I thought the storm wasn't going to get here before Wednesday."

"There was a nor'easter that's gone rogue. It's developing into a bomb cyclone that they're expecting to hit in this area around five o'clock."

Dani looked at her watch. It was almost two. Three

hours, she'd have to hightail it to get back to the lodge before it hit. For sure, Dani didn't have the expertise, the clothing, or the equipment—despite Tiana's insistence that she take the extra bivouac sack in her pack—to survive a freaking bomb cyclone, whatever that was.

"High winds, forty-two inches of snow. Our team is planning to be snowed in for the week back at the lodge."

"And you've lost a whole film crew?"

He put his hand on his chest. "I didn't lose them, ma'am, I'm just tasked with finding them."

Dani wiggled her finger toward Tripwire's map case.

He pulled his map from the plastic protective envelope and handed it to her.

Shifting so they stood side by side and had the same view of the topo map, Dani ran her finger along the trail. "I don't know if this is helpful or not. But at ten, I left the lodge. I took this path here to this branch, and then I headed along this trail here. I saw no one and heard nothing along the way. It's not the easiest of trails. Lots of rock outcroppings to clamber over. The odd root sticking up just enough to catch the tip of your boot. And some issues with dirt and debris covering parts of the trail from where trees fell over. Unless Valor is saying otherwise, I'd consider it cleared."

"I'll call that in. Which trail were you planning to take back?"

Dani moved her finger. "Well, I thought I'd take this lower track so I'm walking along the cliff's edge. But it's five klicks longer than the trail I came off." Normally, back in the States she tried to lay off the military lingo. She knew Tripwire would understand the shorthand klicks for kilometers and how far a kilometer was versus a mile.

"I'd stick to your plan. I came up that trail. It's clear and the slope is easier to manage. You might want to consider taking it at a jog to make sure you get back before this hits. Gale force winds, you can get blinded and turned around quickly."

"Your team isn't going to be searching through a bomb cyclone, is it?" She hugged her arms around herself, feeling the piercing quality of the wind change.

"No, ma'am."

She scowled. "Please don't 'ma'am' me. Just Dani."

Tripwire nodded. "Okay, Dani then. I'm sliding across the ridgeline off trail to check out a couple of possible sites, a cabin and Eagle's Nest, then Valor and I will run the Eagle's Nest trail back to the lodge. We should make it in time." He focused over her shoulder on the cave and his eyes rested on Dani's pack and the little altar inside where Dani had put the palm-sized notebook with Lei Ming's poems. "I'll call your plans in, and command will keep an eye out for you. Would you mind checking in with the search and rescue coordinator when you get back to the lodge so we know you're safe?"

"Yeah. Sure. No worries."

"Maybe I can catch up with you there."

*Mmmm that smile.* Dani knew smiles like that. They often led to wonderful things. But as far as wonderful things went, this was bad timing.

"We could grab a coffee or something?"

Dani sent him a tight-lipped smile. Any week but this week and being snowed in with this hunky rescue guy would be a welcome distraction. This week, though, she'd devoted to mourning. Dani was reticent to give up the time and space she'd eked out to replace it with male companionship. She could get that almost any time and flirting under these circumstances sat wrong.

A week snowed in at the lodge, though, they'd be sharing space. She couldn't just coldly brush him off.

Besides, he had a dog, and dogs were the best medicine. "Thanks for the invitation," she said noncommittally.

Valor pushed up against her leg and sat down, dipping her head then bringing it back up so Dani's hand rested between her ears.

"Valor would obviously enjoy spending some time with you, too."

Dani bent to plant a kiss between Valor's ears and whispered, "Thanks for the hug. I really needed it." She stepped back to the cave entrance. She raised her hand to wave. "Be safe. Good luck," she said, then crawled into the opening to grab her sack, giving Tripwire space to gain command of his K9.

"Thanks, Dani. You, too."

Dani liked his voice, deep and rumbly. Calm and steady. It was the right kind of voice for a K9 handler.

"Valor." He tapped his leg and this time Valor leapt to his side, plastering herself against his left thigh, and straining her head to see her next signal. "Let's get to work. Search."

The two trotted off through the woods.

Dani felt cold and alone with them gone.

"No time for that," she said, grabbing at her backpack and slinging it on. She eyed her walking sticks, *take them or leave them?* She'd take them for now. If she found them burdensome, she'd lean them up where they'd be easily found, and she'd tell the lodge manager where they could be retrieved when the snow melted. Surely, they'd understand the situation.

With her backpack adjusted into place, Dani tipped her head back and called toward the sky. "I love you, Lei Ming. I'm so sorry you're gone!"

And that would be the best Dani could do by way of pilgrimages for now.

Dani took off at a measured trot.

A bomb cyclone was heading her way.

That was terrifying.

# Chapter 11

*Trip*

He compressed the button on the radio attached to his left shoulder. "Tripwire." Trip stepped around the far side of the outcropping that formed Hermit's Cave and was now heading through the woods on his second task. With the carpeting of leaves coming up to his knees in some places, this wasn't great terrain for moving fast, dotted as it was with debris-covered holes and roots. The very last thing Trip needed was to twist an ankle or wrench a knee. It would pull team members off the search to rescue *him*, putting the missing Berlin Tracy team in jeopardy.

He felt the urgency of the moment.

*Slow means fast.* A SEAL mantra. This scenario was why that was etched into a SEAL's brain. *Don't let*

*the "go" hormones get the better of you. Stay in your
head. Keep control.*

He waited for a break in the radio traffic, then
pressed the button a second time. "Tripwire," he said.

"Go for TOC." TOC stood for tactical operations
center, another term for command. Bob and Noah
manned the center. They put all the other members of
the team out on the search since the window of opportunity was closing.

"Tripwire. I made it up to Hermit's Cave. There
was a lodge guest there named Dani Addams. I repeat,
Dani Addams."

"Noah. Dani Addams, copy."

"Tripwire. I'm wondering if the lodge manager
made a census of the guests and has accounted for all
of them. We may have a lot more folks than just the
photography crew out on the trails. Addams had no
idea about the weather conditions. She left out before
the change in the storm's trajectory."

"Copy. I'll talk to the manager about the issue.
Which trail is Addams taking down the mountain?"

"Outer ring trail from Hermit's Cave. She had a
good pair of hiking boots that looked worn in. She's
not a newbie day hiker. I suggested she jog the distance,
and she agreed. She looked like she was fit and could
do that safely. If she pushes, Addams should be back
at the lodge before the bomb cyclone hits. I asked her
to check in with you when she gets there. She agreed
to do that."

"Noah. Copy. We've got her on our whiteboard.
We'll get a reminder sign taped up on her lodge room
door."

"Tripwire. Valor and I are heading toward the log cabin now. Our second task area."

"Noah. You hit the needed timing for the first location. If you maintain your speed, you should be fine, getting back before things get unmanageable. Let me know what you find at the cabin. Over."

"Tripwire. Wilco. Over and out."

Valor hadn't put her nose in the wind. Nothing of interest. She'd trot off and trot back. She kept looking back in the direction of Hermit's Cave.

"You liked her, didn't you?" Trip said when he caught Valor's eye. "I did, too." He lifted his elbow to protect his face as he crashed through a curtain of briars. "I think she liked you better than me, though. Maybe I'm feeling a little jealous. I certainly didn't get hugged and rubbed like you did. The advantages of being a dog."

Valor wagged her tail in the gentle back and forth that said she was having a good time, but there were no scents that were grabbing her attention. The wind was coming straight in from the east over the cliff's edge.

Trip decided to keep Valor nearby until they'd checked out the cabin. He gave her the flanking signal.

"Maybe Dani will take me up on my coffee offer. I thought dinner was too much, don't you think?"

Valor sent him a glance.

"Under the circumstances and all. Strange guy showing up and you. You were kind of forward, crawling in the lady's lap that way. She was a good sport about it. Some folks don't like German shepherds."

Valor looked up at him again, both eyebrows raised.

"I know. Hard to understand. But not everyone is comfortable around big strong dogs with sharp teeth like Dani was. I'm going to let it go this time. But just so you know, that's not allowed."

Valor dropped her head.

"It's okay. Like I said, Dani seemed to enjoy giving you some loving." He stopped and lifted his binoculars to take a quick three sixty of the area. Finding nothing, he moved on.

Valor trotted beside Tripwire's long-legged gait.

Trip's head was on a swivel looking for any signs of the missing people.

Crowd of them like that? They shouldn't be so hard to find if they'd stuck to the trails.

Valor looked up at him with a little smile and her tongue dangling out the side of her mouth. When they got to the cabin, Trip would get her a bowl of water. He wondered if Dani had given Valor any treats. He felt sure she would have told him, or he would have seen wrappers or something if she had.

"You know, I felt a good dose of chemistry when I shook Dani's hand. I haven't felt this way in a long time. And I'm counting on you being my wingman. WingK9. I figure, if she likes me over a cup of coffee, she might let that spool out to a meal. Something tells me that if you were there, you could clear the way for me to get to know her better." He glanced down at Valor. "She had nice eyes. Didn't she?"

Her gaze had been intelligent, direct, and unwavering. Trip could understand how a lone female would feel concerned about a big guy coming up on her that far from others. She hadn't seemed scared. If he'd gotten that vibe, Trip would have backed away and made sure Dani heard him talking with TOC, so she knew he was under their supervision and that TOC knew she was there with him.

Accountability might have made her feel safer.

She said she was Major Dani Addams. But he'd known women that would give themselves a military rank as a security device. Like wearing a fake wedding ring to wave off unwanted advances.

He didn't think he'd been that guy.

She'd seemed cool with everything from his sudden appearance, to his warning about getting back to the lodge—okay, she'd seemed a little nervous when he said there was a bomb cyclone, but that was understandable—to Valor getting overly friendly. "Yeah, what was that all about, huh, Valor? I've never seen you act that way before. Ever."

Tripwire was using Ranger beads to keep track of his pace count. He had his GPS tracker backing him up, but he liked to do things old school when it came to navigation. Trip learned the hard way that redundancy was key. The stupidest mistakes could get him into the world of hurt. Even if it was fairly primitive, Trip had been counting his strides and using Ranger beads—a manual counting tool used to keep track of distance traveled through his pace count—since he was back in high school, learning how to navigate the mountains. It felt natural. As he slid another bead down the string, Trip stopped to scan the horizon.

The metal handrail secured into the rock should be up around here. He was told the steps themselves had been carved out of the cliff's side.

Trip tugged out Valor's lead and attached it to her collar as he went to inspect closer to the edge. He was wary and careful as he placed his feet. The manager had explained to the team that the area had experienced landslides. Rocks and trees were easily dislodged, the effect of the odd weather they'd experienced over the last year. There was a waiver all the guests signed as they got their room keys that they'd been warned of the dangers and assumed the risk.

On his way up the outer ring of the Hermit's Cave trail, he had seen places where rocks had been dis-placed and trees uprooted.

The trail itself had seemed solid and clear, or Trip-wire would have encouraged Dani to take a different route than the one she'd already planned.

Valor and Trip came up to the edge, and Trip could see the cabin below. Tracing up from it, he found the stairs came out another twenty meters to the north.

It was an interesting place to put a cabin. On this part of the mountain there were basically three levels, the roadway, far below them; the top of the mountain with its hiking trails; and a shelf that ran, say, four stories below him. Here, where the cabin was built, tucked up against the cliff wall, the land extended out a good thirty yards, maybe more. A lot of work putting those stairs in. He'd be sure to ask around about the history when he got back to the lodge.

Trip lifted his binoculars, focusing on the cabin and surrounding plateau. It was a cute little log cabin with a stovepipe. No smoke. Stack of logs. He'd been told that it wasn't occupied at present, and he had permis-sion to search the area. But he didn't see anyone. Cer-tainly not fourteen someones.

He'd ask command if they wanted him to go down and do a thorough search.

His radio hissed then "TOC for Tripwire."

He depressed the button. "Go for Tripwire."

"Noah. Sitrep?" Noah was asking for an update.

"Tripwire. Valor and I have reached the coordinates for the cabin stairs. I have my binoculars trained on the cabin, and it looks dark. No signs of activity."

"Noah. If you're out from under the tree canopy, can you try Bob on the satellite phone? Over."

"Tripwire. Wilco. Out."

Trip signaled Valor to a down stay, then shrugged off his pack. Opening the inside protected pocket, he pulled out the satellite phone and flicked the antenna up. He dialed in to Bob's satellite phone.

Their cellphones lost their range in the lodge guest parking lot.

"Bob."

"Tripwire here. Noah asked me to call."

"Where are you now?"

"On the cliff's edge near the stairs for the cabin."

"I'm trying to make a tasking decision. I may need to reroute you. Take a seat. I need your input."

"All right." Tripwire lowered to sit on the rock with a hand on Valor's scruff. He turned his back to the wind and dipped his head to listen past the gusts of wind that set the naked trees moaning as they bent.

"The woman that you came across out on Hermit's Cave, Dani Addams. Did you watch her hike out of there?"

"Negative. She's taking the lower path, Hermit's Cave trail, back to the lodge. She was going to try to jog parts of the trail back, so I'd guess she'd get there about the three-hour mark. She'll be back well before the storm."

"We've documented that. I wanted to get a handle

on her demeanor while you were with her. You said you didn't see her leave?"

"Nothing remarkable on her end. Valor wasn't following my commands when I was up there. I'm not sure what to attribute that to."

"Like how?"

"When she made the find, Valor didn't come back and alert. Instead, she barked her alert—the way she's trained to do when she's finding small children—and stayed with Dani. I found Valor sitting on Dani's lap, giving her a full body hug."

"Huh. Have you ever seen Valor do that before?"

"Never. I'm mentioning it now, because Dani seemed to have an affinity for dogs and knew that Valor wasn't responding to my commands, so she went into the cave when I was getting Valor back in work mode."

"You checked her boots. Did she have anything else with her?"

"A day pack. It looked like it was stuffed full. She was wearing layers. It looked like her pants were weather resistant with a fleece lining. On her top, I could see a base layer, a fleece layer, and a wilderness parka layer. She didn't have a hat on her head, but the coat had a hood. All of her clothing that I saw were reputable outdoors labels." Trip stopped. He hoped Bob would read that for what it was, his giving her a once-over before he sent a civilian out to face the storm. Okay, he might have paid a little more attention than normal. She was damned cute. And she had crawled into the cave with her butt in the air.

"Did you see anything else up there with her? Anything besides that she had the proper equipment?"

"Inside the cave it looked like a little altar of sorts was set up. Looked like a candle and some stones, and I saw one of those little notebooks that fit in your pocket. She didn't mention it so I couldn't say if it was hers or something someone set up earlier on."

"But Valor was acting odd…" Bob paused. "She never acted that way before. That's my sticking point."

A chill spread through Trip's system. "Roger."

"The sheriff got a call in from Dani's mom, she thinks Dani might be suicidal."

"Suicide?" That came at Trip like a sucker punch to the gut. "Okay, that reframes what you're asking me. I thought you were worried about her ability to get back. Dani didn't have a despondent affect at all. Her face was animated—not overly so. Her tone changed with her emotions. She was clean, prepared, and appropriate." He thought how she had answered his invitation of coffee with a 'thank you.' Not to say that that was an incorrect answer, she didn't owe him the time of day. Did she say thank you because she wasn't planning to be available? Wasn't planning to be alive? Man, that seemed wrong. "She wanted off the mountain as in down the trail. By rerouting me, are you thinking about sending me to catch up with Dani instead of heading to Eagle's Nest?"

At Iniquus they ran things as a team. Even if Bob and Noah ran the TOC and Ridge was the commander, they discussed and came to shared conclusions.

"What are you seeing at the cabin?" Bob asked.

"With binoculars, it looks lonely."

"Copy. Okay, we need to work the problem. We're shorthanded with a very limited time frame and a devastating end if we don't accomplish our mission. We're talking fourteen folks out on the trails. If you clear Eagle's Nest, with Dani Addams's information about the inner loop trail, we'll have run all of the known trails on the east side of the mountain. Eagle's Nest is starred as one of the coordinates where Harper Katz had suggested they try for sunset views. It's top of our list for you to be at the exact time you'd get there if you stayed on mission."

"There's no way someone's thinking spectacular sunset today. Too gray. Too much cloud cover."

"You're closest available to a known location and a possible despondent woman—an active duty Army major. Let's talk it through. People change their minds. You know that. But from what Mother Addams told the sheriff, I agree it looks like Dani set out this morning to end it."

Trip looked down at Valor. Had she picked up on something subtle that Trip had missed? "It's a hard call. Lives on the line. What did the mother say exactly? I think I might need some convincing about Dani."

# *Chapter 12*

### *Dani*

Blisters were forming on Dani's heels. She knew she should stop, dig out her first aid kit, and put on some moleskin. The longer she delayed taking action, the worse shape her feet would be.

Hobbling down this path was incompatible to survival.

She needed to stop.

Her body didn't want to listen to reason. Her body wanted off the mountain and into the shelter of the lodge.

Was the lodge enough shelter?

A bomb cyclone didn't sound like something that would ignore a building. It sounded like a kind of supervillain in a comic book. The kind of nemesis that scoffed at the humans' screams for help as it thundered through the towns, leaving destruction in its wake.

"Stop! This panic is going to get me killed!" Dani screamed it aloud, but the wind pulled it from her mouth and sent it flying into the trees before the words could reach her ears.

She scanned the woods and limped toward a boulder. Perched on the outcropping, she arched back to shuffle her pack off her shoulders, Dani remembered the admonishment of the desk guy not to hang out near the rocks lest they slide. "Stick to the paths where you're safe."

She'd had to sign an acknowledgment of inherent risk. She'd chuckled as she scrawled her signature across the page. She'd flown into D.C. from her base in Afghanistan, for Heaven's sake! Danger? Here? In the mountains of Virginia?

Laughable.

Dani had figured that the kinds of folks who came to five-star lodges nestled deep in the mountains were the kinds of folks who were litigious at heart. That was probably a prejudice, but not one that would require meaningful inner debate. At the time, Dani imagined that a lot of the guests were doctors and lawyers and their ilk. Dani would have bet that she and Tiana were the only active duty military who'd been through the doors in a while.

But then, there was a whole search and rescue team. Of course, now she knew they were out here working, and the lost people would probably be picking up their tab. Dani pulled the first aid kit from the side pocket of her pack and placed it under her thigh to make sure a gust of wind didn't carry it off and scatter the contents.

A whole week snowed in.

Dani couldn't afford that. The five-star accommodations, even off-season, was way out of an Army major's budget. She wondered if they'd cut her a deal since no new guests would be coming in, and she didn't have a choice.

She was thinking ahead when she should have her mind focused on her present circumstances.

The sky had changed from sunny to gray in the hour since she'd been jogging the trail. Two more hours of push and she'd be down.

Tiny pin pricks of ice stung her face and the temperatures were definitely on a slide.

Quick as she could, Dani unlaced her boot and rolled her socks down to her toes. There was a mega blister wrapping the back of her heel.

A surge of adrenaline raced through her system.

It wasn't a full-blown anxiety attack. She wasn't freaking out.

But she was alone.

All by herself with the wind and the woods…and the cold. She zipped her jacket up to her neck. She wouldn't waste energy on fear. She was dressed well enough as things stood now. She had options if she was getting too cold. She could wrap her torso with her Mylar emergency blanket. There were a couple of handwarmers in the pack, but she hadn't checked their expiration date. If temperatures continued to plummet, they'd help her get down the trail.

For now, jogging kept her warm enough, but she could feel her base layer growing damp from her exertion sweat. Okay, probably some fear sweat, too.

*Bomb cyclone.*

Dani doctored her heels then threw the kit back in her pack.

*What would I do if I lose trail visibility?* she wondered as she pulled first her liner sock then her wool hiking sock on, slid her foot back into the boot, then knotted the laces tight.

She was running next to a sheer drop-off. If the trail turned, and she didn't see that it turned, she could jog right off the edge into nothingness.

What a terrible way to die, to be flung into the sky like a skydiver leaping from a plane only to discover they had no parachute. Terminal velocity and no hope. None. No amount of smarts or strength or will to live would stop a fall like that.

Dani didn't want to stop again. She took some pain pills and sucked on her water hose. She took the cookie packets and crammed them in her coat pockets.

Tugging at the Velcro strap that attached her ball cap to the pack, Dani adjusted it onto her head. With stiff fingers, Dani grabbed up her ponytail of shoulder-length brown curls; she shoved it through the hole in the back.

The visor would protect her a bit from the wind and ice. Though, that wasn't bad yet, just intermittent tiny pricks. The wind though was full of debris.

Dani scooped up her parka hood, settled it over the ball cap, and cinched it down tightly against the wind.

Things were getting a little wilder. A little woolier.

The trees bent low with a moan then snapped back in place.

Cracking, falling, thudding noises echoed from deeper in the woods.

Thank goodness for Tripwire. Not only had he

warned her about this weather, but he'd steered her to this trail.

He was right, the decline was less steep. The trail wider, with no tripping hazards. And she was on the eastern side of the mountain, which meant the wind blew the trees away from her. She wasn't afraid of one falling on her and trapping her under its weight. If that didn't kill her right away, she'd surely be dead by morning.

Had she gone down on the same path from this morning, she'd be in the thick of those trees, bending and breaking, toppling and crashing as their roots dislodged from the waterlogged ground.

Dani stood, testing the feel of her first aid administrations. Better, she decided.

She slung her day pack on her shoulders, adjusting it into place. Reaching around, she grabbed the belts that wrapped her hips and then the ones that strapped across her sternum. Dani snapped each securely in place.

She jerked then stilled at the sound of a tree falling in the distance, the cracks of branches from a neighboring tree took the impact of the fall then succumbed to the weight. Crack after crack, then the final *fwump* as it came to rest on the forest floor.

She took in a breath and blew it out again as she tugged the pack straps tighter to keep the wind from finding space between her and the bag and to keep it from rubbing.

Dani reached for her walking sticks.

One more check that the hurricane whistles were securely in place. One more pat down to remind herself of what piece of equipment had been moved to which of her pockets. One more deep breath, and she stepped back onto the trail.

Taking off at a jog, Dani fought to keep herself from giving in to the adrenaline that spiked her system. She couldn't sprint the whole way back. She'd run out of steam.

*Stay in your head, Dani. Slow and steady wins the race.* Dani knew this from her long days at the operating table. She wanted desperately to save the K9s and give them the best possible shot at returning to duty and to their handlers. But if she let the pressure of time get in the way, it clouded her thinking. She could *not* allow for bad outcomes.

When a handler lost their dog, it was a horrible thing.

"I get that now that I've lost you, Daisey," Dani said as she squinted up at the sky. "I wasn't ready for either Lei Ming or you to die. That it happened on the same day, in the same hour? Too much. *Way* too much." She closed her eyes and shook her head. "I try to comfort myself that you and Lei Ming were together crossing over, but it doesn't seem right to me. There's some kind of disconnect, Daisey."

She was thinking about the moments before the accident. Daisey had suddenly turned around on the seat and tapped Dani with her paw, looked right into her eyes. Dani had laughed. "Oh, I love you too, Daisey. Always and forever."

Dani thought Daisey tried to convey something to her that she couldn't get.

Daisey knew it was coming. Dani was convinced of that.

"It was like you could see the other side with so

much more clarity. Like when I said I loved you that last time, that you were fine going. You'd done what you came there for and now the task was done." Dani panted between words. Emotions and exertion. She needed to stop trying to do both. It was sucking her energy.

Dani was plain exhausted from today.

Wrung completely out, and she had hours to go to survive.

And *still* her mind played the same song on repeat. "You knew you were going. Nothing will ever convince me otherwise. You were fine that you were going. I'm convinced of that, too. It didn't feel like you were fine leaving me. You will never leave me."

She touched her hand to her heart then planted her stick again. "You live in here. But I need your terrible breath in my face, waking me up from my nightmares. Your giving me the rhythm of my day… Having you in spirit is a gift. It's not the same thing, you know, baby? It seemed so easy for you though. There was death, and you walked toward it nonchalantly."

Dani ducked her head against a gust.

"They told me that Lei Ming fought to her last breath. Not that I'm blaming you, Daisey. What do I know? I couldn't see you. But the sergeant that was with Lei Ming said she fought to her last breath, past her last breath. When she was still conscious but no longer able to take in air. It was quick, though. They said it happened fast. She didn't suffer long." Dani chewed on her lip as she rounded the curve and shortened her stride down a sharper incline, planting her sticks and leaning on them heavily.

*You died. You died. You died.* Each iteration was hammered into the trail as her feet hit the ground.

*You died.*

This was a torrent, a flood, a tsunami.

And now that she'd let the monster grief out of its cage, here she was, facing it full force at the same time she was blazing into this new crisis.

"I'm learning how to exist without you constantly by my side." She gasped past the pain that shot across her chest. She bent double, hands on knees, the full-blown stomach punch of her loss catching her breath and seizing her lungs.

She had to wait it out.

Dani had no control over the grief.

It was probably a mistake to try to pack the months of grief down into her system, waiting for a more pragmatic time to deal with them. Even though her sorrow had leaked out bit by bit, in retrospect, she should have given herself daily time to let it flow.

"I'll be honest," she whispered as she picked up her sticks, again. "I have never experienced this level of pain—physical or emotional—before in my life." She forced herself to stand. "Sometimes, Daisey, it creeps up on me and attacks me, and I can hardly stay upright." She took a couple of tentative steps forward. "I forget to breathe. I know you're with me. I sense you here. I think you're with me now."

She panted as she jogged up an incline.

"I believe you sent Valor over to Hermit's Cave. I do. Without her signaling to Tripwire, I would never have known that I was in dire straits. Thank you." And instead of the cadence of "You're dead," hammering through Dani's brain, she now kept her cadence with "thank you." It was better fuel for getting her out of the storm and back to the lodge.

A dog to dog message. Yes, Dani was going to believe that because it was a balm to think that Daisey was watching out for her still. Cared for her still.

Dani might have chalked Valor's appearance up to happenstance except that Valor's behavior had obviously confused Tripwire.

Valor. *Oh my gosh, what a beautiful dog.* "She has that same thing as you had, Daisey, that motherly nurturing quality warming her eyes."

Trip had said she was acting out of training, but she must not have been acting out of character because he called her Little Mama.

Everyone called Dani's dog "Nurse Daisey."

Dani had never had a working dog sit in her lap and give her a contented hug before.

Thoughts of Daisey watching over her, and her magical interaction with Valor, gave her hope. She needed it. Even in the last few minutes the weather was worsening. The wind had changed direction slightly and now pressed against her. She couldn't jog here. She'd just have to lean into it.

It slowed her descent.

She tried to calculate the time it would take her to get down at this pace.

At least she wasn't on the ground.

She pictured herself on her belly, crawling to the lodge door like those old characters of a cartoon crawling through the desert to an oasis.

Then she was back to her image of the bomb cyclone as a Marvel supervillain.

Dani had no idea what a bomb cyclone was. In her

mind she conjured the terrible dust storms called ha-boobs that happened when a thunderstorm in the arid lands collapsed. The intense winds were filled with debris. She couldn't see anything but brown. It filled her nose and lungs and choked her. They were terri-fying. Add a roadside bomb to a haboob and that was the image Dani's mind conjured.

And there she was alone. With no buildings to pro-tect her and no help. Alone.

And that became her new walking word. Each step forward, "Alone. Alone. Alone."

At least they'd know where to go look for her pop-sicle body, should she not make it back.

She instinctively reached again for her phone to check radar.

No connectivity out here.

And no phone.

Dani had left her cell on the bed when she tiptoed out of the room and turned out the lights so Tiana could get some sleep.

Dani thought maybe this storm coming in was the thing that triggered Tiana's migraine.

The headaches were new, so Dani didn't know. It might not be weather related at all. It could be emo-tional distress.

If Tiana woke up and felt better, she might have gone to get some food. She'd see the SAR TOC in full swing. She'd hear about the storm, and she would freak the hell out.

Sure, Tripwire had said he'd call her location and direction into the command center. They'd be able to reassure Tiana that Dani knew about the storm and was on her way back. That they were keeping track of her.

That should calm Tiana down.

Dani encouraged herself along.

*When I get back to the lodge, I'm going to soak in a tub. I'm going to wash my hair and get perfectly clean. I'm going to do it right away.* Who knew what the lodge had by way of backup generators? And if they had the generators, did they have enough gas to run them?

She stopped with a stitch in her side. Gasping. Maybe a cookie. A sip of water would keep her going. She had to move faster. She had to get off this damned mountain!

She took a breath and forced her body forward again.

"I owe myself the tallest stiffest drink *when* I get down to the lodge."

She pressed down hard on the *when* because her brain had wanted to say "if."

# *Chapter 13*

*Trip*

"TOC for Tripwire." It was his radio not the sat phone.

"Go for Tripwire."

"TOC. We've done our calculations. Based on the storm's trajectory and timing and your location, we're going to send you back to Hermit's Cave. We want a status report once you get there. Over."

"Tripwire. Rerouting to Hermit's Cave. Over and out."

He turned and patted his leg for Valor.

This time, instead of the "slow means fast" trot through the woods, Tripwire ran. He ran as hard and as fast as his legs would take him.

He signaled Valor out in front with her keen senses. He trusted her to lead him.

"Trace," he called out to keep her on task, performing one of her tracking skills, tracing their way back to where they'd come from.

Valor kept her pace connected to Trip's, never too close, never too far out.

Now, when a life might well be on the line, all the hours and days and months of practice could be paying off.

If Dani's mom was right, if Dani meant to take her life after losing her best friend and the dog of her heart in a vehicle crash, if the pressures of her job and deployments were pressing too hard...

Trip had buddies who hadn't made it. He and Valor had just been to Tony Branson's funeral back in Washington in January. Tony and he had been through Hell Week together, but Tony had been assigned to Norfolk, where Trip had been assigned to Coronado. They'd lost contact until they got to K9 training together. Trip was assigned to Rory and Tony had Argo.

Argo was looking for IEDs when he stepped on a plate. He lost his life. Tony lost a leg.

Of the two, Tony said he missed his dog most.

A dog of the heart can break you in ways you never knew you could be broken.

Trip felt sure if Argo had made it through the explosion, and they had retired together, Tony would still be here.

Instead, there was the funeral. And pain was part of his legacy.

His wife Marybeth. His daughters Riley and Charlotte. He had sat to the right of the altar with other K9 teams and watched as Marybeth squeezed newborn Charlotte so hard that the infant screamed.

Lynx, one of the Iniquus Strike Force team members, and Reaper's wife, Kate, took the children out so Marybeth could grieve openly without trying to crush it down for the children.

In Trip's experience, when you shove grief emotions down it condenses them, makes them dense and sticky as they brew in the system.

Sometimes, duty required it, to get the job done. But man, the consequences…

Dani's mom had told TOC that Dani had gone back to work as usual on her base in Afghanistan following the accident that killed her friend and her dog, postponing her grief until her leave request came through, and she could get back to the states for Lei Ming's memorial.

Last night, Dani had spent the night at her mother's home. According to her mom, Dani seemed "off" in a way that a mother would know. And though Dani was supposed to pick up another friend, someone from the Army who had known Lei Ming, and they were to head to Ohio in a rental car, that had sounded like a lie to Dani's mom.

This story paralleled too many stories from Tripwire's sphere.

Trip had a hard time picturing Dani as despondent.

But Tony's dying by suicide had been a shock to everyone. No one had seen it coming.

Trip pushed himself to run harder, faster, whipping through briar vines, spreading his arms wide to maintain his balance on the uneven terrain.

If there was a chance that Dani was sitting there, undecided, wavering, he had to get to her.

He just prayed he wouldn't be too late.

# Chapter 14
## Dani

They wouldn't have the lodge fire that night. That was a given. And that was a shame, that had been the thing that Dani had offered herself as an encouragement since this morning.

On the way up the mountain, emotions would roil through her, whipping her around, making her feel like she couldn't survive them, then those feelings would ebb, and she'd remind herself of the peace she'd get with a hot toddy, the crackling fire, and the solace of the bare limbed forest around her.

Tripwire had offered her a coffee. That could be just as pleasant. His eyes were warm and caring, just like Valor's had been. Like peas in a pod. They both had latent power. Strong. Smart. Kind.

A coffee might be nice.

The fire pit with a hot toddy, though, would be even better.

Surely, they'd have them again once the storm passed.

Dani stopped again, leaning on her sticks. Self-recriminating. Beseeching herself to keep on. The stops were coming more and more frequent. Dani was used to sixteen-hour days on her feet doing physical work. But she didn't have to fight the wind.

This day felt like it had been going on forever.

The drive starting at five this morning. Her mom's face pinched with worry. Then Tiana being ill and the solo hours-long sob fest of a climb. A brief respite from the crap when Tripwire and Valor came on the scene. His kindness and support… Now, she was back to the battle, fighting the wind as she jogged the path down again.

Exhausted.

"You can sleep for twenty-four hours straight. I promise," she told herself as she propelled herself forward again.

At least she had gravity helping to pull her down the mountainside.

Tripwire would be back at the lodge with Valor about the time she got there. Maybe he'd let Valor lie on her feet and warm them the way that Daisey had just a short time ago.

Dani angled her head to speak to the sky. *I liked Tripwire, Daisey. I mean like-liked. I felt the buzz and sizzle of a connection. What did you think of him? Bad timing, right?*

She was on an emotional journey. Planned. Prepared

for. Paid for with incredible effort of getting through her job and taking care of the military working dogs who depended on her good care, pushing aside the need to fall apart on the job, in the communal show-ers, in the women's tent. There had been no good place to go to release.

Yeah. At any other time, it might have been fun to have a fling. *That* body. She blew out a breath. He was spectacular. And he was a dog guy.

*Bad timing.*

Still, a week snowed in was a long time. And she loved Tiana, but Tiana had her own mourning to do. Her own soul searching. While they shared the loss of Lei Ming, Tiana harbored an enormous amount of guilt; she had to. She was driving their vehicle when it crashed. She'd never said that she blamed herself for Lei Ming and Daisey's deaths. But if Dani was wres-tling with the idea that she'd killed Daisey by grabbing at her collar, how could Tiana not have doubts about the role she played?

Maybe she had some survivor's guilt like Dani had.

Maybe the new migraines weren't from the physi-cal impact of the accident but from the emotional one.

Hard to tell. Tiana wasn't talking much.

A week without a break from Tiana was unhealthy.

She huffed out her breath. Maybe she could go faster if she dropped the walking sticks? Maybe she could go faster if she ate the cookies. Or had a rocket pack strapped on with turbo boosters.

What if she fell? Twisted her ankle or wrenched her knee? She'd have to crawl back to the lodge. The sticks would be good to have for emergency first aid. She'd keep the sticks.

Get back.

Stop by and tell search and rescue command that she made it in; they didn't need to worry about her.

Then she'd see if she could offer her services to the K9s that would be heading back from the field. She could give them a once-over, for safety's sake, if they didn't have a veterinarian of their own deployed with them.

Then bath.

Then... Tripwire?

Her feet pounding down the trail finding a steady cadence, Dani's mind flitted to Tiana. Did she know about the storm now? She'd be pacing and wringing her hands the way she did.

Dani's mind went back to the Army tent. The three of them—Lei Ming, Tiana, and she—lying on their cots, Lei Ming reading one of her poems. Lei Ming stabbed a finger onto her place on the page, stopping to tell them, as she did almost daily, "I'm not going to make it home."

*Again*, Dani had thought with a mental eye roll.

This time Lei Ming had sat up and looked at Dani. "I'll never see Hermit Cave again. I need you to do something for me. After I'm dead, would you go there for me? Would you tell the cave good-bye and thank the space for inspiring me?"

Lei Ming had been more riled than she normally was.

Dani had learned through repetition that she couldn't convince Lei Ming that this was just anxiety, and she'd be fine. "I promise. No worries," Dani had said. That repetition had taught her that the argument was never won and not worth the extra breath. Making the promise was the best way to soothe Lei Ming.

"You, too." Lei Ming turned. "Tiana, you have to go and say good-bye for me. Promise, okay?"

"Sure," Tiana had said without looking up.

It was a worn-out conversation. Discounted as lying somewhere between unlikely to absurd that Lei Ming wouldn't go home.

Dani jabbed her walking stick into the ground.

It went deeper than she'd expected.

Stumbling forward, Dani flailed her arms out.

Tossed into the air. It was the car accident all over again. She was tumbling and rolling. Her body had no sense of up or down, left or right. There was dust and dirt and rocks amidst a sense of freefalling.

Dani could only see brown and gray in her visual field. She grabbed at what was in front of her. Handfuls of dirt. Nothing solid or supportive.

A sudden jarring stop.

She lay on her stomach, her legs spread eagle. Her arms out like Superman.

The air rained dirt and rocks.

# Chapter 15

*Trip*

As they approached the backside of Hermit's Cave, Tripwire used a hand signal to direct Valor to flank him.

He then signaled silent mode.

Trip stopped to catch his breath. The last thing he wanted to do was run up on Dani and startle her. He needed to keep things chill.

He was well practiced with biofeedback and was efficient at reducing his heart rate and breathing pattern. In the field, this was a necessary skill. It meant he could get his firearm on target and shoot accurately without a stutter or tremor that would put those around his target in danger.

Trip rounded the rocks then leaned across to check the cave, moving stealthily lest Dani had a gun.

It was empty.

"Dani?" he said conversationally. Cool. Composed. He let his focus blur as he focused on listening.

"Dani?" he called out. Friendly. Relaxed. "Dani, you here? I got rerouted. I'm heading down the mountain. Would you like to come with Valor and me?" He emphasized Valor's name.

Why hadn't he asked more questions about Valor's weird behavior?

He ducked into the cave and saw the altar.

An aluminum cup had once been a tealight now burned down to nothing. There was a pattern of gemstones, but with the dusting of fine powder on them, Trip thought they'd probably been here a while. The pink rock was clean and slightly out of place. He could imagine Dani coming up on this and picking up the rock, then putting it back with the others.

There was a small black notebook, the kind he had in one of his cargo pockets, ready to write down random coordinates or notes. He scowled as he picked it up. He didn't want to find Dani's suicide note. Didn't want to read how he'd failed her.

He flipped it open anyway.

Poems.

Page after page of poems written in a neat geometric handwriting.

The words he was skimming over were dark, depressed, soul searching. He put it back where he'd found it.

With a gesture to signal Valor she was to remain

in the cave in a down stay, Trip walked to the barrier and stepped over.

The wind whipped up the wall, making his clothes billow and flap like they had when he was jumping out of the plane this morning.

This morning?

Hard to believe he was living that same day.

He came to his knees, then flattened onto his stomach. With his binoculars, Trip searched the length of the cliff, across each scrub of tree, each jutting lip of dirt, all the way to the bottom.

He took in a breath, held it, then forced himself to rework the area.

Dani had been wearing various shades of gray. Not even a fleck of color. She could be blending, especially if she got hung up in an odd angle.

Crawling backward away from the cliff's edge, Trip stood and made his way back to the cave where he could get out of the wind and hopefully hear better as he called in his findings to Command.

Radio chatter had been almost non-existent. Every once in a while, one of his Cerberus teammates had called in the successful completion of some point on their tasking sheet. Other than that, nada.

Ridge had said that Zeus was taking a mini break. He'd followed the trail to three spots where tracks showed multiple people. If it was that team or not, they'd have to trust Zeus's nose. Ridge said it looked like they were meandering but keeping close to various trails. It was just hard to tell which order they took those trails. No clues were solid enough that he wanted to move resources in his direction.

It didn't bode well for Berlin Tracy and her missing

camera crew. The longer the searchers were out, the farther away from the lodge they moved, the harder it would be to get people—untrained in dangerous conditions and possibly without the physical stamina to handle the distance—down the mountain at the speed that would be required to beat the storm.

Pressed into the cave's opening next to Valor, Trip toggled his radio. "Tripwire for TOC."

"Go for TOC."

"Tripwire. I'm back at Hermit's Cave. Dani is no longer at this location. I've done a visual sweep of the cliff's side. There is no sign of Dani Addams below my location."

"Bob. Copy. What's that area look like?"

"I can tell you that if…" And he stopped. He couldn't bring himself to say the words aloud. "If Dani jumped…" He coughed, then said, "If anyone were going over this cliffside, they wouldn't fall to the roadway. No sense in sending a vehicle down the road. There's a wide ledge. At this point, I'd say ten meters wide. Guessing, it looks about four stories from my elevation down to that ledge." He pulled the plastic case around to read the topographical rings. "Looking at my topo map, that's true wrapping from the cabin about three-quarters of the way back to the lodge. Over."

"Bob. No note? The backpack is gone?"

"Tripwire. The backpack *is* gone. Inside the cave I saw a small altar-like structure, a burned candle, and colored stones. There's a small notebook with poetry. Flipping through, I didn't see a page that looked like a goodbye letter and no page that included a signature. I can't identify this as belonging to Dani." He stalled on calling her Dani Addams. In this moment, it felt too distancing and unemotional.

Using a whole name was the way they referred to search subjects at Iniquus. Emotional distance was supposed to allow team members to operate in a pragmatic, clear-headed way. But he'd held Dani's hand, looked into her eyes, *felt* the chemistry. "I never saw the notebook in her hand. It could have been left by someone else. The cave is deep enough to protect the inside, where the altar is placed, from the elements."

"Bob. What do you propose for next actions?"

"Tripwire. Based on what I'm seeing here, my guess is that Dani followed through on the decisions she made to take the cliff-side path down. The wind is hitting the cliff and there are some serious intermittent gusts. There is the off chance that jogging beside the cliff worried her, and she headed toward the interior loop of the Hermit's Cave trail. The trail she ascended to this site. She might have felt more secure there because it had some familiarity and perhaps some protection from the wind. My proposed next action would be to put Valor's nose on the ground and follow the path. Hopefully, I can catch up to Dani and accompany her to the lodge safely."

"Bob. Copy. Standby for instruction."

Standing by wasn't at all what Trip wanted, but he said, "Tripwire. Standing by."

While he waited, Trip turned his attention to Valor. She had her nose in the air sniffing deeply. Dani's scent must still be in here.

Just to see what happened next, Trip said, "Valor, find Dani. Search."

Valor scuffled up and rolled herself out of the cave past Trip to the pad of land jutting out of the pathway.

Her nose went to the ground, and she headed back toward the track Dani had taken up to the trail end.

Before Trip could call her back, Valor turned and retraced her steps. Her nose was hard at work, snuffling the ground. The scent still detectable despite the gusts. Valor sniffed the cave then followed the track over to the railing that protected sightseers from tumbling down accidently.

Her nose traced down to the center. Her tail stood in a high flag, which told Trip she was on the scent.

Trip's stomach dropped.

"There? There on the ledge?"

Valor sat. Her signal that yes, Dani had put her hands on the rail.

Was Dani looking over at the beauty of the valley, or had she put her hands there to climb over and end it?

Trip was aware that the wishful-thinking and processing part of his brain might have faltered while he was doing his binocular search.

It was possible.

He was human.

Even now, he could readily admit he had no desire to find Dani's body lying below.

He shrugged off his pack and dug out his FLIR camera. This device helped their team pick up heat signatures in hard to reach areas. Instead of climbing through thick briars or into an earthquake toppled building, they could reliably use the cameras to check the space for heat in the shape of a human being.

If Dani had jumped—*God, that thought!* If she had gone over the cliff's edge, her body would still be warm. He closed his eyes and expelled the air from his lungs. He desperately didn't want to have been the last person to have spoken to her. The last person to have had a chance to make a difference and to have just walked away when his dog was acting all kinds of weird and protective of her.

Trip remembered listening to a podcast about a guy who had worked at a suicide call center. He said that it was mostly slow working there, and he did a lot of reading. People who called in wanted to talk. On occasion, he'd been given permission to reach out to a family member to go over and help the person get to the hospital. One night, he got a call from a girl. A twenty-something graduate student. He did his job, which was to listen. The girl had been interesting, clever, and on an otherwise boring night, the call made the time pass quickly. After some time, it sounded like she might have been drinking alcohol. His gut reaction was that she'd been feeling lonely, didn't want to drink alone... They talked for well over an hour. Lightly flirting. But her slurring had gotten worse. And worse. And then she'd said the thing that is the number one tell for someone who has decided to die by suicide. She said, "I just can't deal with the pain anymore."

Trip remembered that podcast like it was yesterday.

The guy working at the suicide prevention call center had asked her the next thing in a script of things they could and could not say. "Are you thinking of causing yourself harm?"

"Yes, that's why I called you," she'd said.

"Did you already do something that would cause you harm?" Even as he repeated his words years later, his voice quivered with emotion.

"Yes." Her voice was becoming difficult to understand.

"Please, tell me what you've done." He continued down the script on his computer, typing in her words as he heard them. Now that she'd said the danger close words, the guy pressed the key that would record their interaction. His supervisors would want to hear if what she said and what he heard were the same thing. They often weren't. Brains were nuts like that.

The guy had described how sweaty his palms were. How hard it was to breathe. How his foot jackhammered the floor and his scalp prickled at his failure to read the situation.

The grad student gave him the name and number of pills and the amount of alcohol she'd knocked back before she'd called. She knew she was going to die; she just didn't want to die alone.

The case worker had looked up the combination in his computer program. "That's not compatible with survival."

She said nothing.

"Could I please send help to you? Can I send a paramedic to your address?" When he asked, he could hardly get his words out, he was choking on his own saliva. His fear was palpable. He felt like he was losing a friend. They'd made a connection.

"Yes," she whispered. And that was the last thing she said to him. He sat on the phone with the line open until he heard sirens, heard the fire and paramedic bang on the door, move into the room.

Some guy came over the phone, "We've got her." And hung up.

And that was it.

Numb, the case worker went home.

HIPAA meant that her medical information couldn't be shared with him.

He did the thing he wasn't allowed to do. He knew her name, Sharon Amelia Glover, Sherry—Trip was surprised that he remembered the woman's full name.

The worker looked her up on Instagram.

And there he found all of the posts.

The condolences.

The grief.

Sherry had died.

The dude never went back to his job. Didn't call or anything, just never showed up.

He was haunted every day of his life. Questioned himself. Did he do the wrong thing? Did she die because of him? And he said that all he could do was to keep repeating the mantra, "There's nothing I can do about it now." It was the only thing that helped to keep him sane.

Valor barked, startling Trip.

Tripwire realized he was lying there, holding the FLIR camera, not looking. He was deep down in his bones terrified that he had been the last person to have talked to Dani. That he would be in that podcast guy's shoes, haunted by his choices.

He extended the camera out and pressed the buttons.

"Valor, is Dani down the cliff?" he asked as he carefully moved the camera inch by inch over the possible fall areas, focusing on the screen, looking for a change in temperature value.

Valor barked three times and took off down the trail. Came back, barked three times and took off again.

"Valor, down. Stay," he commanded.

He reached for his radio when he heard, "Clear the net. Clear the net. Clear the net." It was the signal that all non-emergency radio traffic needed to cease. Trip pulled out his notebook and pencil ready to write down the coordinates.

"Go for TOC."

"Ridge. Subjects found with injuries. I am Ridge, plus fourteen, plus K9 Zeus." He read out his coordinates, and Trip found them on his map. They were miles away from his location on the far side of the lodge where a stream carried water from the ridge to the valley below. It would be swollen with all of the rain they'd been getting.

"TOC. Copy. Status report."

"Ridge. The group was descending a bank without rappelling gear while carrying their equipment. They were unable to negotiate the steep incline. Injuries sustained. The wounded can walk out with significant support. Technical ropes required to get the subjects back up to the trail for exfil."

"How many support team members do you need?"

"Given the time and injuries to legs and ankles, I'm requesting all available to location. Over."

"TOC to Ridge. I will be rerouting teams to your location. Over and out."

Trip felt cold wash over him. He needed to find out if Dani was okay. He didn't want to be part of that rescue team.

"TOC for Tripwire."

"Go for Tripwire." Trip clenched his teeth.

"TOC. Proceed to lodge via eastern cliff trail to see if you can't locate Dani Addams. We need you pressing hard. The clock is ticking. That route is much longer than the trail coming back from Eagle's Nest. You're going to be racing that trail to beat the storm. Over."

"Copy. Over and Out."

Permission granted. That was a weight off his chest. "Valor."

She stood, body held rigid with excitement, knowing she was going to get a work command.

"Find Dani. Search."

Bob told him to push hard, and he would, but not for his safety.

He had to catch up to Dani and make sure she made it back alive.

# Chapter 16

## Dani

She was pinned. Trapped. The dirt and dust of Afghanistan filled her nostrils, her mouth, and throat. Her lungs.

Dani flexed her hand. There was no dog collar. She panicked and reached, patted, coughed, and screamed out, "Daisey!"

It took her long minutes before she realized she wasn't under the vehicle at her base. That had been months ago.

Lei Ming was dead. Daisey was dead.

*What's happening?*

Dani pressed her palms into the ground, pushing herself up. She didn't budge. Something incredibly heavy pressed onto her back.

She tried to shift her weight to the side, fighting for relief from the pain stabbing into her right hip. But that just made things worse.

She stilled. Breathed.

Ice pelted her face as she tipped her head back trying to understand what had happened.

Dani rested her cheek on the ground, closed her eyes, and tried to remember what had occurred moments before. She had been jogging, thinking about her promise to Lei Ming. She'd planted her stick. It kept sliding in, and Dani had leaned on it with her weight and momentum, trying to catch her balance as she'd stumbled forward.

Then the fall.

She was in Virginia in the woods around Wild Mountain Lodge.

There was a massive storm heading her way.

Dani reoriented herself to the problem at hand.

When an injured K9 arrived in her surgical center, it was almost always with an overwhelming, catastrophic set of injuries. The only way forward was to evaluate the situation, pick a place, and start.

Dani assessed her present situation: She was pinned. There was a bomb cyclone.

And unless Dani could figure some way out of this mess, she'd come here to die.

Pushing against the weight on top of her was getting her nowhere.

She had to figure out what the problem was to solve it.

How could she get out from under the landslide?

Her fingers flexed against the surface, feeling the soil and rocks. She turned her head to the left and tipped it back as far as possible. There was a line of demarcation, brown then muddled gray.

Dirt then what? Sky?

She turned and tipped in the other direction. Brown then gray. A different shade of gray. A solid gray.

"Okay. Situation," she said aloud to focus herself. "I'm most probably lying on a ledge with cliff below. Cliff above. No equipment and a bomb cyclone heading my way. Alone. And no communications."

She tried to drag herself forward but, no. She was pinned in place.

"The Iniquus search team is on the mountain combing the trails, not for me, but someone might stumble by," she encouraged herself.

She blew out forcefully through her nose, hoping to clear her nostrils of the tickling debris. It made her sneeze, and that sneeze crunched her lungs against whatever had her wedged so tightly.

It wasn't true that they'd stumble by. Tripwire and Valor were working the trails from this far-east edge, clearing toward the west. He said he was going to check Eagle's Nest, then he'd run that trail to the lodge. Dani had looked at that trail; it was well west of here.

The team members must be spread out, searching their task areas all along the mountain ridge.

It was quite a system that the lodge had built up and maintained over the decades. It was one of their biggest calling cards on the website that Dani had looked through yesterday after she'd reached her mom's house.

Wow, that was yesterday?

It seemed like so much life had been lived in such a short period of time.

Dani tried flexing at her ankle. That too was a no.

She had sensation in her feet and hands. She could wiggle her toes and fingers. It gave her hope that she didn't have a major spinal injury.

It made her less worried that she couldn't bend her legs at the knee. The weight was too heavy, she told herself. That incapability wasn't because she was paralyzed.

Pinned, just like at the crash. That had taken a team of rescuers to get her free. And she was the last one they worked on. First, they rescued Tiana, who was bleeding profusely, and then Lei Ming. Since Dani was the only one conscious, the soldiers had left her for later.

From where she lay under the wreckage, there had been boots. Lots of boots and dust. Lots of yelling.

Lots.

And here, nothing. She was her only hope.

Okay.

Alone but not forgotten. Her name *was* on the Iniquus list. Tripwire had radioed her position into the TOC, and her trail had been identified. If it weren't for that, she might have tried to cut across and get on her earlier trail.

Pro, it was farther away from the wind.

Con, there were trees crashing down.

Pro, she wouldn't have been on the side of a cliff that gave way.

Con, if this happened over there—a rockslide or a downed tree—it would take a lot longer for them to find her.

Granted, dogs have great noses, but the wind was crazy.

They'd have her name on the board, she clung to that

thought like a lifeline. Iniquus expected her to blow through the doors about the same time as the storm pounded into the mountain.

They'd know she was out here somewhere between the cave and the lodge. They'd know what trail she was on. The rocks and dirt on top of her might be thick enough to shield her from the wind and insulate her from the cold. She could probably get her mouth to her water tube. If she was careful, it should be enough to drink for several days. Tiana had made her fill the reservoir all the way up.

Wait. Tripwire said they expected forty-two inches of snow.

She'd be buried alive.

People could survive under avalanche snow, there was air between the flakes. But not for long. Forty minutes or more and the survival rate was nearly zero. Best shot was having a dog snuffle your scent and dig with their paws until they got you free.

And that was a fifteen-minute window.

Dani knew this from her veterinary work she'd conducted with a military mush team, competing in Alaska. Dani remembered the specialized clothing they all used to prevent frostbite.

She remembered the pain and the fatigue of being out in that kind of cold for long periods of time. The sled team trained in those temperatures. Dani was stationed at Lackland Air Force Base in San Antonio, Texas, and deployed to the Middle East and once to Africa. Those were temperature extremes that lay on opposite ends of the continuum.

And that's where she had been three days ago, Afghanistan—not horrible, the temperatures were in the forties just like they had been here this morning.

While Dani kept pushing those kinds of mundane non-threatening thoughts forward in her consciousness, she worked to get her arms free. Pressing her hands out, she moved an inch. Bending her elbow, she retracted an inch. Thrusting out, she got another half inch, retracting, pushing, retracting, pushing...inch by inch, Dani worked to develop a tunnel for her arms to move free. With that, if nothing else, she could brush away the snow accumulation.

She was grateful for her ball cap tightly cinched under the parka hood. It had protected her face and head as far as she could tell. And would help when the precipitation came down in earnest.

Hey, maybe the bomb cyclone winds would whip the debris off and free her.

But say she was free; how would she get off the cliff's ledge?

*One crisis at a time.* She coughed hard, gathered saliva in her mouth, washed it around and tried to spit out the grit that had packed into her teeth and gums.

The wind blew it back at her face.

"That was damned stupid. You've got to stop with the stupid. You're trapped. Think!"

Ever since the accident, small spaces, and the idea that she couldn't get out, had freaked Dani out. A newly introduced claustrophobia.

Panic rose in her throat, and she dropped her mouth open, screaming. She heard it like an observer at a play. *Look at her screaming her head off in this wind. No one's out here. That's a stupid way to use your voice and your energy.*

*Dani, you should listen to that inner voice and shut up.*

She clamped her teeth together, extinguishing the last note.

"It's unfair, you know, Daisey," she said as she rotated her shoulders, working to develop more space for her lungs to expand. "If I was going to die trapped, why couldn't I have died with you and Lei Ming. I had a couple extra months of life, but was it worth it? All this pain and heart agony, what was the purpose?"

The pressure on her back was unsupportable. Her spine was like a dry stick ready to snap. She turned her head this way and that, trying to relieve the pain.

Dani stopped, laying her head down, panting.

As she stilled, Dani sensed Daisey there with her. She smelled Daisey's warm breath on her face.

Dani refused to open her eyes and see that it was a hallucination.

She was remembering being out at a state park, Dani threw the Frisbee, and Daisey raced and leaped with joy, caught it between her teeth, and paraded back to hand it to Dani. Daisey had been completely full of herself, fully embracing the magnificent beast that she was.

They had been visiting with some friends in Texas. The dad had taken the kids to the pool and while Dani was throwing the Frisbee, she could hear the kids playing, happily calling "Marco!"

"Polo!" and the lifeguard's whistle seemed to blow without cease.

Her hurricane whistles!

Dani twisted to see if she could get her mouth onto one of the whistles she had attached to the loops on her pack straps.

She blew loud and long, grateful that these hurricane whistles had a pitch designed to cut through raging winds.

Dani stopped, breathless. Was anyone even within hearing distance?

"Daisey, baby. I need your help. Can you go and talk to Valor? She's the German shepherd who was with me earlier. Can you tell her that I need help? She's searching for people. And I'm not in her scent cone down here... But Valor and Tripwire are pretty much my only hope right now. Can you go get Valor for me? Please?" She drew in a painful breath. "Daisey, I'm depending on you. Get Valor. Get her here quick!"

# Chapter 17

*Trip*

Valor moved off the trail to a boulder just past the tree line. She spent time sniffing a low spot. The right height for someone to sit and catch their breath.

Tripwire scanned the woods for movement, wishing that Dani had been wearing blaze orange or bright blue, something that would make her stand out against the landscape. He squatted to examine the ground. The damp soil was a perfect track trap, a place where shoe prints were easy to read. She'd been here.

No telling how long ago.

Man, he hoped that Dani had stayed on the cliff trail and hadn't decided at this point to cut across to the other side of the cave loop.

He pulled Valor's collapsible water bowl from a side

pocket on his pack and filled it with the water reservoir's hose.

Valor's tongue hung long as she panted.

Trip had to order her to drink. She didn't like to eat or drink or rest when she was on the scent. All she wanted to do was track the subject.

It was up to Tripwire to manage her wellbeing.

He unwrapped a protein bar and munched it down while he studied his topo map. It was the same one Dani had in the map bag attached to her pack strap. He checked his GPS coordinates then found his location on the inner loop trail. He and Valor had made good time getting here. He was pleased. With that anyway.

He was unhappy that Dani might have left this path to be trouncing through the woods off trail. That's how people became disoriented and lost.

Trip hadn't seen any navigation equipment with her. It might have been stored in her pack. Still, it would be a time-consuming mistake to have rerouted.

He focused on the elevation lines traced in red on his map. Yeah, if he was going to attempt to change trails, this would be the place. It was in a saddle of land with a constant altitude. No ups and downs in the terrain was always easier on a body.

The radio chatter was picking up. Another team announced their arrival to the injured subjects' coordinates.

Ridge had been triaging the group, calling in their names, vitals, and injuries. One of them sounded like they'd need to be packed out.

When there was a break in traffic, Trip called in his coordinates and his concerns about Dani's track. He let TOC know that he and Valor were regrouping, so Bob and Noah would understand why their GPS markers weren't in motion for several minutes.

While Iniquus searchers called in their GPS coordinates, it was to verify that their numbers lined up with the computer readouts. He and Valor were moving white symbols sliding across the map on a computer screen back at the field base. All the dogs and searchers had GPS tracking units on them. But Murphy's Law meant you had to plan for malfunctions.

"TOC. If you veer off that cliff trail, I need you to call that in. Over."

"Tripwire. Wilco. Over and out."

Trip would give Valor another couple of minutes of rest, then he'd see what her nose told him about Dani's direction of travel.

Suddenly, Valor's body went rigid, her water bowl forgotten. Her ears were up, rotating, sweeping for a sound.

Valor's nose lifted into the wind, her head oscillated, searching the air.

Tripwire let her work.

Valor pinned her eyes toward the trail. She was all ears, now.

Reading her body language, Valor had locked on to something significant.

"Search," Trip commanded, scooping up her bowl, dumping the water and thrusting it into his pack in one fluid movement.

Valor raced down the trail.

There was no way Tripwire could keep up with her. No way. When she locked on, she was a fur rocket.

Valor had been trained to work off lead. Sometimes, she wore a camera that fed back to Trip's phone. On some assignments, she wore a communications collar, so Trip could hear what was happening around Valor. That equipment was especially helpful if she had to crawl into a tight space in a collapsed building, finding folks who were pinned underneath the rubble. With that device, Trip could talk to the person, assess them, reassure them, and command Valor. Today, though, given that their task was to run a "hasty" down known trails, the teams had left the extra weight in their vehicles.

The only safety mechanism that Trip deployed today was the GPS tracker on her collar.

As long as the storm ceiling stayed high enough, and he maintained a radio frequency, Trip would be able to find Valor.

Tripwire ran a steady pace. With the wind carrying sounds with it, Valor could be picking up something from very far away.

He was right to have made that decision.

It was a good half hour later that Trip heard Valor's three sharp barks in the distance.

After Valor's first real-world find, where she'd trotted out of the woods dangling the toddler by the seat of the pants, Tripwire had needed to figure out how best to handle those situations.

Each dog had their own personality. Some dogs you could train to come back, alert the find, and guide the handler to the lost person.

Not Mama, and Trip knew that.

Typically, yes. If she found human remains, or an adult who was medically stable, Valor would give them a swipe of the tongue then haul ass back to Trip where she'd sit and wave her paw, while her tail thumped the ground. That was her "find" signal.

Trip would command, "Lead." This meant that Trip would follow her, but she had to make sure she kept to a pace that Trip could match.

But if Valor came up on a subject that was a child or who was severely ill or injured, she *refused* to leave them.

On searches where there was a high likelihood of an adult being in bad shape and every time they were searching for a child, Valor wore a camera and communications equipment on her vest.

Under such circumstances, Trip trained Valor to send up a distress call of three sharp barks. Wait five minutes, then bark again.

It was the same three sharp barks signal that Valor had sounded at Hermit's Cave.

At the cave, he hadn't been that far behind her, Trip had easily followed her distress call to the overlook.

In hindsight, Trip reinterpreted that scene. Valor had barked this morning when she found Dani. She had crawled into Dani's lap and was giving Dani a full body hug.

Valor would not leave Dani when Trip issued a command.

Why hadn't he figured it out? It was so obvious what had happened now that Bob had told him about the concerns for her mental health.

At the time, Tripwire saw zero signs that there was anything amiss. He still wasn't convinced. Dani had been too responsive toward him. He thought he'd seen something in her eyes and felt something when their hands touched. They'd shaken hands and not released. It wasn't like she was clinging to his hand; it was a relaxed, friendly, almost familiar moment.

He felt at home with her.

He thought—hoped—she might be experiencing the same tingle of interest. The same chemistry of attraction. The same sense of…the only word he could come up with was belonging. But, man, thoughts like that had never been part of Trip's life.

If he were right about the chemistry that seemed to dance between them, that would mean Dani was engaged in life. "You don't get a sizzle when you're despondent," he muttered under his breath.

That was Trip's experience anyway. He'd gone through it. It was still fresh, that bleak time when he got sick with a stupid dustborne fungal infection that screwed up his life.

It was ironic as hell that it wasn't a bullet or bomb that took him out of the game, but a microscopic enemy that he'd breathed in.

Trip was told that not only was his illness taking him off his SEAL team for good, but that his K9, Rory, had been reassigned to Delta Force. Rory was the dog of Trip's heart. They were tightly bonded. *Tight*. Then his hospitalization…

Yeah, those were dark days.

There was this cute little nurse who had been flirty and offered her phone number. She'd been exactly his type, too—a curvy girl, brown hair with soft natural curls, a full kissable mouth, intelligent caring eyes… Trip realized he was describing Dani.

But with Dani, he'd come vibrantly awake, aware.

By contrast, he'd felt nothing for the nurse during that dark time. Her smiles intruded on his grief. Her chatter had been sandpaper across his psyche. He just didn't want to deal with her.

If he was comparing himself when he'd felt his darkest to what he'd experienced with Dani...yeah, it was hard to believe Dani was despondent. That she'd meant to harm herself.

His buddy Tony's wife hadn't thought anything was wrong, and Marybeth had known him best.

The guy from the podcast who was a professional at dealing with people who were suicidal missed the clues, too.

He had just met Dani. He knew nothing about her except that somehow in a very short space of time, she'd wiggled her way into his system. He had to get to her and make sure she got back to the lodge safe and sound.

His radio broke squelch.

"TOC for Tripwire."

He reached up to press the radio button. "Go for Trip."

"TOC. We're getting a GPS signal from Valor. She's been stationary for five minutes."

"Tripwire. Copy. Are her coordinates on my trail?"

"TOC. Affirmative. When you get to Valor, call it in. Over."

"Tripwire. Wilco. Over and out."

Tripwire picked up the pace, running full tilt down the trail.

He heard it, three barks. Even at this distance, they sounded frantic.

"Please be Dani," he said on an exhale. "Please be all right."

* * *

When Tripwire got Valor in his view, his stomach dropped.

Valor's paws were on the edge of the cliff, leaning out. Her body trembled. She'd bark the way she was taught and wait five minutes to bark again. She'd done it correctly the entire time it took Trip to reach her.

*Man, no matter what, when we get back to civilization, two big juicy steaks, Valor.*

When he thought that, Valor looked his way. She stomped her paw impatiently and barked right at him.

Now, Trip was close enough to see a chunk of the trail was missing.

He was unbuckling his pack as he ran and dropped it to the ground when he came parallel. Trip worried that the ground where Valor was standing would go too. "Valor, back."

Valor turned her head and barked at him, ignoring his command. It had to be Dani down there. Valor never ignored a command.

"I know. I'm here. I'll help her. Back!"

He kept his attention lightly on Valor to make sure she'd comply as he dumped his gear from his pack. Grabbing up his rappel harness, he picked through his rappelling anchors to find one that would slip into the cracks of a nearby outcropping of rock. Clipping a carabiner through the anchor loop, Trip attached a rope to that and then to him.

The first rule of rescue was not to become part of the problem. Trip needed to make sure that if more ground gave way, he wasn't down the side of a cliff with no way to get back up.

On his belly, dispersing his weight, he slithered toward the edge.

If Dani was down there, if she'd survived the fall, he didn't want to send any more rocks tumbling on to her.

He peered over the edge.

There was a ledge jutting out of the cliff, about six meters below. There was a pile of rubble that had been part of the path. If Dani was alive, it was only because this lip existed. The apron below that was a long way down. It would have been unsurvivable.

Trip didn't see Dani.

Balancing on his elbows, he brought his binoculars up and adjusted the focus.

Valor belly crawled up beside him, draping her paws over the edge. Her head hung; her tongue lolled out. Valor chomped at the air, then she sent out three sharp barks as she looked at the earth that had once been a trail.

Trip didn't see any limbs. Even with the binoculars, he still didn't see any part of Dani.

She had to be down there. Tripwire trusted his dog.

What if she was under all of that? She'd have suffocated. There was little chance she was alive.

When he scooted backward, Valor did the same. Trip signaled Valor over to the rocks and put her in a down stay. He needed to be hard focused, and he couldn't have Valor's safety distracting him.

Reading Valor's tight muscles and anxious eyes, that was Dani down there. There was something about her that had a strange effect on his dog.

Trip's hand moved over his equipment until he landed on the FLIR camera.

Valor saw it and barked her approval. She was no

longer alerting to the subject; she knew Trip was in rescue mode.

Valor stopped, her ears up with attention.

Trip heard it, three soft, high-pitched whistles coming from below.

Trip cupped his hands around his mouth. "Dani! We're here. We've got you. Hold on! I'm coming!"

# Chapter 18

*Trip*

"Clear the net. Clear the net. Clear the net."

"Go for TOC."

"Tripwire. We have a bit of a problem out here."

"TOC. Coordinates and sitrep."

Tripwire read the GPS coordinates to Bob. With his brain racing, searching for options and best practices in this situation, Trip caught Bob up with what he had seen below.

"TOC. And you heard her blow the whistle? She's alive. We go from there. I need you down with her getting a clear idea of what we're dealing with. All other Iniquus operators are actively engaged in rescue efforts. Local authorities are actively involved with the area residents. As you look over the situation, keep in mind, for the time being, you are the only one available. I'm going to work with Noah, to get the newest weather information and come up with solutions, so we're out in front with recommendations when you radio in."

"Trip. Copy."

"TOC. Trip, this is hard to say, brother, and it's going to be even harder for you to hear. Be prepared. I may have to order you back to the lodge without performing a rescue."

Trip failed to respond. How could he? Leave Dani out here to die? *Hell* no.

"TOC. I need to hear that you will comply. I will only order you back if there are no other solutions. It all depends on what you find when you get down to her. How badly she's hurt. If you can get her freed up. Walking wounded is a very different scenario from someone who needs a medivac helo to a trauma hospital."

Trip would *not* say Wilco. "Trip. I'd better get down there then. Over and out."

Catching up his helmet from where it lay on the ground, and strapping it into place, Trip looked down at Valor. "Any other rescue, and I would trust you in that down stay. This woman is throwing you off your training." He glanced at the tree. "If I tied you here, and I got snagged up somehow, that could put you in danger once the storm hits. I'd never do that." He grabbed two locking carabiners and attached them to the D rings on Valor's search and rescue vest.

The vest was constructed to be lightweight and breathable, protective as Valor ran through dangerous environments, keeping anything from stabbing into her, be it a sharp stick or a bad guy's knife. It was also designed so the handler could attach the dog to his pack for climbs and descents. It was very similar to the rigging Hugo was in that morning during the wind catastrophe that slammed Pierre into the plane's wing.

*This storm is the shit gift that keeps on giving.*

He pushed his concern for Pierre to the back of his mind. Pierre was being helped by the best trauma professionals to be had. Trip needed to focus here on being the best at rescue.

"Hell of a day." Trip kept his tone even. No stress. He needed his brain to be clear thinking. You show up, and you work the problem in front of you.

This was a day on the job.

It didn't really feel that way to Trip. This felt personal in a way he'd never experienced before. It worried him. Personal made for mistakes. He needed to be in his head, thinking, tactically accurate.

Too much was at stake.

Valor wagged her whole body with excitement when she saw the rope bag in his hand. She gave him a yip of agreement; that's what she wanted to have happen.

Valor loved rappelling. But Trip could tell from the rigidity of her muscles and the vigilant twitch of her ears, she also wanted to be with Dani. "You and me both, Little Mama. It's going to take me a second to get us set up. We don't need to add stupid to the day."

Valor lay down as if she understood and was willing to wait patiently.

The one anchor he'd attached in the rock was fine for crawling up to the edge of the cliff, but if he was going to add his full body weight plus Valor's body weight, and possibly Dani's body weight, he had better make sure he had redundancy. If this boulder was to give as had been the case all over this ridge today, then something else needed to keep them from plummeting. From the situation with the crew down in the creek, to the path seeming to disintegrate under Dani's weight, Trip didn't trust the terrain.

He stalked to a separate outcropping, found a crack and tested the rocks for movement. He slid an anchor in. Sometimes called a chock, the anchors were shaped like pyramids, wide at the base and becoming narrower toward the O ring. When he angled the wedge into a crack, the width of the base caught and held the load.

Trip walked back to a third boulder and placed another anchor. *Three times the charm.*

From his pack, he picked out his rappelling line. The length would give him options to select the best route off the ledge, be it up to the lodge trail, again, or be it down to the apron below. Measuring off his map, that apron looked about ten yards wide at this location. It might be the best place for them to wait for his team to pick them off the side of the mountain. It might be the way that he could get gear up from below—a gurney and backboard.

It all depended on how badly Dani was injured. And that all depended on how she took that ride down to the ledge.

Man, that was a long way to fall. As he prepped his ropes, Trip sorted through his biggest concerns. He could deal with broken or crushed limbs. Damage to the vertebral column was a big worry. Head injuries. Internal bleeding. For those issues, she'd need a trauma doctor just like Bob had said over the radio.

And while they had been able to pack Pierre up and

send him off in a helo, that simply wasn't an option anymore today.

Time was against them.

He couldn't see a way to beat the bomb cyclone back to the lodge. Both Dani and Valor were depending on Trip's right actions.

Sliding the end of his rope through the O ring on his first anchor, then tracing the figure eight knot back through the loops, Trip pulled a quick backup knot at the end to prevent the figure eight from slipping. He yanked on it to check that all was secure.

Moving with practiced dexterity, he connected in the other two anchors with clove hitches.

Trip gathered his supplies into his pack. "Ready to go, Valor?" He threw his pack straps over his shoulders and strapped them down tight as he maneuvered over to Valor.

Squatting, Trip hooked her into his harness. Trip looked over his shoulder at her expectant face. "Ready to go for a ride? Go save Dani?"

Valor gave a sharp bark of impatience.

Dropping over the side of the cliff with gale force winds sliding up the sheer side was going to be a trick.

He didn't like the way the trees lay almost to the ground then popped up between gusts. He especially didn't like the instability of the trail.

He called out, "I'm coming, Dani, hold on."

Trip had been on many a search mission where he was working as a solo team with his K9 partner, but he was on his own in the rescue mission and that made everything exponentially more dangerous.

He attached his belay device. Left hand forward,

right hand in a fist at his low back, he took a few tentative steps backward. "Here we go, Mama."

Valor dangled off the ground, her weight pulling at his hips. As a team, they were much more practiced at this than they had been with Valor hanging on Trip's front skydiving this morning. He twisted his head to check on her. This was the first time she'd been off the ground since he'd played rocket man on his high-speed chase to save Pierre.

To be honest, Trip had been concerned about how that first jump was going to affect Valor's training, and if she'd developed a fear, if he would be able to build trust again.

Valor's ability to stay with Iniquus's tactical search and rescue team was dependent on Valor's ability to go everywhere Trip wanted to go and perform every task Trip was asked to perform.

If Valor balked at doing the job, if she didn't think it was fun, he'd have to hand her off to another Iniquus search operator. Trip would be training a new K9 for the job.

Going over this cliff was a huge deal.

Trip found himself holding his breath.

He stepped to the edge, his heels hanging over the void, his toes holding his weight. "Ready, Mama?" He kept his tone in that neutral calm zone.

Just like on that plane this morning, when he was relaxed, she was relaxed. Those other K9s were having stress reactions because their handlers were freaking out.

Slow and steady. Cool as a cucumber, Trip leaned straight back.

He kept a vigilant eye on Valor.

Valor seemed okay. She looked her normal relaxed self. She wasn't pedaled or yawning. Trip had an inkling that Valor wanted to get to Dani and knew this was her only route down.

"Dani, hang tight. Valor and I are coming to you now."

With his right hand out from his body, Trip walked the cliff wall down to the ledge. He was wary of its ability to hold their weight.

But sometimes, you just had to trust in fate.

# Chapter 19

*Trip*

Trip wasn't sure how he was going to manage the scene.

"Dani, I'm here. I'm here with you. Can you speak?"

"Yes." It wasn't as strong a response as he'd hoped, barely audible.

"Outstanding." He knelt and unhooked Valor from his harness. "Give me a second to get out of my rigging."

"Okay." Her voice wavered like someone on the edge of consciousness.

He couldn't see her. But her head must be toward the other edge of the shelf. If she was actually under those rocks, it was a miracle that she could get enough oxygen into her lungs to speak at all. Trip worked at his pack clasps. Catching Valor's gaze, he signaled her into a down stay, whispering, "Mama, you have to let me do my job. Do you understand?" He rested his pack up against the wall where his gear should be safe.

Valor lifted her lip like she was going to growl at him, her eyes were both anxious and commanding. Trip had never seen her this way before and was trying to read these new signals. Was this fear from coming down the cliff side after this morning's FUBAR jump training or was this about Dani?

Valor stomped her foot impatiently looking from the debris pile to Trip and back again to the debris pile.

Okay, this was about Dani.

That was good news. Trip would take a win where he could find it. Valor was fine with the rappel, and Dani was alive and talking. So far so good.

He needed to go about this methodically.

First step, Trip needed Valor under control. This shelf was entirely too narrow for mistakes. "If I can't trust you to stay out of my way, I'm going to have to take you down to the apron below us and climb back up. That will slow my helping Dani. Don't do that."

Valor climbed the debris to the cliff wall where Trip had leaned his pack and lay next to it, curling into a tight ball and pulling her tail over her head, protecting it from the wind.

"Thanks, Valor. Stay."

Now, was the moment of truth. Could he get Dani free and to safety all by himself? And could he do it before the storm reached them?

Trip's gaze studied the debris pile as he rounded toward where he'd heard Dani's voice.

*There she is.*

Her tear-streaked face was turned toward him, her head protected with a ball cap and cinched parka hood.

It looked like she'd been working to get her arms free. There were valleys of dirt and stones on either side of her hands.

Trip lay down so they were face to face.

In this wind, he didn't want her to have to use any more of her energy communicating with him than was necessary.

"Hey there. Valor told me you were down here. Curious place to come hang out with the storm coming in. I thought we'd decided you'd head to the lodge instead of camping out."

She smiled weakly. Her eyes closed against the dust that swirled with the air.

He reached for her wrist to find her pulse. It looked like she had been doing her best to shift the debris and get herself free. "Hey, Dani, do you remember me and my dog? What's my name?"

"Tripwire and Valor."

"Can you tell me where you are? What happened?" He watched the second hand tracing around the dial while he counted. Her pulse was rapid, weak, and thready. It could be something dangerous like internal bleeding. It could also be low blood pressure caused by the weight on top of her.

"I was jogging along, then I was flying through the air, and now I'm here."

"And here is…?"

"The Wild Mountain Lodge." She licked her lips. "What time is it?"

He checked his watch. "Three thirty."

"Is the storm still hitting at five?" She curled her

fingers into his pants' leg like she was afraid that he'd disappear.

"Last I heard from our weather guy, things weren't going to get really bad until a bit later than that. We have a little time to figure this situation out."

Dani had answered the next two questions in his assessment of her mental awareness on her own. Not only would her inability to answer clearly be a sign of traumatic shock, but it could also help him assess if Dani had sustained internal damage from the fall or the hits she took as the debris piled on top of her.

She moved her hold to the sleeve of his shirt and pulled on it. "Stop assessing me. You need to get back to the lodge. You still have time to get to safety. Go."

Movement pulled Trip's attention to Valor.

Valor was disobeying, again. But if she were to disobey, this was the perfect way to do it. She was on her belly, edging her way between the debris and the cliff wall. Valor crawled all the way up until she lay head to head with Dani then pushed her nose against Dani's hood.

Dani rocked her head back and turned to Valor to receive a vigorous tongue bath.

"Okay, that's enough, Valor. I need to check on Dani's wellbeing."

"Ha!" Dani laughed out as she turned back to him. Her right hand reaching into Valor's fur.

Trip thought her touching Valor would be good medicine. Stabilizing.

"Can you feel your fingers and toes?" he asked. "Have you tried wiggling them?"

"I can, and I have. Other than what you see with my

hands and head, I haven't made much progress getting myself out of this situation."

"You're doing great for having an unexpected flight." As he looked the situation over, it seemed that she must have slid down the side of the cliff and was now wedged between the cliff's wall and a rock outcropping. A sizable chunk of trail was balanced on a cliff ridge and that outcropping, like a tabletop. How much pushed into Dani, it was impossible to tell.

"I'm going to call this in, and we're going to come up with a solution."

"The solution, Tripwire," she said sternly, "is that you get Valor and get the heck down the mountain."

"I have to call this in." Trip reached down to where her hand was curled into the fabric of his sleeve and slid his hand into hers. He experienced the same tingle he had when they had met hours before at Hermit's Cave. He pressed into his forearm, so he could get himself into a squat without losing that contact.

Valor was watching him with a keen eye. When she saw him getting up, Valor made low throaty moaning noises.

"I've got her, Valor. I need you to give me a minute."

When there was a break in the radio traffic, Trip called in "Tripwire for TOC."

"Go for TOC."

"Trip. I'm with the subject. She's awake, alert, and oriented by four." He repeated the findings of her mental status as he looked up the cliff wall. "The trail gave way, and she fell approximately fifteen feet. She's trapped under the landslide. Her shoulders and above are clear of debris. From what assessments I can do right now, she doesn't seem to have taken a severe blow to the head. Her pupils are equal and reactive to light. She reports movement and sensation in her fingers and toes."

"TOC. When you say debris what are we talking here?"

Trip squeezed Dani's hand then released their hold. Shifting around, using his free hand to touch the various rocks. "Tripwire. Okay, she's lying prone. Her chest and abdomen seem to be protected by the way a boulder landed and is supported by surrounding rocks." He tried to thrust his hand between the bolder and her back but couldn't get his fingers in. "She's wedged in there tight. Her hips and legs are under about two feet of debris." Trip wished he could take a picture and send it on. But with no cell service, that option meant he couldn't get engineering feedback from Bob.

"TOC. Is there any way she could be dragged out the front? You said her head and arms are clear?"

"Tripwire. Affirmative. She has cleared her head and shoulders. She's a foot from the drop-off. I wouldn't be able to get enough leverage hanging from a line."

"TOC. And what about her legs? Could she go backward?"

Trip rounded to the other side of the lip to get a better look. He rested his hand on his head while he evaluated. "Tripwire. On this side I would have about six feet of working space. If I were to try to get her out going backward, I'd have to rig something to stabilize that boulder over her back." He let his finger off the radio button. "Dani, are you still wearing a day pack?"

"Yes," she whispered.

He compressed the button. "Trip. I was reaffirming with Dani. She's got her pack on. It wouldn't be a smooth tug, there are ways for her to get snagged up. I'm looking at this hunk of the path that's resting here. I don't want to make the structure unstable and have it collapse on her. It's too big for me to lift, and her head would be under there."

This situation needed a whole tactical rescue crew up here. If this storm was at all survivable, he'd advocate for just that and set up a shelter around her where they could wait it out.

This situation was just like a skydive when he'd decided his parachute wasn't going to deploy, once he cut away, his one shot at survival was the emergency chute. Trip would pull the toggle and pray things worked out.

"Trip. I don't see any other way. Getting her out the back is going to be the only thing I can do with the equipment I have on hand."

"TOC. Look over the lip of the ledge. You should see the apron ring that we were discussing earlier. How far down is it?"

"Tripwire. Standby." Trip was a little anxious about putting weight on the edge of this shelf. He didn't trust any of this to hold. He moved back to his rigging and reattached the lines dangling from the anchors far above his head.

He clipped in and waited to catch Valor's attention. Trip reminded Valor with a hand signal that she was in a down stay.

The lines tight in his hands, Trip backed toward the edge where he looked over his shoulder. He pressed the radio button with his chin. "Tripwire. I'd say that's a good twenty yards. I can see road below. I have enough line to get down to the apron. I do not. Repeat. I do *not* have enough line to get us anywhere near that road."

"TOC. Copy. Looking at your GPS coordinates and the distances, our recommendation is for you to go down instead of up and make your way to the cabin. We're told it's a sturdy structure that's maintained. There's a key under the mat. You have permission to access the structure and use what items you need until we can perform an extraction. Dani's condition will help us make that decision of when in the storm cycle that will be. Over."

Trip knew what Bob was saying without saying it. If Dani was stable, they wouldn't come until the weather had calmed. If she was in bad shape, they'd take bigger risks. Trip needed to get Dani out sooner rather than later. And, if he couldn't get her out in time, he'd be told to abandon her.

No *fucking* way he'd ever follow through with that order.

# *Chapter 20*

*Trip*

"Here's the plan, Dani," Trip called as he drew his folding shovel from his pack. "I'm going to dig you out from your feet to the boulder. This stuff back here looks like I can move it off you. Then we can assess the best means of getting you free." He thrust the shovel blade into the dirt, leaving it standing as he reached to get a sizable rock off the top of the pile and chuck it over the edge. "We'll come up with a strategy when I can see the structure and if you've sustained injuries."

"Okay... Tripwire?"

"Yup." He scooped up his first shovel of dirt working just beyond where he thought he'd find the soles of her boots. He was worried that she'd broken her ankles or legs in the fall. He'd want to get those splinted before the painkilling protection that adrenaline offered wore off.

"You can always leave and save yourself. Once it starts icing, this side of the mountain is going to melt away. I'm certain of it. My walking stick slid into the ground like a straw into a milkshake. Slid right on in. Best I can assess, it created a wedge, when I lost my balance it became a crowbar that broke off that part of the trail. If I hadn't used the walking sticks, just jogged along, I don't think this would have happened. But if that's what the ground is like… You're risking yourself and Valor being on this ledge with me."

Trip didn't respond, he focused on digging without slicing the shovel blade into her legs. He felt like there was an hourglass over his head pouring out time, moving the storm closer.

"Honestly," Dani whispered. "I'm appreciative. I'm hopeful. Thank you so much. But I'm not down with your dying beside me. First drop of rain, you need to be scrambling back up to solid land and—"

"And leave you here?"

"I'm not the kind of person who would want someone and their K9 to put their lives on the line for me. If I'm mostly out and pointed in the right direction. If you leave me a…some webbing, and you leave the line in place, you said it would reach down to the apron, right? Yeah, I can get to the cabin, and you can get to the lodge. When things clear up, you can send in the troops."

"You know that's not how things work."

Dani whispered, "I'm uncomfortable with the circumstances. Hero cloaks aside…"

"I can't even imagine how uncomfortable you are

right now." She wanted him to go back to the lodge and leave her. Trip could read that in one of two ways. That she was suicidal, and this was a longer death than jumping, but just as sure. Or that she was brave as hell and not willing to endanger someone else's life with the chance of saving her own.

He shoveled into the dirt, throwing it back over his shoulder.

At this angle, he didn't have a watchful eye on Dani. Even if it sucked at her reserves and taxed her oxygen levels, he needed her to be talking to him so he could keep tabs on her wellbeing. Her thready pulse had him worried. He didn't mention it to Bob because Dani had been listening. There was no sense in making matters worse by creating even more anxiety.

Bob knew this was life or death—for everyone. The entire Berlin Tracy group with their injuries, his teammates that were fighting to get them back to the lodge, Dani, and him. It was bad all over the mountain. They had to handle this like all the mass disasters they'd responded to: Work the problem in front of them, keep the bigger picture in their head.

He couldn't keep an eye on her and work. Trip needed to make sure he didn't move something that had a chain reaction, roll a stone onto her, and then not know that Dani was being crushed and suffocated while he kept at his work. Clearing out the back, then rounding back to her head to find she'd expired.

A chill dragged itself through his system. He shook it off. "My job is to dig. Your job is to talk to me."

"Just stream of consciousness stuff? You don't want that. Believe me. This is a dark day. All my thoughts are poison to my system. I'll tell you what, let's talk about dogs. You're on a search team. Does each member handle a dog?"

"Yes, that's right. Have you heard of Iniquus?"

"I'm a major with the Army, home on leave from my deployment to Afghanistan, so yeah. I've run into quite a few of the Iniquus operators in theater."

"What do you do for the Army, Major?"

"Please, I'm playing civilian today. Use Dani. I'm a veterinary surgeon. I mostly work with Special Operations Forces K9. Though I did work on an Iniquus K9 a few years back. The outcome wasn't what we'd hoped, unfortunately. So Iniquus…?"

"Iniquus has a K9 force called Cerberus Tactical K9. We cross-train the dogs. We can, for example, attach to one of the tactical operations forces and head out on a mission as K9 support when warranted. We do security, bomb sniffing, drug sniffing, parades, diplomats, celebrities."

"Have you ever secured anyone famous?"

"I couldn't say so even if I did. It's part of our contract. But I personally don't do much of that. I'm dedicated to the search and rescue side of things. We train and deploy to mass disaster."

"Is that why you're in the area?"

"In a way. We were on a two-week training mission, working with international teams we've hooked up with on different deployments. We're sharing tactics and learning how best to work together. Valor's been training with the fast rope all week. She loves it."

"Such a good girl." She changed her tone to talk to Valor. "I bet Tripwire owes you a big treat. You deserve one. Don't you, sweet girl?"

Trip found himself grinning as he listened to Dani using her cutesy baby talk voice on Valor.

"We were out on a training evolution when Headquarters told us to get out of Dodge and head here to ride out the storm."

"So this search was something you happened upon? You weren't brought in?"

"Someone staying at the lodge and her photography crew set out this morning, same as you, before the storm took the sudden turn. Their group's manager stayed back at the lodge while the others went on the photoshoot. When their manager saw our manager with his K9, she talked to him and hired us on."

"It's a miracle. Miracle on the mountain. They should make a documentary."

"I'll sign on to that title. We just need to make sure it holds true."

After that, things fell silent except for the scrape of Trip's shovel and the whistle of the wind gusts.

He let her rest for a moment then said, "I need you to keep talking. That's your job."

"I can't think of anything to say. Tell me about your team. Their dogs. You said your manager had a K9 with him."

"Our TOC commander and logistics guy's name is Bob."

"Real name or call name?"

"Call name, because—"

"Let me guess," she said. "He likes to fish?"

"Ha, yeah, he does like to fish. But no, that's not the reason he got the call sign."

"He's bad at swimming? His wife cuts his hair?"

"Funny, I'll tell him you said that. But again, no. His name is Marshall Palindrome."

"Oh, that's terrible."

"Want to hear what's worse?"

"Yeah. Yow. That's my boot. You're down to my foot now."

"Sorry, but good. Now that I know where you are in this pile. Let me get this off the bottom of your leg, and you can flex at the knee, maybe get some circulation going." He slid the shovel in the dirt farther up the pile.

"What was worse about Bob Palindrome?"

"His wife's name is Anna. A.N.N.A."

"No H? It's a palindrome, too? And his K9?"

"No H and it's happenstance. They married before he joined the Marines. He handles K9 Evo."

"Boo. It doesn't fit the pattern."

"Evo came with that name. Short for Evolution. But Bob calls him Eve. E.V.E. so he fits with the family."

"And it doesn't lower the dog's testosterone levels, cause he's a mighty dog."

"Exactly. We have a gal on the team that just got married and that necessitated a change in call signs."

"Because something good happened? Or to go with her new last name?"

"Her legal maiden name is Theresa Hellen Elliot, and she married a guy named Dan Butler."

"Okay."

"Her call sign, now, is Didit."

"Didit? Wait—You used her full name."

"Theresa Hellen Elliot."

"Initials T.H.E. Butler and har har har. The Butler Didit. I bet you guys were cooking that up for a while."

"It's a good one."

"Bob and Didit." She panted. "Who else?"

"Noah."

"Navy guy? Religious guy? Likes to buy things in pairs?"

"Weather guy."

"You're kidding. N.O.A.A.?"

"It was spelled that way, but that became too confusing for those Air Force hot shots. They ended up spelling it N.O.A.H."

"There's a story there."

"He was a pretty badass Air Force pilot. His goal was to fly into hurricanes."

"He'll be jazzed about this."

"If everyone gets home okay, he will."

"Wait. You were hired on for a mission. Did they find everyone?"

"Now that I've found you, everyone's been accounted for."

"And they're headed back safe and sound?"

"They ran into a similar problem as you did, I think. I know they need technical rescue to get them back up to a trail."

"Technical meaning ropes in this case?"

"Right. And some first aid support. They sustained injuries—walking wounded. They'll be okay. The team lit off in their direction to get them back. Zeus, our best K9 tracker, got to them first."

"Don't you be jealous that Tripwire said that, Valor. You have the best ears of the bunch. You're my hero pupper, aren't you, beautiful girl?"

"Two more shovels, and you should be able to bend your legs."

"Ah that'll be a relief. Maybe get this pain in my back from stabbing me."

That worried Trip. He had no idea how she'd be doing under all of that. And adrenaline could mask the most heinous of injuries, so Dani wouldn't know either.

"Tell me more about Noah and his K9," Dani said. "How did he get that name?"

"Noah's got a science degree in weather, which is important for our search and rescue team. We often get hired to go into high risk areas at high risk times to help get folks out. Being able to take advantage of a window of opportunity, of course, makes a huge difference. Noah helps Bob manage TOC, communications, tracking operators, writing tasking sheets. It's a big job."

"Does he have a dog?"

"Yep. Hairyman, or as I call him Sloberus Maximus."

"Ha, big breed? St. Bernard?"

"Newfoundland. Noah uses him for stability. He has a bit of vertigo from ear damage. Too many bombs at too close a range."

"I'm sorry about that. Newfies are such amazing dogs."

"I've learned a lot about them from working near Hairyman. They have those webbed feet and water-resistant coats. After Noah told us about that, we thought it might be cool to have a water rescue dog on the team. First time we took him to the river to see what he would naturally do around water, Hairyman dove in and swam straight out. He was moving, too. Focused. I'd seen that so many times when a search and rescue dog got the scent, nothing could call that dog off. Single minded. A couple of us grabbed paddles, pushed the kayaks into the water, and followed him."

"Oh this is good. What was Hairyman going after?"

"Around the bend, I saw a canoe overturned. Paddling harder to catch up, I rounded the boat to find a mother pushing her toddler baby and eight-year-old girl onto Hairyman's back. Her head was barely above the water. She was out of go juice." Tripwire would never get over a dog's capacity to help. To figure out the problem and jump into the situation.

"Amazing. K9 miracle workers."

"Can you feel my hands on you?"

"Yes. You're brushing off my ass."

Tripwire chuckled. "Sorry to be so forward."

"Forward away! I mean…you know. Do what's necessary."

Trip might have found that invitation to be a fun tease. But there was a rip in her pants and blood soaked into the fabric. "I'm going to squeeze down your leg. I need you to tell me if there's any pain."

"Okay, while you're feeling me up, let me tell you that while you've been working down there, I've been thinking through the problem. If the thing that's wedging me under the rock is my pack, it would be good if you could just pull that out and then I'd have the space."

"Those were my thoughts. Even if I sliced a hole in the bottom and emptied the contents, it'll make a difference."

"While you've been digging me out back there, I was able to get the sternum strap undone and get the shoulder straps pulled out of their doohickeys. The only thing holding to me now would be the hip strap."

He stepped on either side of her, kneeling to strad-dle her.

"You know, I usually don't let guys do this kind of thing on a first date."

He smiled at that. If she was thinking this was a first date, it was a hell of a "How I met my..." story. "I don't usually make advances of this kind...circum-stances being what they are..." Yup, it was the kind of story you'd tell your grandkids later in life. It brushed through Trip's psyche that he'd just imagined Dani in his long-distance future. He'd never had those kinds of thoughts before. He set that line of thinking aside for another time and focused in. "You're going to feel my hands. I'm going to try to get the strap unhooked. I'd rather not try to slice it when I can't see what I'm doing."

"Agreed. Thank you. And careful now, I'm ticklish."

His smile turned to a grin. *Yeah, I like her.* And he amended that to *Yeah, I like her spunk,* because the podcast dude had said how much he enjoyed the call on the suicide prevention line and talking to the woman he was mildly flirting with. Then it all went to shit.

# Chapter 21

*Dani*

Her pack was off. Dani took a couple of deep inhales of air. "He did it, Valor, Tripwire got me out."

"Almost, anyway. I need your feedback. If you tightened your muscles, and I grabbed your ankles but didn't lift them, just eased you out by pulling straight. How do you think that would work?"

"I could try to squirm back."

"I'd like to keep your spine straight."

"Okay, pull away." She gave Valor a scratch beneath her chin. "See you in a minute."

Slowly and steadily, she was sliding. "What are we doing after I'm free? Up or down the cliff?"

"Down. And then five klicks to a cabin." He used klick to mean kilometer.

Five klicks being just over three miles, a much
shorter distance, according to Bob's calculations, than
following the winding trail above, which was almost
twice as far from this point.

"If you're ambulatory," he said, "and we can push,
in this wind I'd say an hour's walk. That will give us a
few minutes to do what needs to be done."

"Battening down the hatches?"

"If there are hatches to be battened, rest assured
that will happen. Now, when I say cabin, I'd lower my
expectations way down. If we have four walls and a
stable roof, we're going to call it a win."

Her head was clear of the tunnel, and Dani could
have sobbed in relief.

"Checking your spine. Yell out if I hurt you."

"How about I just press back into child's pose, keeping my spine as rigid as possible and see how that
feels?"

"You're the doctor."

"Veterinarian. But yeah, I have an idea how mammals are put together."

"Slow and steady." He had one hand on her shoulder and the other rested gently on her hip as if when
she started to break, he was ready to hold her pieces
together.

She pushed into her hands, bending at her hips. Her
knees pressed against sharp rock. It hurt, but it was
the good kind of hurt. The kind of hurt that could be
relieved easily.

Dani lifted onto her hands and knees where she did
a couple of cat and camels.

"Good?"

Dani lifted her head to find herself looking into

bright blue eyes, filled with concern. They took her breath away.

"Easy now. Give it a second. Actually, in this little space, that's a good position for me to check you over. May I have permission to do that?"

"Sure," she said. She didn't really feel like she needed to be checked over. But a handsome rescue guy wanted to palpate? She wasn't going to stop him.

Dani closed her eyes. She had an ex-special ops guy helping her. She was so lucky. He could have been someone without skills or without a pack filled with survival gear, armed only with good intentions.

It could have been no one at all.

She could very well have faced the storm alone.

And died.

Life was tenuous, just look at Lei Ming. And Daisey. *I can't go there right now. Can't.*

She had promised herself she'd take the top off the bottle and let the pressure of her grief escape.

This hike and everything that went with it had been like shaking a champagne bottle, popping the cork and discovering the force sent her emotions spraying out uncontrollably with no good chance she could shove the cork in until the onslaught was released.

This wasn't the time for processing emotions.

She wasn't the only one at risk. Trip and Valor came after her to save her sorry ass. Now, she'd put them at risk, too. It was one thing to be endangered but being the cause for someone else to put themselves in harm's way? That was a weird sensation. It did funky things in her system.

She didn't like it.

"Your back is cut up, abrasions... Pain scale one to ten, how are you?"

"I'm at a one hundred percent—I don't care, get me the hell out of here."

"I read you loud and clear. All right, you have a cut down your right thigh. The blood coagulated, so you're not bleeding, but it's packed with dirt. When we get safe, we'll need to get that cleaned out."

She sat back on her heels, pulling her tops back down into place. The wind and cold had made her skin brighten with pain. She didn't need the distraction. This situation was still life or death.

It was weird to think that.

That she was in a situation where it wasn't at all a given that things would turn out well. That the three of them, Valor, Tripwire, and she might not make it through.

Dani watched Tripwire sling his backpack on and latch it into place. "I'm going to take Valor down to the apron below us. I'll climb back up and take you down. Good?"

She gave him a salute.

*Good? Not yet. Getting there.*

He chirruped. "Valor. Rappel."

Valor trotted right over to stand still and confident behind Tripwire as he clipped her to his rigging.

"Back in a minute," he said, grabbing his line. He leaned back over the edge of the ledge and disappeared out of sight.

To distract herself, Dani gathered up her own pack and threaded the straps back together and put it on. She was really going to do this. She was willingly going to go over the edge of a cliff.

What choice did she have?

She took a sip of water from the reservoir hose, swished it around, and spat it out. This time she was smart enough to turn her back to the wind.

She was taking another swig as Tripwire's head came over the edge again.

*Here we go. My turn.*

Tripwire crooked a come-here finger, and Dani stepped closer to where he was kneeling on one knee, tugging a length of webbing from one of his cargo pockets. He must have left his pack with Valor below.

He started winding the webbing around her waist and between her thighs. "You learned rappelling in boot, remember?"

"I worked diligently to forget. You've got to remember. I didn't join up to throw my body out of planes or over walls. I joined to take care of dogs."

Dani's system was going haywire. She squeezed her eyes shut. *Maybe these crazy butterflies in her stomach are love,* she joked. Though a man as skilled and kind and handsome as Tripwire certainly could make a woman fall in love at first sight, she knew better. Heights terrified Dani, and her body was in freak out mode.

*It might feel like the same thing, falling in love and dropping over the edge of a cliff in a windstorm.* Dani had never been in love before, so she had no reference for that sensation.

"The configuration I just made for you is called a hasty. In just a second, we're going to be connected at the hips. No matter what happens, you're not going to slip away from me. I've got you. I'll keep you safe."

She nodded her head but didn't open her eyes until she felt his hands on either side of her face.

"You're okay. I swear I won't let anything bad happen to you."

She bobbled her head.

"Thirty seconds, and we'll be done. You can leave your eyes shut the whole way."

Tripwire was maneuvering the lines, getting them straight from way up on the original trail. She wondered how he'd secured them. Would they hold?

Sure, he'd just gone down with Valor and climbed back up again. But Dani weighed a significant amount more than Valor did.

"I saw a YouTube of this old lady," Dani said. "She went skydiving for her birthday. As she was heading out of the plane she choked. The guy she was going down tandem with had to pry her fingers from the door frame."

"Yeah? Did she have a good time once she was in the air?" He was back by her side, attaching rings from his harness to the one he'd made for her out of webbing and knots.

"Hell no, she didn't. She wasn't attached to the guy's harness, so she was slipping away from him. Her pants were coming off. She was fighting for her life. The guy was pressing on her ankles to keep her from dying. It was horrible. I would never skydive."

"Valor did just this morning," he said.

"She's far braver than I am."

"You're plenty brave. You're going to be fine. I need you to do your part though, okay?"

Dani heard Valor barking below her, and Dani turned to look down at her. Wayyyy down.

Trip tightened his grip around her as she trembled against him. "It's only about two—two and a half stories down. Not enough to kill you, just enough to break both your legs."

She sent him a stink eye. "Reassuring."

"All you have to do is hug me. Tuck your head down, so you aren't looking, and hum a song for me. And I'll tell you when we're down."

"Okay."

"Okay?"

"Except for the humming part. I can't do that. We're going to be lucky if I can get down without peeing all over myself."

"Since you're going to be wrapped around me, I'd really appreciate it if that didn't happen."

"I can't make any guarantees. I'll do my best. Promise."

"Thank you." His eyes were laughing, and there was a twitch of mirth at the corner of his mouth. "I need you to lift your legs and wrap them around my waist. Cling on tight around my neck. We're going to do this on three. Ready?" He tipped his chin down and raised his brows.

"No." Her voice was a bit shaky as she reached up to wrap her arms around his neck. He was too tall. Sure, for a kiss this was great, just like she thought when they met. He was "stand on your toes and tip your head back" tall. But for this? She was too short. This didn't feel safe.

He reached down, wrapping his hands around her waist, and lifted her up like she was a feather.

She was *far* from a feather.

Dani was regretting the sausage biscuits she ate for breakfast...and last night's all you could eat buffet.

He didn't even grunt as she swung her legs to wrap around him. Dani had seen couples do this move in movies. It wasn't a configuration she'd ever maneuvered herself into before. But at least here, she could get a good grip around his neck.

He patted her arm. "Dani? A little air please?"

"Oh! Sorry."

"Tuck in."

Dani brought her head down and hid her face in the curve of his neck. She started humming. Not beautifully. This wasn't a time for ballads—as if Dani had a ballad in her. No, this was a single note that she hummed until she was out of breath, then she sucked in a lungful of air and hummed that one out too. She focused on the sound and making it as loud as the wind that whipped against them.

There was barking.

The barking was getting louder.

And louder.

And then beside her.

Then there was a rough tongue reaching around her neck, lapping at her.

They weren't moving anymore and after a long moment, Dani realized Trip was sitting on the ground hugging her, and she was crying. Yup. Sitting in his lap wrapped around the poor man like an anaconda. Sobbing.

For a split second, she was back at the crash. She was there in the wreckage. And she felt Daisey lick her. And for that stutter in her brain. She thought, "Trip-wire's here, he'll get you, Daisey-Doodle. You'll live."

"Hey. Hey. Hey." Tripwire smoothed a hand down her back, then cradling her head, he tipped her back so she could see his face. So calm, still with that bit of humor in his eyes. "We're down. You're okay."

Dani tried to remember that she was a major in the Army. Sure, she'd promised herself this time to fall apart. But circumstances change. And she needed to stuff these emotions.

She tried.

She tried hard.

Finally, with a hitched inhale, she was able to nod her head.

He swiped her tears with his thumbs, and for a moment Dani thought he was going to kiss her.

If he kissed her, she'd be good with that. That would be really nice, actually. She could do physical attraction. She'd just have to put the emotional attraction somewhere else, a back shelf somewhere. This wasn't the right time for that.

Dani closed her eyes, ready for it.

"Dani?"

She popped her eyes back open.

"Things are picking up with the storm. We've got about an hour's hike, and we need to secure ourselves the best we can. Are you ready?"

*Alrighty, then!* Her face prickled as she blushed.

She'd read that wrong.

Holding still, she waited as he unhooked her from his harness, then she clambered up from his lap.

Today was going much suckier than she'd anticipated. And she'd anticipated a horror of a day.

She winced as she adjusted her pack.

"I've got it." Tripwire held out his hand.

She looked at him dubiously. He already had a pack. "I'm worried about your back. We have a three-mile hike."

He had a point. Her back felt like she'd jacked it up but good during the fall. Dani unsnapped the straps and handed it over to him. "Thank you."

He bobbled it up and down. "It's heavy. What have you got in here?"

"Survival ten. Survival twenty, actually. Hiking alone… Just in case, I doubled up."

His eyes looked troubled as he asked, "Any weapons? A gun?"

She shook her head. "I had a can of bear spray when I started off, but it isn't on its loop now. Do you think we'll need weapons?" She slapped a hand out, grabbing his arm. "Do you think there will be bears?"

"Doubtful." He chuckled as he hugged the pack to his chest and pulled the straps on, wearing his own pack across his back and her pack across his front. He looked like a soldier ready to head outside the wire in the war zone.

The image wasn't wrong.

Mother Nature was a formidable enemy.

# Chapter 22

### Dani


Trip paused as he radioed their progress to the TOC. Now that Tripwire, Valor, and she were all on the apron that skirted between the top of the mountain and the road below, Tripwire could give a better assessment of their situation.

For sure the road would be the best possible way out of this mess. They could simply send a car and pick them up, turn around and hightail it back to the lodge. There simply wasn't enough line. Tripwire's rope barely got them this far down.

At least now that she was accounted for, they'd be able to tell Tiana that she was safe. Well, safer.

One less piece of guilt—since Dani had survived the slide off the mountaintop surprisingly well, it meant that the Iniquus team wouldn't fight through the storm to get to them. They'd wait until conditions improved.

The temperatures had been dropping all day, now that she was out from under the dirt pile, Dani realized how drastic the change had become.

As Dani's teeth chattered, she crossed her arms over her chest, hugging herself tightly.

On the good side, the wind had seemed to die down for the moment.

Tripwire pointed to Valor as he spoke over his comms.

Dani understood what he was suggesting; Valor had a fur coat. Up against the cliff wall, Dani took a knee, and Valor moved in front of her, blocking what wind swirled toward them. It helped. Her arms hugging Valor helped, too.

Valor gave her a long tongue swipe.

"Tripwire. What does the storm picture look like, Noah?"

Noah was their weather guy, Dani reminded herself.

"Noah. Expect temperatures in the low twenties. The storm is breaking into three bands. The first band will reach us in about an hour and a half. Caution. Do not—I repeat—do *not* depend on these time frames as specific or correct. This is an unpredictable storm. The radar indicates we're in a lull. The first band is hurricane force winds that will last for twelve to sixteen hours. As the winds die down, we'll get a break. Then, the next band comes in about an hour later with heavier snow. We expect that same forty-plus inches— as predicted earlier—for the mountain regions. And the third band will be ice. The storm should move off in forty-eight to seventy-two hours. We'll check conditions for exfil at that time. The staircase right behind the cabin is our plan. The lodge has snowmobiles. We can drive those out, throw lines down to you as an assist, and you three can walk up those stairs. Over."

Iniquus didn't know anything about the cabin where they were headed other than that they had permission to use it and anything they needed there, a key hid under the mat, and it was supposed to be primitive but structurally solid.

Dani had been preparing herself to make it through the bomb cyclone by sheltering under a pile of dirt, so a cabin, in comparison, sounded like Nirvana. "For me at least," she told Valor. "I feel badly about you and Tripwire."

"Bob. We need to stay informed about Dani's condition, check in on a regular basis with a sitrep. If her status changes, we'll work to meet the need."

*Yeah, that's not going to happen.* She'd already put Tripwire and Valor in danger. She wouldn't allow others to take a substantial risk for her.

"Tripwire. Wilco."

"Bob. On our end your radio transmission is breaking up. Communications issues are anticipated. We'll do our best under the circumstances. Let us know when you get to the cabin. Over."

"Tripwire. Wilco. Over and out." He indicated to the north with the blade of his hand as he walked toward her. "Five klicks, and you can lie down. About an hour. That will give me a few minutes to—"

"Batten down the hatches."

"Exactly." He reached a hand down to help her stand, then ruffled Valor's scruff. "Come on, Valor. Stay close to Dani."

Dani stumbled right out of the gate. She felt a little lightheaded and thought it was about the anxiety of their situation more than about any concussion she might have sustained. She hoped so anyway.

As she faltered, Trip grabbed hold of her arm and sent her a worried look. She was going to label this his "Dani-look" like he thought she was going to break into pieces, and he'd be standing there needing to clean up the mess.

"I'm okay. Just getting my sea legs after the land gave out, and I took the unexpected trip down. Ha ha! Get it, Tripwire? The 'trip'...?" And she acted out tripping, then skated her hands out like she was flying in a plane...taking a trip... She was a moron. And she could stop babbling at any time.

"You've had a rough time. Would it be okay if I held your hand as we walk? It would make me feel better." He slipped his hand around hers. Warm and gentle.

Maybe she hadn't actually tripped. Maybe it was more like a Freudian slip? Maybe her body was betraying what it hoped would happen. Yeah, she could admit that to herself, she wanted to hold Trip's hand as they walked along.

"Sure," she said, then rolled her eyes at herself. Poor Tripwire out here in the woods with his dog, trying to do a heroic deed. And here she was emotional and needy and not...just not...not good. She wasn't good. Dani hurt in every way she thought someone could hurt.

*You're an Army major, suck it up, buttercup.*

Her knees buckled.

Okay, maybe the dizzy *was* because she fell head over heels off a cliff and not because she was falling head over heels for this handsome ex-operator. Or maybe the two things could happen simultaneously.

"Whoa there." Trip stepped closer and tucked her against his body, wrapping his arm around her. He sent a look in the direction they were heading. "The farther you can walk the better, time wise. But if you're too hurt, I can throw you over my shoulder. You have to tell me what's going on for you. I can't guess."

Dani blinked at him. She couldn't imagine doing that to anyone, asking them to heft all of her over their shoulder and hike for an hour.

Whatever his background was with special operations, he would have gone through something like the SEALs did during their whole Hell Week thing where they carried logs over their heads for something like a hundred hours straight—but they had their team members helping them out.

"Hell no, you're not going to throw me over your shoulder," she said. "I hated training that in boot camp. It makes all my blood rush to my head. I'm fine. Fine-ish. I'd appreciate the support of your arm, though."

"Sure."

She turned and slid her arm around his waist under his pack, gripping one of the loops in his waistband to hold her in place.

Okay, who was she kidding? Maybe his arm helped balance her a bit. But Dani just liked the feel of it. Liked to be close to him.

She'd been sure she was going to die just minutes ago, stuck on the ledge alone on the side of a cliff, and now she wasn't. Of course it felt good to have support in all the connotations of the word.

They walked a few paces in perfect sync, moving together with ease.

Dani needed to be careful here.

Tripwire had entered the scene when she was at an emotional weak spot. She was reconsidering her thoughts about him since they met at Hermit's Cave, and they were dangerous.

Granted, not as dangerous as their present situation.

But assuming they'd pull through and got to go on to live another day, Dani would be heading back to Afghanistan. Tripwire would be here. There was nothing but more pain in that scenario.

Dani had tried long distance relationships before, and they just plain sucked. She was in enough pain; she didn't need to add salt to her wounds.

Huh, she was thinking in terms of relationships. *Bad move, Dani.*

That wasn't what was happening here; Tripwire was rescuing her.

Dani needed to get out of her head and think other thoughts. Like, for example, she didn't even know this guy's name. "Now you," she said.

"Now me, what?"

"We were talking about some of your teammates' names. Tripwire? What's the story behind that one?"

"There's a bit of a story. My first mission handling a K9, he sat down in front of a booby trap that would have sent us all home to the good Lord. He saved the entire team. My name memorializes our getting back to base that night. Until then, I was Trip. All the way through boot, though, I was hoping they'd call me Mr. President."

"Mr. President?" She chuckled. "When you said

that, your southern accent was shining through. What's your given name?"

"Harrison Augustus Williams III." He sent her a grin and a pop of his brow.

Dani had to process that for a minute. "Williams comma Harrison. William Henry Harrison. Mr. President would be a stretch. It wouldn't work anyway. The military would put a kibosh on it."

He'd been Trip through boot. Dani thought "Trip and Valor" worked better together than "Tripwire and Valor". Names needed to sound right when spoken together, like "Trip and Dani" sounded better in her ear than "Tripwire and Dani".

Dani was vaguely aware that in her thoughts she was making them into a *something* that required their names to be linked. She let it brush through her consciousness as she said, "Harrison Williams the third. The third, that's the 'trip' or is there a good story behind it?"

"The third making me 'Trip'? Could be. I don't recall when folks started calling me Trip. I do remember that round about second grade I was in a play at school. *Three Billy Goats Gruff.*"

"Were you the troll?"

"Nope. I was a goat. Me and my best bud Timmy and that other kid. My line in the play was 'trip.'"

"What?"

"As we went over the bridge, I said 'trip' then Timmy would say 'trap.' So it went 'Trip. Trap. Trip. Trap.' And then the troll guy...gal. It was a girl, Victoria."

"Victoria the troll? You're making this up."

"Hand to my heart. 'Trip. Trap. Trip. Trap. Who's

that walking over my bridge?' And then, we'd all say together, 'It is we, the three billy goats gruff.' After that, everyone called me 'Trip' and called Timmy 'Trap' or 'Trapper.' Timmy's mom *hated* that."

Dani glanced up at him. "Does your mom call you Trip, too?"

He caught her eye. A slow smile spread across his face. "No, my mom calls me Precious."

Dani snorted.

They walked in silence for a while. Even with the exertion, it was getting colder. Dani had dressed in layers, but she'd anticipated upper forties all day, not freezing temperatures. Dani's teeth chattered. Trip squeezed her arm then stepped away from her, dropping his pack.

From the back pocket, Trip dug out a chemical hand warmer pack that he shook then wrapped in a bandana. He instructed her to slide it down her shirt. "Let's see if that warms you up. I can't have you going into shock." He trapped her chin between his thumb and forefinger, tipping her head back so he could study her face. "Is it helping?"

"My teeth aren't rattling anymore. Thank you."

They set off arm in arm. Their pace steady. The quiet, though, allowed her brain to run bomb cyclone scenarios and none of them had happy outcomes. Despite the miracle of Trip dropping down the side of the cliff to her rescue, her imagination was still picturing this fiasco in doomsday imagery.

"Okay, let's talk. Take our thoughts off the hike." Trip must have been reading her mind. "Dani. We were talking about call signs. Do veterinarians have those?"

"They just call me Major Addams. Back in boot camp, they called me 'Wednesday'."

"Wednesday Addams? I don't see it."

"No? Resting bitchface, dark sense of humor?"

"I've seen that meme, it also says Wednesday is smarter than the rest and a leader."

"That seemed *way* too tip of the tongue. You memorize memes?" She bit down on the pain shooting down her leg. She felt a trickle of moisture tracing from thigh to sock. The cut Trip told her about must have opened back up.

"Yeah, well, my mom sends them to me, and then she likes to discuss," he said.

"She sent you a meme about Wednesday Addams?"

"Yup. She said that she dreamed that I was getting ready to marry Wednesday Addams—which then makes me finding a woman hanging off the side of a cliff out in the middle of nowhere—who happens to be named Wednesday Addams—seem kind of freaky, don't you think?"

Did she think this was the beginning of a relationship that was prognosticated fate?

She didn't need to answer; Trip had asked it as a rhetorical question. She kept walking as Trip unfolded his story.

"—the whole Addams family was coming for dinner that night. In the dream, Mom had called me, upset because she didn't think her ceilings were high enough for Lurch, and she'd wanted to know if he was coming, too. She wasn't sure what to cook and what to wear. Morticia Addams was so elegant and lovely, and here she was, a South Carolinian woman who liked her cheese grits and crab cakes."

"Low Country food. Delicious. What did your mom think about you marrying into the Addams family?"

"Nervous mostly. Mom grew up in a time when bullying was acceptable, and Mom has a birth defect. One of her arms didn't form properly. She gets nervous around people judging and teasing her. Staring. It makes her self-conscious and by nature she's an introvert. Normally, she doesn't like anyone coming over. But interestingly, the way she told the story, Mom seemed excited to have my future in-laws for dinner. She just wanted everything to be nice for them."

"Yeah? What did that look like?"

"That was my question, too. She said she cut the heads off a vase full of roses and left the stems in the center of the table, leaving the flowers where they fell so they could wilt and dry out. She used my grandmother's crystal goblets and got black linens off Amazon and had them one day shipped."

"Festive."

He smiled.

"And highly detailed."

"She's an artist. She likes to describe the images in her head. You'd like her, I think. I can see the two of you getting along."

He looked down at her, and Dani wondered if he heard that the way she had, that he was thinking about her meeting his mom. She found herself smiling back at him.

"Your face is so familiar to me. I feel like we've met. I'm trying to remember how I would know you, though. I feel certain that if we *had* met, I couldn't have forgotten you."

# *Chapter 23*

### *Dani*

Dani had to stop and put her hands on her knees. Her jaw hung open as she panted past the pain shooting down her sciatic nerve.

Trip took a knee so he could see her face. "When you can, tell me what's happening."

She lifted a hand and batted it through the air as if she could just wipe this all away. She was not going to be a damsel. She was not going to slow their progress and put Trip and Valor in more danger. She needed her body to cooperate just a little while longer. If she could get to the cabin, and they were safe, it didn't matter if she curled up in a corner and wept.

Dani struggled to stand.

Trip's hand rested on her shoulder, a stabilizing force.

She blew out past pursed lips and nodded.

"Better?"

"Good," she fibbed. "Pain came and went." She looked ahead and didn't see anything but gray cliff brushing near her shoulder, and off to her right, sky. They were clinging to the cliffside in the hopes that the apron wouldn't fall away. Unless they were fortunate enough to hit another shelf, they'd die. And Dani had used up that good luck card already today.

Dani wanted to wipe the concern from Trip's eyes. She slid into his outstretched arm and started off again, angling her head down so he couldn't see her wince. It was everything she could do not to hobble and drag on him. "You said you recognize me? And how is that, soldier?"

"Sailor. I was in the Navy."

"So not through the military, then."

"You know better than that."

"SEAL?" She squinted up at him then dropped her gaze again, knowing he'd tried to read her, and the pain that must be shining in her eyes might have him bend down and toss her over his shoulder, caveman style.

"I'm a retired SEAL, yep."

"You're young to have left the Teams."

"It wasn't in my plan to get out so soon, but I had a bout with valley fever."

Valley fever came from a fungus in desert sand. Military working dogs went out to the southwest in the United States to acclimatize to dry desert heat conditions. Before the K9s were accepted for deployment, they had to move through a desert training evolution and a subsequent examination by Dani or one of her fellow veterinarians. On occasion, one of the K9s contracted valley fever out on the training grounds. The only thing she could do for the dogs was treat the symptoms and cross her fingers.

Not being a people doctor, Dani was less familiar with how it affected humans. For K9 or human there was no cure. You either beat it or you didn't. And if you beat it, it could reduce your lung function for life.

"Shit." It was the only thing that came to mind to say.

"Yup. That about sums it up." He looked over at Valor. "Mama, I'm going as fast as I can. If you'd let up on the whining, I'd sure appreciate it."

Valor gave him a growling bark rebuke.

"She's anxious about the storm." Dani wiggled her fingers on the top of Valor's head.

"She's not the only one." Trip stopped talking as his focus went to the horizon.

Dani jiggled her hand where her fingers hooked into his belt loop. "Keep talking. It's keeping me sane."

He looked down at her until he caught Dani's gaze. Something worried and dark moved into his eyes, and Dani had no way to interpret it. She felt sure that if she asked, he'd obfuscate.

"Maybe we have a friend in common—are you married? Dating?" he asked, switching them back to the "How do I know you?" conversation.

"I'm single. You?"

"Nope, not seeing anyone. Never been married."

She looked down to hide her smile. "Lone ranger type?"

"In the K9 world, we say lone wolf."

Dani laughed. "Cute."

"Thank you."

She rolled her eyes. "Your being single is by design?"

"More or less."

When he came down the cliff wall to save her, then she'd wrapped her legs around him while he got them down here to the apron, then holding her hand…all of those things could very easily be Tripwire doing the rescue part of his search and rescue job. Wrapping her in his arm stabilized her so he didn't have to heft her bulk up onto his shoulders and hike for an hour in a windstorm while handling his dog…

*She* had felt a connection.

*She* had sensed chemistry brewing.

*She* had enjoyed the repartee, had felt a kinship. A… more than companionability. Maybe that was all her.

A blush rose up from Dani's chest. Man, would it be embarrassing if she'd had those thoughts, and he had no interest. *Wait. He asked me for coffee up at Hermit's Cave.* An invitation that could also be interpreted as a friendly gesture with no other interest attached to it.

No matter what his thoughts and feelings, her own thoughts were ill-timed, Dani reminded herself.

"Have you ever been in love before?" She squeezed her arm around his waist. "That was forward of me. As I heard that pop out of my mouth, I realized I quite possibly stepped over a line. Fair warning, that might happen a lot. One, I don't, on the best of days, have a great filter. I usually work with dogs, and they don't give a rip what I say to them. And two, since you saved my life, and now we're on this adventure together, I feel like normal social constructs are kind of out the window. Fallen over a cliff if you will."

He chuckled, his voice warm and intimate. "I don't mind answering your questions, Dani." They took a few more paces before he said, "I've cared for women in my life, but I haven't put myself out there for a long-haul relationship."

"You equate relationships with truck driving?"

"Long distances, bumpy roads, the occasional swear-filled breakdown on the side of a dark highway in a thunderstorm. Beautiful vistas, discomfort, boredom, excitement, new discoveries, the radio turned up loud belting out a song with pure joy—yeah, there are a lot of reasons that would be an apt metaphor. There's a sweet spot, I think, for SEALs to get married. In my experience, it's easier if they met their wives before they made it onto the Teams. It needed to be a done deal before they made the plan, otherwise, it might be selfish."

Dani tipped her head.

"The rate of divorce is high. We're gone around three hundred days a year. It's hard to make a relationship work in sixty days. The births missed, the anniversaries and holidays, the puking and stitches. When you're only around for sixty days out of a whole year, nothing can be a little moment, everything has to have significance. The sweet is extra sweet. The fights are extra vicious. Something I've observed." He swung his body, throwing his hands up against the rock, blocking a huge gust of bitter wind from her and Valor.

"Oh." She breathed out as he leaned in close, pressing against her, his head ducked down.

She hugged as tightly to him as her pack would

allow, one hand laced through Valor's collar, terrified that they would be swept off this narrow apron of land.

They waited it out, hunkering there together.

The punch of wind was gone as quick as it came.

Trip lowered his arms around her. They paused a moment longer, then Trip pressed away.

Heads bent, they were back on their trek, and back to their conversation.

"SEAL relationships," he said, taking off where they had been interrupted. "Kids, they've got their moms to be the stabilizing force, the one that polishes up their dad's image and covers over the dads not being there in person but in spirit. It's a conflict for the family—pride and understanding, self-recrimination for wanting more. I can't judge what other people think and feel, but for me, it was the wrong road."

"You know, those men not being around, might just be how the men wanted their lives constructed. Women too, I'm not discriminating. It could have had zero to do with being on the SEAL team. The Navy guy might like the dualism of deployment and homelife." Dani had to stop again. "I saw that to be true in some instances in theater." That last sentence squeaked out from behind the pain, clawing at her lower back.

"Breathe into it." He lifted his free hand from his lower belly up to his chin demonstrating a slow inhale, then sliding his hand back down to his abdomen.

"Lamaze training?"

"Experience."

Dani noticed Trip had shortened his stride and slowed the pace. And while she appreciated it—it did help her—it also worried her.

They were racing against the bomb cyclone.

They operated on Mother Nature's timetable not their own.

"My mom had a theory," she said. "My mom seems to always have a theory. This theory is about marriage. She believes no one should get married before they are twenty-eight years old and early thirties is best."

"She'd approve of my choices then. I just had my thirtieth birthday."

"Me, too. I'm a January baby. You?"

"Groundhog Day," he said.

"So I'm the older wiser one."

"Without a doubt. Did your mom have a reason for this theory of hers?"

"The adult brain doesn't fully form until twenty-five. According to Mom, you shouldn't even be dating the person you end up marrying until you are entering that relationship with a fully formed adult brain. If you picked your dating partner earlier, you were choosing with your juvenile brain, and you would have established the relationship—and by that she means norms—as a child-brain. The norms lock you into being who you were prior to being a fully formed adult-brain. With friends and family, it's one thing. It's different, she says, with partners of the heart. You need a nice fresh adult relationship once you've grown into your new adult brain."

"Huh. I don't think I've heard this before."

"For the context of this conversation, imagine marrying someone with an eighteen-year-old brain as a military professional heading off to boot camp. You're doing fine in your relationship when you deploy. During that year you're gone, let's say you turned twenty-five. You get back to hug your spouse, and you realize you're a completely different person, and you no longer fit together. In the olden days, you had to suck it up. Mom says that's why 1950's housewives met their husbands at the door with a cocktail. If they took the edge off at the beginning of the evening, they could get through it."

"Sounds horrible."

"Mom has a dark side to her thoughts. Also, she's a neuroeducation specialist."

"Has her theory affected your relationships?" he asked.

She thought she might see the cabin on the horizon. She pointed and waited for his nod before she responded. She thought she should make some kind of joke about her relationship status, but before she could think of anything clever, she said, "The Army life more than my mom's theories, I guess. I'm deployed a lot, and the people I meet are as well. We're always pinging in different directions. You know this. It makes things hard. For me, I just never found the person who I clicked with. I've never met someone that I thought, yup, he's my one and only. Or to use your trucking metaphor, the one that I wanted to sit in a cab next to for the next sixty years. We're alike in that sense."

He pulled her a little tighter to his side in a hug. "I'm thinking we're alike in many senses."

# Chapter 24

*Trip*

Trip stooped to reach under the doormat and retrieve the key that he handed up to Dani. The winds whipping past were loud enough now that it made it difficult to hear each other. Their last fifteen minutes of walking, they bent over, using their heads to cut a path forward. They'd stopped talking; it was hard to hear each other without yelling, and that took too much energy.

Dani unlocked the door. As she turned the handle, the wind used the opportunity to blow the door open, sending Dani stumbling into the tiny one roomed cabin.

Trip caught her by the hips as he pushed inside, grabbed the door, and shoved it shut. They were both gasping to catch their breaths.

Valor laced between them.

Trip reached up and pressed the button on his radio. "Tripwire for TOC. Over."

In return, he got radio static.

"Tripwire for TOC. How do you read?"

Again, static. It was an inevitability in these storm conditions that they'd lose their connection. He would have liked to report that they'd made it to the cabin. And to let Bob and Noah know Dani was not in as good a shape as she wanted him to believe.

She was being a good soldier, but not a great injured rescue.

In order to make the best call for right action, they needed the clearest correct assessment. Dani was lying about her pain.

"Tripwire for TOC. If you can hear me, Trip, Dani and Valor have made it to the cabin where we are preparing to bivouac. Repeat. Tripwire, Dani Addams, K9 Valor have reached the cabin. Over and out."

He focused on Dani, her lips were rolled in, and she was blinking her eyes like she was trying to take it all in.

"Dani." Trip pulled off their packs, dropping them by the wall. "Can you get Valor some water, please?" He pulled out Valor's collapsible bowl and handed it to her. "On the way in, I saw a woodpile. I'm going to get that in and stacked before this thing gets any worse."

She gave him a thumbs-up.

On his way out, he put his hand on the wall, inspecting the construction. There were some major beams making up the bones of the structure, the tree trunks that made up the walls were a good foot in diameter, the beams almost twice as wide. It looked like they'd been here for a while, decades. He hoped the wood wasn't dried and ready to snap with the pressure it was about to take.

"You need to batten down the hatches, too," she reminded him.

He gave her a grin and moved out into the wind.

The trek from cabin to woodpile was a battle against the wind that whipped his clothes and tried to knock him off his feet. Trip gathered an armload of aged hardwood. These would burn long and hot, with little smoke, a bonus if the wind rammed the venting air back down the stovepipe.

Back at the cabin, he kicked the door three times in lieu of knocking.

The door pulled open, he moved in, the door shut behind him.

"Just drop them, we'll be neat later," she said.

He glanced up and all the cabinets stood open. Jarred candles were now lit and positioned around the room.

"Is there a bathroom?" he asked, picking through a pocket on his pack and pulling out a pair of safety goggles that he tugged into place, then a ball cap, then his hood that he cinched down, just as Dani had done earlier.

She turned and pointed toward a faint light from a half open door in the back. "Toilet and shower, I have the water dripping to keep it from freezing. There are two fifty-five-gallon plastic tanks in there. Full, but I don't know how long the water's been in there." She pointed to the bowl of water Valor was lapping. "I used the water from my reservoir bladder. It's fresh."

Trip raised his hand to say he took that information in and was headed back out to get more wood.

The air had an odd quality to it. The sky looked like a bruise—purple with streaks of yellowing green. Trip pressed his way back to the woodpile. He either needed to get this in the cabin or over the edge. Very soon these fire logs would become missiles, and Trip just wasn't sure about the solidity of the roof.

He saw a flash of orange and realized Dani was fighting against a plastic toboggan.

With a push kick, Trip stomped the sled to the ground then stood in the center to keep it from blowing away.

She leaned in, cupping her hands between her mouth and his ear. "I found this and thought it would make fewer trips."

He nodded, then bent to lay the wood on the sled to help hold it down. Trip reached for the rope she had wound around her hand and pointed her back to the cabin.

Staying upright against this wind was a core workout. Dani didn't need any more strain on her body.

The night was fully upon them. In the short time he'd been moving wood, the sky had turned black with no sign of moon.

The wind made angry howling noises. Above them, trees crashed down, unable to withstand the onslaught. Trip just hoped the wind didn't hurtle them over the cliff's edge and down on the cabin roof. Not many roofs could withstand that force.

With the last of the wood inside, Trip slammed the door then lowered a beam across it, letting it rest on the iron elbow, securely attached to the wall. An old-fashioned locking system that would keep almost anything from beating its way in.

On his last trip out, he'd examined the shutters on either side of the front window. They were hinged and had slide locks that could be secured from the inside.

"How are you finding things?" Trip asked as he shucked his coat and hat.

Dani pointed to the kitchen area where she had closed the cabinet doors and had placed items in neat piles. "Food wise, there are a bunch of canned goods. We won't starve. It won't be delicious, but we're used to military cafeterias. You take what you can get. I have some gorp and granola bars from my pack. I didn't claw through your stuff."

"I have some MREs in mine. We'll do fine." His eye landed on a bucket of water sitting atop the wood oven. The oven door was open, a fire danced inside. Already, the heat took the nip out of the air.

She followed his line of focus. "I figure we should boil the water before we use it."

"Food, water, fire, roof. I think we'll get through this." He moved to the window, threw up the sash, and wrestled the shutters closed. Locked them, shut the window, locked that. It was another layer of protection, but it felt a little too little against a whole lot of lot.

Once he got everything in place, he'd start to put together contingency plans. Sitting here on an apron of land, halfway between up and down on a cliff in a storm that would be setting records for ferocity, yeah, it was going to take some creativity to come up with a viable Plan B.

Right now, he had nada.

"I found a can opener and some dog food for Valor.

I checked the sell by date, and it's still good. No dents. I think it's safe."

He turned, taking in the one-room cabin. It felt oddly domestic. The candle and firelight. The little brown table and two ladder-back chairs. A futon sofa that when pulled out would be a bed. And that was about it.

It could have been a scene out of the log cabin days. Pioneers facing whatever life threw at them.

With the other three shutters and windows latched, Trip said, "Hatches have been battened, Major." He gave the room a final glance. "I think we're as prepared as we can be."

As if on cue, the howl of wind grew louder.

Dani was on her knees, getting the wood stacked.

He didn't love that, what with her back injury and all. It needed to be weighed with what helped her psychologically. Sometimes being proactive made all the difference in the world. And frankly, there was little else they could do to be proactive.

*If Dani's feeling despondent, her actively working toward survival must be a good thing, right?*

There had been several times now that Trip could interpret her behaviors and her words as red flags.

"Dani, I need you to stop that. Your leg is bleeding, again. Let's get that taken care of."

He decided the best way to answer his own questions about her possible mental fragility was a straightforward conversation, and he'd have it.

First things first.

# *Chapter 25*

### *Dani*

Dani had no good way to see her wounds. Her fingers counted numerous rips in the back of her pants. When she got back to her computer, she was going to send the company a huge thank you letter for the quality of her clothing. They had done an admirable job protecting her from the rocky slide.

Slide was a good way to describe the experience. Looking back, she remembered the sensation of being in a water park, and almost a straight plummet with the water gushing around her, only in this case it had been soil.

When Trip had been out gathering wood, she had folded herself into different angles to see if that helped her assess the damage to her leg. In the butterfly stretch with the soles of her feet together, letting her thighs fall toward the floor, Dani could see that her pants were blood soaked, dried, soaked again, and were now a kind of crusty damp. But she couldn't see the injury.

It was just in a bad spot.

A mirror would help. But the only one she saw in this tiny cabin was one that was fixed to the wall in the bathroom, and too high up to be of service.

"I need to get to your leg wound," Trip called as he scrubbed his hands in the bathroom. "You don't happen to have a change of clothes in your pack, do you? Your pants are ripped and there's quite a bit of blood." He came in and watched her stack the last two logs against the front wall.

"And it's in a strange place. I was going to do something about it myself, but I can't see to make sure I got it properly irrigated."

"How do you want to do this?" He pulled a black plastic leaf bag from his pack, and a first aid kit. The kit was much bigger than the one she carried, much more comprehensive. Dani's little kit was there for bee stings and blisters. Trip carried his into the woods to save people's lives. Once again, gratitude flowed through her system, not just that someone showed up, but that the someone was equipped and capable. And Trip Williams.

"I'm an Army gal, not a lot of modesty left. I could just drop trou and let you deal with it."

He pulled the futon sofa until it lay flat forming a double bed. "Sounds like the easiest plan." He plucked a knife from his tactical pants' pocket and slit the bag open, he laid it over the bed, making a more sterile environment for her and protecting the futon. On top of that he laid a towel he'd brought with him from the bathroom.

Meanwhile, Dani untied her boots and yanked them off, setting them by the woodpile. She scooped off her socks, shoving them into her boots for later.

The fire had warmed the room to toasty. Barefooted was fine. She stripped off her fleece shirt, powdery with dirt.

Trip maintained good focal discipline while she unbuttoned her pants, unzipped them, and wiggled them off. Dani wasn't sure she appreciated that—and yet, what could he do in such a situation? Ogle her?

From his first aid kit, Trip produced a water bottle with an irrigation spout along with a packet of sterile water. He pulled the elastic for his head lamp over his head. It looked as clean and professional as one could hope for under such circumstances.

He turned to her now.

She stood there in a shirt just long enough to cover the triangle of her panties. Her pretty panties. At least she wasn't wearing her comfy utilitarian ones today.

Trip's gaze traveled slowly down her body to her feet and slowly back up again.

It wasn't a sexy sweep; it was a medically assessing sweep. And once again, Dani felt a niggle of disappointment. Who wants to be alone and half-naked in front of a handsome guy and his mind was thinking, "How damaged is she?"

Trip was probably wondering how he made it through his work on the Teams just to find himself here on the edge of a cliff, in a musty old cabin that might well be whisked off the mountain any minute now by the bomb cyclone.

A terrible way for a warrior to go. Too much essence of Wizard of Oz.

She bet he was wishing he was at the lodge with a fat steak and a beer, confident as the storm crashed around them. If he'd gone on to Eagle's Nest and then down that trail, he'd be there.

What turned him around?

Valor pressed against her thighs.

When she reached down to rub Valor's ears, Dani closed her eyes.

Dani remembered reaching out for Daisey's collar, her fingers sliding past the fur. The determined fist. Was that the reason Daisey was dead? Should she have let Daisey fly clear?

Today, under the debris pile, should Dani have just accepted her fate and not blown the whistle?

Were her decisions life threatening for this man and his dog just like they might have been for Daisey?

"Are there any cuts on your chest or abdomen?" Trip's voice yanked her from her thoughts.

"No. When I was sliding down, I kind of went into a tuck that seemed to protect my face and core. I think the damage to my legs and back happened after I landed. My backpack took a lot of that. It's my thighs and lower back…"

"Okay. I think we'll take this in steps." He pulled on a pair of nitrile gloves. "If you bend over the bed, it'll be the most practical way to irrigate." He moved to the galley kitchen and snatched up the rectangular plastic bin. He brought it back and set it on the floor, then held his hand out.

Okay, Dani would admit that on their walk, she

had entertained some pictures of just this scenario, her bending over the bed at Trip's request.

Him coming up behind her.

This was *so* not the sexy scene she'd envisioned.

She kneeled on the floor, bending over the bed, thinking, whelp, at least I'm wearing a pair of my favorite panties. Not gray, no holes or stains. She was relieved of that humiliation. A girl can't really come back from a guy's first visual being of the granny panties.

*Not the time. Not the place. Set the "Trip is revving my engines" thoughts aside*, she admonished herself.

Trip slowly slid her shirt up to her bra strap, and Dani had to shake her head at how two scenarios could have exactly the same moves and such different motivations.

"Oh, Dani," he said softly.

Yup, same scenario, different motivations.

"How bad does it look?"

"Raw. Painful. I'm going to get this cleaned up and dressed. We'll try to stave off an infection."

She rolled her eyes. The guy was bent behind her ass and thinking infections. Marvelous.

"I'll start at the top and work my way down."

"Thanks."

"Okay. What works for you, talking to keep you distracted? Not talking so you can cuss at me into the pillow?" He slid down to kneel beside her. Their thighs touching. His headlamp switched on with a click so he could see clearly in the candlelit cabin.

"Let's start by talking, but if I turn my head, and you hear mumbling, realize I've moved on to the cussing part of the show."

"Squirting disinfectant cleanser."

"K." It was cold and stung. Dani curled her fingers into the pillow and tried not to flinch.

"Now, I'm going to scrub with a cotton cloth."

She felt the cloth near her ribs.

"I don't want to hurt you, Dani. I'll try to be gentle."

Yup, two scenarios, different motivation. "K." Dani pushed her face under her arm so she could grimace privately.

"What are you known for on base?" Trip asked. "If I were asking about you, what would someone tell me about you outside of your work?"

To be honest, there wasn't a whole lot that Dani did outside of work. Dani lived her job. She had to say something. "I… I am known for my plethora of weird facts."

"Yeah? Give me one."

"Uhm, okay. Wolf fact. When a wolf sticks out its tongue, it's to show submissiveness." Why Dani was telling Trip about being submissive while she was in this position was something she'd take up with Freud on a different day. "It helps to keep peace in the pack. It's a phenomenon like yawning in humans. Sort of."

"That's kinda job specific."

"I guess. How about this one—there's a tree called the 'sandbox tree.' It grows down in the Amazon and is covered with poison spikes. It grows these fruits that look like the sugar pumpkins people decorate their tables with for Thanksgiving. Unlike most other plants, the sandbox tree's fruit doesn't fall off when it gets ripe to decay on the ground and fertilize their seed. Instead, the sandbox tree's fruit dries on the plant. Then, it will explode with a huge boom and shoot its seeds out. It can shoot them long distances. It's one of the most dangerous plants in the world." Okay, Dani knew what she'd tell Freud about pulling up that strange fact, she was sure that soon the air was going to be filled with dangerous projectiles of the bomb cyclone sort.

"As weird as that fact is, I know it's true. I was a victim of said explosion. It wasn't my favorite night."

Dani twisted around so she could see Trip's face. "Are you kidding me?"

He grimaced. "Sadly, no. I was in the Amazon rain-forest training with our allies. There was one of those sandbox trees, say, sixty meters away. I had no idea the sandbox tree even existed. We heard a bang, and the group we were training took off running to hide behind large trunks. It didn't sound like ammunition. My team had no idea what was happening. We flattened to the ground while we figured it out—I thought maybe the guys were razzing us—some Amazon joke. But that thought lasted a split second. The dried fruit from the tree, I found out later, had exploded and was shooting the seeds out."

"Those seeds are projectiles going a hundred and sixty miles per hour."

"Felt like it. Each one was like getting hit by a rubber bullet."

She shook her head—she didn't know what that felt like.

"It left huge bruises and welts but none of us had one break through the skin. The men we were with had gotten a tree between them and the incoming projectiles. They were all fine."

"What did you do going forward? Were there a bunch of those trees in your area?"

"Yes, lots of the trees. Several more explosions of

dried fruit. What did we do? Ran like hell. Got paranoid. Walked around picking out an escape route, ready to bolt."

"Is that the weirdest attack Mother Nature has thrown at you? Not weather wise."

"Mother Nature attack like—flora and fauna?"

"Yeah. Like the sandbox tree."

"No, sadly, I've had weirder."

Squinching her face up and burying it in the pillow as Trip scrubbed a particularly tender spot, she asked, "Did this have something to do with a K9?"

"Nope."

"Tell."

"Nope."

"Come on, how bad could it be?" she taunted. "Certainly not as bad as having tiny particles of grit scrubbed from your cuts."

"Bad."

"Hint?"

"No."

Dani couldn't make out from his voice if he was playing or if he wanted to change the conversation. She wished she could see his face to read it. But she was invested in burying her nose in the pillow and hanging on. "Where were you?"

"Same trip."

"Plant or animal? Are we playing 20 questions now?"

"Might as well, we have hours if not days here in the cabin."

"Plant or animal?" she asked again.

He paused while he squirted water from his bottle,

catching the drips with a gentle stroke of the towel down her side. "Animal."

"Mammals, birds, fish, reptiles, amphibians?"

"You're really going to make me say?"

"Yup."

"Fish, I think. That cut looks clean. I'm dabbing on some antibiotic cream."

She nodded. "Fish, but you're not sure."

"Yeah, I don't know. I'm moving on to the next cut. This is disinfectant soap, expect a sting."

Dani rolled her eyes up as she searched through her memory. Amazon animal that could be a fish or not. So obviously water... She shook her head. "Nope. Holy hell! Ow." She paused until he put the bottle down. "I need another hint. You don't have to tell me what happened if it's embarrassing, just the name of the organism."

He took a deep breath. "Candiru." Then he rubbed her cut with the cloth.

"What?" Her voice squeaked out, part pain, part incredulity. "No. That didn't happen. What I know about the candiru is that it's sometimes known as the 'penis fish.'" She twisted to look at him. "Myth has it that the candiru can lodge itself in the urethra of people who are urinating in the water."

He nodded slowly.

"You decided against a condom when you went into the Amazon water?"

"I didn't go in the water."

She blinked. "You were peeing? And it swam... That's a myth!" She pointed at the ground and then at his crotch. "A candiru is said to swim up a urine stream and right into a guy's dick. But that makes no sense.

Why would it want to swim into your penis anyway?"
She winced. "I've read when it gets inside a human
penis it lodges itself in place with sharp barbs while it
feasts from the inside."

"Yeah." He pursed his lips and shook his head. "No
need to remind me of that."

She laughed. Gallows' humor. This sounded hor-
rific. "What happened?"

"I was taking a leak. Things...happened. I freaked
and jumped back, clamping down on...things. Their
commander pulls his machete from his pack and said
that the only way to prevent the candiru from reaching my bladder—where it would cause inflammation
and ultimately death—was to instantly amputate my
dick. He's got his machete two handed up over his
head ready to slice down on my penis. Am I really
telling you this?"

Despite Dani's best efforts, she could not lift her
gaze from Trip's zipper. "Oh my god!"

"Luckily, there was a guy who grew up near those
waters, he said not to chop off my penis just yet. He
said I should keep my grip as tight as I could, that he'd
be back. Off he goes."

"What were you doing?"

"Sweating. I'm quite attached to my penis. This is
a weird conversation." He squirted more disinfecting
solution on her back and went back to his task.

"You can't change the subject until I hear how you
got the parasite out of you."

"The local guy comes back out of the forest with his
hands full of leaves. He went to the fire circle where
he brewed them up."

"You trusted him to drink it? I mean... I guess if

I were a guy, and I was weighing whether to trust the herbs or slice off my penis—"

"It wasn't meant for drinking."

Once again, she was pointing at his crotch. "You soaked your penis in it?"

"Yup, for two hours. I sat there with a bowl of stinky liquid balanced on a log, holding myself in place and waiting for the candiru to get irritated enough that it would swim out."

She looked up at him, eyes wide. "And everything is okay?"

A slow smile spread across his face. "Yeah, everything's fine. I peed some blood, took some antibiotics just in case, and made sure never to take a leak into Amazonian water again. Now, can we change the subject? I'm kinda done with you looking at my dick with pity in your eyes."

"The candiru is a myth. There is absolutely no proof that it exists."

He sent her a wink.

Dani sighed as she turned her head back into the pillow.

"Ointment." Cool balm was slicked over the cut with gentle fingers. "I'm going to start on your thigh. It's going to sting. It's a deeper gash. I have steristrips to pull it back together."

"Thank you."

"Three. Two. One."

"Agh!" Dani gritted her teeth together.

"This time, it's just plain water. Ready?"

"Okay. Go. Keep talking though. It's your turn. What's the thing folks would tell me about you?" she asked.

"Haven't got one."

"You must have. Is it embarrassing? It can't be any more embarrassing than sitting there with the training team holding your dick in a bowl."

"I knew I'd regret telling you that story. You're going to remember that."

"*Forever.* You're going to have to tell me something else to distract me from those images."

"I don't have much to my life beyond dogs and work and work with dogs."

"That wasn't always true," Dani prodded.

"How about this. I can sing. I was in a band."

"Fan girls throwing their bodies at you?"

"That was the motivation if not the reality."

Dani thought his voice was beautifully smooth, so low and resonant, he probably had a gorgeous singing voice. "What instrument did you play?"

"Lead guitar."

"Nice. Will you sing something for me?"

"I'll tell you what, when we get back to the lodge, I'll grab my guitar, and I'll sing you a couple songs. But fair warning, I'm mediocre on a good day."

# *Chapter 26*

### *Trip*

"There." Trip pulled Dani's shirt down over her hips. If he had to stare at her round ass bent over the bed that way for another minute, he'd have to throw himself outside and stand in the storm to regain control. Luckily, he'd had his hard-on arranged so it wasn't visible when Dani spun around and stared at his dick during the candiru story.

Why he had decided to tell her that particular story at the time when she was splayed out like that so trustingly... Trip guessed he was just marrying his dick thoughts with his danger thoughts and that's what his mouth served up. "That's going to leave a scar on your thigh. I'm sorry."

She crawled up to lie on the bed, then turned over to

look at him. She had to be aware that her shirt would inch up to her belly. Blue silk with lace. Not really hiking panties, but he wasn't complaining. He just needed to keep his head right.

Both heads.

This was not the time or place, and it certainly wasn't the situation to be getting physical.

And if that didn't stop him from seeing where that smile of hers might take him, he didn't pack a condom in his rescue kit. Go figure. And he had a strict "wrap it" rule.

Trip focused on taking the tub of water to the sink and cleaning that out.

"I once had a SEAL in my surgical theater," she said. "He was bleeding from multiple sites. I tried to kick him out—to go get help. I told him he could come back afterwards to check on his dog."

"That didn't go down very well."

"It didn't go down at all. He told me I'd have to knock him out to get him to leave. I was afraid he was going to bleed out."

"What did you do?"

"I bent him over a stool and sewed him up. No anesthesia, no meds to help the pain. Because I'm a vet, I can't do medications for humans. I cleaned him and sewed him."

As Trip walked back her way, she patted the bed next to her.

Warm fire. Half-naked woman—Smart. Brave. Clever. Dog lover. She was his type from head to foot. Especially her heart-shaped ass.

Trip had been attracted to Dani up at Hermit's Cave. Getting to know her. Enjoying their banter. The ease of being with her. His comfort level being around her. They clicked.

He had to be careful.

His mind was back to the podcast and the guy enjoying the connection he made with that woman on the other end of the phone line.

Trip hadn't seen anything about her behavior that was outside the norm. Compared with other rescues, he'd say she was rocking this crisis like a champ.

He didn't know if she was hiding her despondency from him. Like she hid her physical pain.

Bruising and cuts aside, she'd come out of the fall in good shape. Her words were spoken clearly. Her sentences made sense. She had both short term and long-term memory intact. Nothing screwy about her pupils.

Still, Trip was vigilant.

If Dani needed help, he'd make sure she got it. And he wasn't going to complicate things by…complicating things.

Lying down next to her on the futon was *not* a good idea.

The only other place to sit was the kitchen chairs that looked old and wobbly, like they wouldn't hold his weight.

He focused himself back on her story about the SEAL.

"I asked him how he could handle the pain." She lowered her voice to imitate a man's. "'Ma'am, this buttercup has learned to suck it.'"

"Weird line of thought." He posted his hands on his hips. "Is that what you're doing? How much pain are you in?"

"A good amount. It doesn't feel like anything to

be all that worried about. A soak in a hot bath, a stiff drink." She looked up at him through her fringe of lashes. "Some time relaxing in bed."

One part of his mind went straight to Dani in bed. Sweaty. Tangled in sheets.

And the other part told him to simmer the hell down.

He stood there, trying to figure out the logistics of where he should go. He wished she had a fresh pair of leggings or something so that little bit of blue satin, that looked so inviting to stroke, wasn't peeping out from under her shirt.

He focused on putting together his first aid kit, stowing it back in his pack. When he looked up, she had a strange look on her face. "What was your train of thought then?"

"SEALs belong in water. And here you are on the side of a mountain. That's what I was thinking." She rolled off the bed and headed toward the galley kitchen.

"Ah, well I was a mountain guy before I was a SEAL guy."

She lifted a candle and was peering into the upper cabinets.

"What are you looking for?"

"I need a drink." She stood on her toes and tipped her head back. "All the way down the trail toward the lodge, I promised myself a hot bath and a stiff drink. The hot bath is out. I'm hoping for the drink though." She turned to look over her shoulder. "I'll keep promising myself that bath until we get back to the lodge. Enticement. I bet they won't have hot water. Electricity will be out, and they'll be running on a generator." She pulled out a bottle of moonshine.

"Hospital first," Trip said.

"I don't need that." She set the jar on the counter.

"You fell off a cliff. Of course you need a medical check."

"Fine." She turned and headed back to the futon. "But first thing when we're back to civilization, I promised Valor a S.T.E.A.K." She spelled.

Valor's tail thumped the floor. She whined "please!" noises and punctuated it with a bark.

"Valor can spell?" Dani lay down then clucked her tongue, and Valor jumped up and came to lie side by side with Dani.

Perfect. Valor could be the chaperone. "Yep. And read." Trip pulled out his phone. He stretched out on the other side of Valor and scrolled to a picture of Valor sitting on a bed looking extra proud of herself. In front of her was a folded black t-shirt that read "treat" across the width.

Trip spread his fingers on the screen to widen the picture. "That's a T-shirt in front of her," he said, a smile wiggling the corners of his mouth. "Valor and I had been working a new behavior, and she had done it perfectly. I reached for a piece of liver, when a call came in from my mom, Dad was just out of surgery."

Dani sent him a sympathetic hum.

Trip rolled onto his side and rested his head on his posted hand, so he could see Dani in the candlelight. Her eyes, her lips, the cute little scoop of her nose, the luxuriousness of her curves, he wanted to gather her up and feel her in his arms. "Nothing too serious. Dad had some knee issues that they fixed. He's fine." He wiggled the picture of Valor. "I answered the phone talking to Mom, and Valor trotted out of the room.

When I hung up, I found Valor on my bed like that, wagging her tail."

"Because you needed reminding that she'd earned her reward." Dani bent to put her forehead on Valor's. "This is what I call 'mind meld' posturing," she said. "When I do this, I feel like I'm developing emotional intimacy with a dog. In my imagination, from our heads meeting, the K9 knows I'm part of their pack and have their back." She kissed Valor. "We're part of the same pack. Now that you've saved my life, you're my forever friend." She smiled over at Trip. "There were moments when I absolutely trusted that the dog felt the same about me." She rubbed Valor's ears in the high-dollar reward. "You don't need a T-shirt to remind me. When we're back at the lodge, I'm going to get you the biggest, thickest, juiciest, rawest steaks that Trip will allow."

Valor thumped her tail.

"She's racking up quite the treats list. I owe her a steak, too."

Trip's hand reached out to cover Dani's. He couldn't help himself.

Dani flipped her hand over and laced her fingers with his. "Tell me."

"I was on a training mission with the international teams that often get pulled in to deploy to natural disasters. Under those circumstances, airport runways are often destroyed, or roads."

Dani nodded.

"We were training to parachute with the dogs. And this morning was Valor's first jump."

"Yeah, you were telling me Valor did a skydive. Busy day. How'd she do?"

"Surprisingly well under the circumstances."

Dani tipped her head.

"At altitude, we were catching some pretty stiff wind currents. Ridge and Zeus were first to jump. Then, the number two team from Switzerland, Pierre and Hugo, along with Valor and me, we got tossed out the plane door."

"Tossed. Wow." Dani turned to lie down so her other hand was free to comb through Valor's coat. "Did that freak you out, Mama?"

"She did great. The number two team got tagged by the plane's wing, and we had to do a rescue dive to get to them."

"That's crazy. Is that team okay?"

"The handler was in surgery last we were updated, and his K9, Hugo, was flown to a veterinary hospital to fix a compound fracture of his rear leg."

"Scary stuff. And what about Ridge and Zeus?"

"The wind slammed them into the ground a few times before Ridge could cut free. Zeus was fine. They're out on this mission. Zeus was tracking our client's scent. Ridge and Zeus found the lost crew just about the time I was calling in that I'd found you."

"What happened to that group?"

"They went out early this morning to do some scenic shots, they had checked the weather, and it all looked good, just like you did. They had no clue of the change. Around lunch they were setting up for a photo shoot when they took a slide. I'm low on details."

"Agh!"

"I do know they didn't fall as far as you. From the radio traffic, I gathered they were walking wounded. They could make it back to the lodge with help, twisted ankles. Soft tissue damage. Which was good since we don't have the team numbers or the time to get gurneys in there and carry them out. Yeah, that would have been a hot mess."

"They're all back?"

"They weren't when we lost comms. We've got a serious team out there. Highly effective. I have no doubts they've got this covered."

Trip scrolled through the phone and found a picture of their team running through a mud course with their dogs riding on their shoulders.

"You all have smiles on your faces, even the dogs." She spread her fingers and moved the picture around until his face filled the screen. "You look like you might be a little high on adrenaline." She handed the phone back. "I've met my fair share of operators. They eat adrenaline three squares a day."

"I'm not that," he said.

"What?" She quirked a brow.

"An adrenaline junkie. Plenty of my brothers are, but that's not me. I'm pretty sure that's why I got to go to dog school."

"Doggos need a steady temperament. Adrenaline seekers aren't great at the calm and the repetitiveness needed to have a successful K9."

"And you were around plenty of handlers, so you'd know. Calm, steady, dependable are requisite." Was he selling himself to this woman? Was she in the market for a man in her life? He used the time he spent scrolling for another picture to show her to deal with the sudden realization that *he* was in the market.

Trip was thinking about what Dani's mother said about having an adult brain. When he turned thirty last month, he had thought he was settled enough that he wanted someone to care about. He wasn't worried anymore about the jumbled emotional tangle that went with a long-haul relationship. He'd matured past looking for easy and indulgent. He wanted the opportunity to rise to the challenge. To grow from the experience. That was something he knew was different from what his younger brain had wanted.

*He* wanted a relationship.

But with Dani? If she was despondent, it wouldn't matter what he wanted, she'd need to put her focus on wellness.

"So you don't like operators in general," Trip said. "Do you like operators who are K9 handlers?"

"I didn't say I didn't like operators. I just don't want to have a romantic relationship with one. I tried dating K9 handlers. That was a bit of a problem."

"Yeah? How's that."

"Do you watch *Big Bang Theory*?"

He threw his head back and laughed. "The one where Sheldon is training Penny with chocolate?"

She arched a brow. "Poor Penny is sitting on the couch being Penny. When Sheldon didn't like what she did, he'd show his displeasure with a look. When she changed her behavior to being consistent with what he wanted to happen, Sheldon offers her a chocolate. Training her. Telling that you went right to the correct episode."

"Because it's an old joke. Operant conditioning. Positive reinforcement. We all do it on some level."

"And, in my dating experience, this was subliminally true. I bet handlers don't even know they're doing it. I know they're doing it because once you've seen training in action, it's pretty apparent."

"But not meant harmfully."

"Maybe. Maybe not. Depends on the guy."

Trip took note of that. He'd watch himself to make sure he wasn't trying to make Dani into something she was not. They'd just met, as surprising as that thought was; they seemed to fit together like pieces of a puzzle. He couldn't assume that what he wanted was what she wanted.

Big picture, what he wanted most right now was for Dani to be safe.

# Chapter 27

### Dani


Behind the cabin a massive crash echoed large. It sounded like the world coming to an end. Dani turned to hug Valor to her.

Trip wrapped his arm around them and lowered his forehead to touch hers.

"Mind meld," Dani whispered.

Trip kissed her forehead. "We're going to make it through this."

She looked him in the eye to see if he really believed it.

"We *will* make it through this. Whatever happens, we'll deal with it."

"Okay." Dani had nothing else to offer. She was scared. Petrified. This wasn't the shittiest day of her life—that was the day that Lei Ming and Daisey died. But this was right up there in a close number two slot.

Thank god for Trip and Valor.

"I'd be dead," she whispered.

"Shhh." He pressed his lips to her forehead and took a deep breath in before he released the kiss.

Dani knew that he had come to the same conclusion: If he hadn't been there, she'd be dead.

It was a big deal.

Sometimes a wave of fragility washed over her when she saved a K9 on the operating table. If she hadn't been there, the dog wouldn't have survived. She had never learned how to classify that feeling. It wasn't good. It wasn't bad. It was…overwhelming.

Trip seemed to handle all of this just fine.

"Have you always been this Zen?" Dani asked.

"I was not. I was an angry, rebellious, terror of a teen."

"No."

"True story, when I was twelve, I was already six feet tall."

Dani wrinkled her brow wondering what it would be like to be in junior high and be taller than most adults.

"When I was thirteen, I was my full six foot two and had to shave every morning. I had an adult body that wanted to do adult things. At thirteen, the kinds of adult things I wanted to do were not available. I was too young to handle the amount of testosterone that was flowing through my system."

"That must have been horrible."

"Good side, I beat the crap out of all the little kids I went up against in sports. They'd show up and look at me, and I saw the terror in their eyes. That was powerful for a kid who felt powerless. I was a shit. I can admit that now. I was terrible to everyone. Anger was my go-to setting. My mom thought I was going to end up strung out on drugs, in prison, or dead."

A frown pulled Dani's lips down at the corners. "I can't imagine you like that."

"My dad said that he was going to send me to military school if I didn't come up with a plan to right my ship."

"If you were that angry, you wouldn't have gone along with a parent putting you in military school."

"I came up with a plan. Best thing in the world. I decided to hike the Appalachian Trail."

"You said a while back, that you were a mountain man before you were a sea man. That's a heck of a long ways Georgia to Maine, right? Were you going for a speed record?"

"I had it in mind when I started my plans."

"What was it?"

"Let's see, there's a guy by the name of Joe Mc-Conaughy who did the northbound trail in forty-five days. That's two thousand one hundred and ninety hard earned miles. And a gal named Heather Anderson did it in fifty-four."

"Ha! I knew it. All these years later, you can pull those stats out of your hat. Best of the best goals, you are such a SEAL."

"That was thick with meaning. Now, was it good or bad meaning?"

"Bit of both. So how fast did you do the trail?"

"I set out April first in Georgia, and I was at the trail's end for Fourth of July weekend. Then I yo-yoed. That means I turned around and hiked back the other way. I still had some issues I needed to pound into the trail. Some more time communing with the trees."

"I understand that. That was what I was doing today. Trail time. Tree time. There's solace to be had in the woods."

He looked into her eyes as if trying to read her depths. A question. A worry.

"Two thousand one hundred and ninety miles though. Then back again just as fast?"

He released her hand to slide his fingers through her hair and tucked the strands back behind her ear. "My goal was different on the way back." He rested his hand on her hip. "I had wanted to be a SEAL for a few years at that point. It was my career goal. One of my goals in convincing my parents to let me online school my senior year to get graduated by Christmas and be able to take off was first and foremost to get them off my back. Second was to build my skills, my strength and agility, my mindset so I'd fit in with the Teams. They wouldn't take me as a hothead. My dad was able to convince me of that. I wanted to finish the trip back by the beginning of October, but I ran into some difficulties. I sustained an injury that laid me up for a bit."

"Alone on the trail? What happened? How did you eat and get water?"

"I twisted my knee, and it had swollen up like a watermelon. Since the goal of the trek was to build my body and skills to succeed as a SEAL, no point in doing permanent damage and pushing through just to end my possible military career."

"No, of course not. Not unless you were in life or death straits."

"There are people on the trail. I could have got-

ten help at any point—most any point. Folks offered
to get a team in to rescue me, and I said nah. I was
set up fine. I changed my goal up. I decided to stay.
From where I camped, I could fish. There were plenty
of fish. I rigged a slingshot and got darned good with
it. At sunrise, small animals would come and drink,
rabbits, what have you. I boiled my water so that was
good. The cold mountain stream felt soothing on my
leg. I'd get in and practice holding my breath under-
water. That part of the SEAL training was a cake walk
for me. It washed the anger right out of me. I learned to
be humble. To take each day one task at a time. Yeah.
Good experience. Glad it happened."

"Wasn't your support crew worried? Your family?"

"I sent word with a guy who was a SOBO, a south-
ward-bounder, Maryland to Georgia through hiker,
and I got a message back from a guy that was headed
north bound."

"A NOBO?"

He grinned. "Yeah, we called them NOBOs or
GAMErs Georgia to Maine. I used that communica-
tion system throughout."

"They didn't bring you any supplies?"

Valor leaped off the bed and went to lie on the floor.

Trip moved his pillow from under his head to in
between them.

Dani was getting mixed signals.

"First," he said. "I'd never ask anyone to carry
weight for me. And my new goal was to—"

"See how long you could manage on your own."
This felt like this was an important inflection point in
knowing Trip. "You asked me if being a SEAL was a
good or a bad thing and I said a bit of both. And I guess

I was thinking in terms of relationships." She blushed heatedly but she didn't try to hide that from Trip. "I have friends who are SEALs and were SEALs, and I've found sometimes they can lock onto a goal—this is not meant to be disparaging or even to throw you all into the same pot—but as a generalization—"

"You don't have to be mindful of my feelings, Dani, you can just say stuff to me. I'm not that delicate."

"There's the whole idea of not letting anyone carry your weight for you. That's kind of what relationships are about. Sometimes, I need to lean on you. Sometimes, you need to lean on me. Sometimes, we need to prop each other up. Well, not me and you, those were generalized pronouns." She stopped and blinked. Her mouth was running faster than her brain. "SEALs get a goal in mind, and they head for it with determination. Sometimes, they don't see the impact. I mean, your mom. Did you ask if she was okay through this? You were still young, weren't you?"

"I turned eighteen just before I hit the trail." He tipped his head.

"I sound judgmental. I'm trying to respond to your question about SEALs and as a generalization, I've found that they do what they think is right and that often comes at the expense of those around them. I don't know you, your mom, or your family dynamic. I don't know anything that was part of your discussion prior to your going, or during your trek. You might well have considered the impact on your parents knowing that you were a teenager, injured in the wilds with limited resources and intermittent letter exchanges."

"I didn't. They weren't in my calculus. My goal was to get strong in my mind and my body, so I could be an effective SEAL when I got done. Was that part of a SEAL mindset? Was that being in the narcissist time of my brain development? Probably both. I hope I've evolved as I moved through life."

"Tell me something you learned along the way."

"Biggest takeaway is my philosophy 'one opportunity at a time.'"

"Okay." She laughed. "You said that to me back when you were rescuing me from the cliff."

"On the trail, you can't take it one day at a time. That's too big of a chunk, so you take one task at a time, one obstacle. I had to change the focus of how I looked at things. It wasn't an *obstacle* it was an *opportunity*. An opportunity to get strong, to build skills, to figure out how to work the problem. Every challenge became a kind of a game."

"Your wrenching your knee being a big opportunity then."

"Exactly. I figured things out. Like, I didn't want to lose my fitness sitting on my butt fishing all day, so I rigged a line across the swift part of the river and attached a bungee and used it like an exercise pool. I could swim all day and not go anywhere. I practiced my SEAL stroke and built those skills. I got habituated to long times in cold waters."

"I'm glad you got to be a SEAL at the end of all that."

"It was great. A great life. A great band of brothers. Then there was the valley fever. Finding opportunity in that was harder."

"Does it make you bitter, being forced off the Teams?"

He scratched at the corner of his eye. "Not about

that. It's that I was a K9 handler, and they handed off my dog to another operator."

Dani squeezed the muscles of her face, pulling everything tight. Her hand came to her heart. "God," she breathed out. "I'm so sorry."

Trip pulled out his phone, flipped to a picture.

"That's Rory!" Dani said. "His name was supposed to be Glory—"

"But that's how you pronounce it in dog. Yup, that's him."

"You were Rory's handler? Wow. I've done well checks on Rory. He had a leg wound from a mission in Afghanistan. Rory's assigned to Delta, a fellow named…" She searched her memory, dogs she never forgot, humans were a different story.

"Ty. Yeah. Good guy. I couldn't have picked a better handler for Rory to go work with."

"Other than you."

Trip scraped his teeth over his upper lip. He flipped the phone over and scrolled to find a picture of Ty and Rory lying in a kiddie pool together. "Ty hunted me down when I was in the hospital and told me who he was and that he had Rory. He sends me pictures and video at least once a week, as long as Ty's not downrange. Stories. It helps. Rory's got another two or three years of work in his career if all goes well."

"And then?"

"I already submitted paperwork to adopt him."

"Ty's okay with that?"

"First thing he said when he reached out to me, you've got dibs. If you can take him after he retires you should do that."

Tears welled in Dani's eyes and she touched her hand to her heart.

"Ty being active duty, so adopting's not possible, and Rory's getting on in years now."

"Yeah. Hard all around. I've seen it. Handlers and their bonds are deep, deep, deep."

"You've had a dog like that. You loved Daisey like that."

"Daisey, yes." Her voice was wistful, then she turned confused eyes on him. "How do you know about my dog, Daisey?"

# *Chapter 28*

## *Dani*

Dani's brows drew together. She shifted her head slightly, and unfocused her gaze, thinking through the day's events. There was something not right about this scenario. She looked toward the back of the cabin. "You said you were up on the ridge, and you made it all the way to the stairs to get to this cabin, but you hadn't been in here yet."

Trip moved off the bed to toss a log into the fire. "Yeah. When I headed us here, I wasn't sure how much shelter it was going to provide. Or if it was at all useful before I got the information from TOC. But on my map, there are stairs cut into the cliff, so at least we could get up to the top of the mountain and worst-case

scenario hike the Eagle's Nest trail back to the lodge."
He turned.

"You and I were heading in opposite directions. And there was all that wind."

Their gazes met. Held.

"Even though I was blowing on a hurricane whistle, and even though Valor has incredible hearing, you didn't find me because of my whistling. You were too far away. I lay there—well, it seems like a very long time. It felt like eternity. I was panicking. I was pretty sure that I was going to die." Something was fishy about this scenario. "How did you get on that trail and find me? And how do you know my dog's name?"

"Good," Trip said. "I wanted to have this conversation with you. But I wasn't sure how to broach it."

Dani scowled as she pushed her aching body up to sit cross-legged on the futon, hugging a pillow to her chest.

"When I got up to the cabin stairs, I got a call from Bob."

"He's... That's the guy who runs your TOC."

"Exactly. He called on the sat phone to ask me about your demeanor when I saw you over at Hermit's Cave." He reached for one of the ladder-back chairs, turned it backward and set it in front of her.

She squinted her eyes at him, trying to remember her demeanor. She was petting Valor. Dani had been a little confused about the dog's behavior. She thought Trip was cute. She'd been sad. Then she was frightened by the storm. "My demeanor?"

He sat down, wide legged, arms crossed across the top of the backrest. "The sheriff received a call from your mom. She was afraid you'd gone to Hermit's Cave to end things." His voice was gruff, and he sounded like he was forcing the words out past some internal gate.

"Mom..." Dani looked down, thinking this through. Why in the world would her mom think such a thing? "I was just with her this morning. She knew my plans. I'm driving to Ohio for my dear friend Lei Ming's memorial service. We stopped here at the lodge to fulfill a promise we made to Lei Ming." She lifted her head to look Trip dead in the eye. "I'm bereft, not suicidal. Suicidal?"

Trip's eyes told Dani that he was in his head moving parts around.

"Bob turned you around. You didn't finish your original search area because they sent you back for me. Wow, am I glad that they found that photography crew, and they weren't up at Eagle's Nest. Can you imagine?" Her brows slid up her forehead toward her hairline. "Honestly, can you imagine if no one found the whole group of people because they were at Eagle's Nest taking pretty pictures when this storm hit?" She lifted her hand toward the door. "All of those people would have died...when you and Valor were sent to come after only me." She held up a finger. "I'm grateful I'm alive. Thrilled they are, too." She canted her head. "Suicide?"

Trip studied her face.

Valor looked from one to the other, then jumped up on the bed and put her nose on Dani's knee.

Dani bent to give Valor a kiss and a little scratch between the ears. "Look, if I was trying to die, why would I leave a hiking plan with two people?" It was imperative to Dani that Trip believe she was fine.

He canted his head. "What people?"

"The front desk guy who gave me my map and told me not to lean on the trees because the soil was unstable, that they'd had a couple of incidents where there were landslides and trees randomly toppling over. He gave me the topo map, and I talked to him about my route up and my route down. He's the one who said take the inner loop and swing to the east on the way home. So he knew where I was going. He told me I'd be back in time for dinner, and then there would be a fire in the clearing. And Tiana, of course."

"Tiana is…"

"My friend I'm traveling with. She stayed back at the hotel because she had a migraine."

Trip scowled. "The manager knocked on your room. When no one answered, he let himself in with the key. No one was there."

"Obviously, she was out of the room if the manager went in. Maybe she went to get something to eat. Or she went to sit outside in the cool air."

"She would have seen my team there. Don't you think she'd ask what was going on? Don't you think she'd be worried about you out in the storm and go talk to someone?"

"If she walked by your TOC and asked about what was going on, what would your management team say?"

"We were out looking for the film crew."

"Not me."

"Not until we knew you were in danger."

"You didn't *know* that I was in danger. You *supposed* that. Or *assumed* that. Which ironically…huh, wow." She looked up at the ceiling as tears filled her eyes. "Thanks, Mom. I love you."

It took her a long emotional moment to get herself back together. She petted her hand in long self-soothing strokes down Valor's back.

Valor crept a little farther into Dani's lap.

"Why is that?" Trip's voice was gentle and filled with human kindness but also confusion. "I don't mean why do you love your mom. I mean what was the thought behind you saying it just then."

"I was heading back on the trail that you suggested," Dani said.

"Sorry about that."

"No blame. No shame. You were doing your best to get me back safely. Neither of us would have supposed that the trail would just fall away like that. I was cautious to watch for boulders and not lean on the trees but had no idea that I could be walking along one minute and freefalling the next." She stopped and blinked. "Yeah, that was some wild shit. But as to Mom? She's always had a wicked keen mom's sixth sense. She'd be out grocery shopping or what have you, and I'd think I'd do some naughty thing. The phone would ring. 'Dani? What are you getting yourself up to?' Shut me down more times than not. She must have felt I was in danger. And then her mind would go to reasons why I might be in danger. She, in her creativity, landed on suicide. And I'm going to admit—" she looked up to catch Trip's gaze "—my first reaction was to be thoroughly pissed at her. But now that I'm thinking about it, if my mom did have the feeling that I was in imminent danger, what could she possibly have said to the sheriff to get them out and looking for me other than that I was suicidal? She wouldn't have lied about something like that. She must have considered it. It's the truth, her fears for my safety sent you back to look for me."

"Her phone call saved your life. That's true. Though, you were on the whiteboard back at the lodge. If you hadn't checked in in a reasonable amount of time, we would have gone looking for you."

"But not in time. Not during this bomb cyclone. You'd have to wait. And I would have died. And hence, thank you to the chain of people who helped me survive. The sheriff, Iniquus command, you, and Valor."

"And most importantly your mom."

"Always. Particularly today."

Trip still had that look of confusion in his eyes. Things still felt off between them.

Surely, her whistle blowing was a sign that she wanted to live. She remembered back to them getting ready to hike to the cabin. He'd pointedly asked her if she had a gun.

Her mind had gone to bears.

She was a moron.

He was asking her if he could anticipate her blowing her brains out.

"I told you Mom's a neuroeducation specialist. Very up on all the newest research. Mom had made it very clear that she was worried about me since I joined the Army right out of veterinary school."

Trip nodded. He was definitely in his head churning thoughts around.

"Because I volunteered to deploy for much of my tenure, she believed I was in danger two-fold—once because I was in the military, and also because I'm a veterinarian. There's an epidemic of death by suicide in veterinarian roles."

"But you get to be with dogs all day."

"A lot of veterinary suicides are triggered by stress over finances. In the civilian world, veterinarian school costs lots of money. Then a clinic costs lots of money. People leave bad reviews when their beloved pet dies, which affects being able to attract clients. That's the financial side of things, then there's the emotional side. Euthanizing pets. For me, seeing the horror of the handlers who lost their dogs, especially when they survived the mission unscathed. That the dog died for them. And I understand to some degree. A tiny degree. My dog Daisey was with me at the veterinary hospital—she was part of my work. She was always by my side. She was my stress relief. She woke me up when I was having nightmares. She brought me solace when I was struggling. She was my confidant. I try to put myself in the handlers' head space." She tipped her head. "Did you ever lose a dog?"

"Died? No. But Rory was like one of my limbs, part of my body. I trusted him with my life. I depended on him to keep not just me but my brothers safe. Ty reaching out to me and making sure I knew what was going on with Rory means everything to me. It was hard enough handing Rory over—but I know he's alive and happy. He loves his work. To think of him hurt or killed?" He dragged a hand down his face, rubbing it across his mouth as if trying to erase the sensation those thoughts brought up.

"Yeah. Huge alpha men on their knees, sobbing on a blood-covered floor. I always had them right there in the surgical room. They had to be there. They needed to see the care and effort we made, so they knew that everything that could be done was done. Everything in my power. I did it." Her focus went to petting Valor, her mind back in Afghanistan. "It's hard." She turned back to Trip. "I try to focus on the fact that I'm good at what I do. If I get the K9 to me, they have a very good shot at surviving. The dogs and their handlers are better for me being there. I can't be there for them if I'm dead." She raised a brow, making her point. She had a reason to fight to stay alive.

# Chapter 29

## Dani

"Thank you for your service." Trip paused. "It can sound trite, but I mean that. When I was out with Rory—when things went sideways—in the back of my mind, I knew that if anything happened to him, Rory wouldn't be left in the dust. There would be a helo ride and a veterinarian who specialized in K9 combat injuries. It helped."

"Yeah." She sighed.

"You're an Army major. You're in danger. It goes with the territory. It's odd that your mom would become a helicopter parent all of a sudden."

Dani's brows pulled together. *Yeah, how to explain this to a stranger...* "Mom is anxious. I've learned to accept that as part and parcel to Mom. It didn't come out of nowhere. Smart women are often high anxiety. Mom had a childhood that would exacerbate that. She came from the age of latchkey kids. She was seven turning eight the year my grandma went to work. Mom had to get off the bus by herself as a young girl and walk up the block to pick up her brother, who was four, and walk him back to the house. She was there for hours without an adult around. Grandma wanted to stress the importance of not letting strangers into the house while she was away, so she'd tell my mom, eight years old at the time, these terrible stories of stranger danger. Mom can recite almost word for word the stories, like the one about a woman whose house was in the woods. Someone rang her bell, and she opened the door. These men dragged the woman outside and beat her with glass bottles until she was nearly dead and then drove off. She crawled inside to the phone to call for help."

"That story doesn't make a lot of sense."

"No." Dani chewed on her bottom lip. "It doesn't. Imagine how scared my eight-year-old mom was. She'd come home with her little brother that she was tasked with keeping safe. She thought that anytime a car full of men could pull up, ring the bell, and beat her with glass bottles. She told me stories about how she would hide in the attic with her kid brother, or she'd sit on the sofa watching out the front window, writing down all the license plates of the cars that drove by so the police would know to look for the last license plate on the list should she go missing. She was always scared as a kid. And I'm sure somewhere in there, probably a thousand times over, she promised herself that when she was a mother, she would protect her children."

"And she did."

"Like a grizzly bear on steroids. Now, mind you—" Dani held up a hand "—she always pushed me out of my comfort zone. She'd always say to us, as my sisters and I left to go to a new activity, 'Okay, girls, you're going to go out there, and you're going to suck at this. You are going to be really really bad at this. Expect it.'"

"Wow."

"You'd think 'wow.' I mean, what kind of mother would tell her kids that? It was certainly counter to the norms of the time where everyone was tumbling over themselves to be their kid's best friend and to cement their kids' egos in the positive position. She wasn't doing any of that. It was brave. She got flak for it."

"I don't know. Was it brave or destructive? I mean, telling your kid they were going to suck every time they started something new."

"Yeah, well it lowered my expectations of my performance right off the bat. It gave me permission to be bad, knowing that I could grow with time if I put in the effort. If I thought I was going to run out onto a basketball court, and I was going to look like the people playing at the park? I'd give up. If my first efforts dictated my continued involvement, I'd think I could never do what the other kids could do, and I'd probably give up. The 'you're going to suck *and* if you keep at it you will gradually improve' was kind of genius. I never thought I'd be good at anything stepping in for the first time. It freed me up to make mistakes. And that was another of her philosophies, 'the best lessons come from your mistakes not your successes'."

"She had a lot of those? Philosophies of childrearing?"

"A bored child is a creative child."

"That could go badly."

"Yeah, ask me about the time I tried to bungee off my tree house by holding onto a bungee cord while my sister held the other end."

"No way."

"Yes way. I let go before my sister did and the hook slapped her in the eye."

"Was she blinded?"

"She has good reflexes. She squinched her eye up in time to protect it. The neighbors, who took me in while Mom and Dad rushed Laura to the hospital, were an Italian family. They had dinner ready for everyone when my parents got home. They took one look at Laura and her black eye and put on a Rocky movie."

"Ha. So boredom was something your mom tried to build into your day?"

"Yes. Boredom and dirt. She thought if children weren't filthy at the end of the day, then they weren't out playing enough, play being one of the places where kids could learn best. She's a neuroeducation specialist, remember. But again, while she pushed us to feel comfortable being uncomfortable, she also mama-grizzly-bear-ed the hell out of us. Even as an adult, she sends me articles so I can be aware and nip things in the bud if my thoughts head toward desolate places."

"Like what for example." Trip seemed like he was settling down. Looking less like he'd been sent into a cage to tame a lion without any idea how to do it.

"Recently, one of the articles said that women are four times more likely to try to die by suicide than men, but men were three times more likely to actually die by suicide."

Trip canted his head. "Did it say why?"

"Men are more likely to use a means that was decisive—a gun or jumping. More violent. Women were more likely to try other means, like medication. That's one of the reasons that veterinarians die by suicide, by the way. They have access to very potent medications, and they know how to use them properly to be successful."

Dani's stomach was in knots. She knew Trip was watching her behaviors. The last thing she needed was to get back to the lodge, wrapped in a straitjacket, hauled off to the mental hospital, and have that go on her military record. She was conflicted as hell about her mother's actions.

Yes, without that phone call to the sheriff, Dani would be dead or dying now, but it could mess with her career.

And there below that thought ran the hum of, *Mom, you might have ruined the potential something good happening with me and Trip.* But Dani wasn't acknowledging that hum.

Dani turned to the fire and watched it dance. "I'm thinking about this conversation from the time you let me in on the idea that you were here to save me from myself."

"I—"

She held up her hand to stop him. "Mom, I get. Mom, I'm grateful for. I'm a little less clear about the lodge folks, the sheriff, and the manager. Tiana... That's problematic, isn't it?"

Trip didn't answer. He sat there calmly, letting Dani's mind chew on the gristle of her last thought.

"I checked the weather, and it looked like we were going to be fine when we started out this morning."

"That would be right. This morning, we were skydiving. The weather was a little complicated, not so much that we didn't take novice jumpers on tandem teams. It was while we were in the sky that things shifted and our plans for the training changed. Headquarters sent us here to the lodge—it was the only place nearby that they felt would be safe and had enough rooms."

"What time did you think that the weather had turned?"

"We were rerouted around ten."

"Tiana would have seen it when she was checking her phone in the parking lot. She must have."

Trip didn't respond.

"I left Mom's house at the crack of dawn this morning. I picked up Tiana from her place about an hour west. We were driving here to the lodge because Lei Ming spent her summers here. When she was deployed with us, she made us promise that should she die, that we would come here and do a good-bye hike along her beloved paths. And to read her poetry at Hermit's Cave and Eagle's Nest."

"The black notebook in the cave was Lei Ming's poetry?"

Dani's face turned fierce. While Dani had planned to leave the notebook there for others to read Lei Ming's poems about the Cave, the thought of anyone removing that notebook felt like a violation. "You didn't take it away from there, did you?"

"I left it." He looked toward one of the windows,

rattling violently despite the thick shutters. He turned back to Dani. "It's not there anymore."

Of course not. Silly to get revved up like that over something inconsequential to the big picture. "Tiana and I were going to do the promised hikes today and tomorrow, and then head to Ohio for Lei Ming's memorial service. After that, I was scheduled for some meetings down at Lackland, and then I'd fly back from there to base. Tiana…she didn't tell me her plans after the memorial service. I was going to hand in the rental car at the airport when I flew to Texas." She scratched beside her nose. "When we got here, Tiana checked the weather while I went in and got a room assignment."

"The registration was in your name alone?"

"Yes, I paid for it and registered online. When we arrived, I went in to get the key…"

"One key card."

"No, I got two. Well, they handed me two. I didn't ask for them."

"The desk guy said he was sending a valet to the parking lot, and I told him I'd be at my car. When I went back out, Tiana said the weather looked beautiful for the hike, but there would be a rainstorm Wednesday—same thing I saw this morning when I looked. Tiana had to use the bathroom. I gave her a key to go in since I didn't need help with the bags. A few minutes later, the porter came over with his trolley to bring our gear inside."

"She was in the bathroom when the porter went in the room?" There was a little bit of disbelief in his voice.

Dani ignored it. There was something very wrong with Trip being told that she was suicidal. Something

that felt dangerous to her. Just like when she was faced
with a dog in medical distress, Dani hoped by going
through the steps methodically, she could figure it out.
"Tiana said she had a migraine coming on. She was
seeing auras. She hadn't had migraines as far as I knew,
but after the accident..." She paused and their gazes
met. "I'm sure if you know my dog's name was Daisey, then they would have told you this too—I was in
an accident on base a couple months ago. Tiana was
driving our vehicle. Our friend Lei Ming was killed.
And my dog, Daisey." She stopped and bit down hard
on those emotions. She waited...then sighed out some
of the pain, so she could keep talking this through.

*Something* was definitely wrong with this picture,
something beyond her mom's worries and maternal
intuition. "Tiana hit her head in the crash among her
other injuries. I thought migraines might be one of
the side effects. I didn't know about them until today.
I didn't quiz Tiana on her medical status."

"You decided to hike alone."

"Decided... Tiana asked me to go by myself. She
said that she didn't think she'd be able to do both hikes.
She wanted me to do Hermit's Cave by myself, and she
would do Eagle's Nest with me tomorrow. She wanted
to do Eagle's Nest because that loop is half the distance
of Hermit's Cave. Tiana thought that by tomorrow she'd
be able to do the shorter of the two. And then she got
a little weird."

"Tell me about that." Trip stood to go poke the fire
in the stove. The log he'd put in earlier wasn't catching.

"She's actually been weird for a while—since the
accident. Tiana is a jokester, a belter of songs. Quick
to smile. Quick to tease. Friendly as the day is long.

At least until the accident she was. We were taken to
the hospital, and I was released the same day. She was
in there longer. She wasn't hurt enough to ship her to
Germany or home, so I didn't worry about it. I was
worried about me. The loss..." Dani stared into the
corner. "Tiana hasn't been the same at all. She's like
a whole different person. Which, I'll admit, I appreciated. I didn't want anything bright or happy around me.
I wanted to put my head down, do my job, wait to be
granted leave to fulfill my promises to Lei Ming, and
grieve in private. Tiana stopped talking. I chalked it up
to emotional pain just like I was experiencing. Tiana
didn't even sing in the shower." She looked over to Trip.
"She was known for her shower singing. People would
bring chairs and sit outside like they were going to a
concert. She has a beautiful voice. Amazing voice."

Dani rubbed her hands in her lap, staring down at
her fingers. "Remember how you said my pack was
heavy? I don't carry a pack like that. I carry survival
ten, because I'm not suicidal." She realized as the word
left her mouth that it was inappropriate under these circumstances. "Tiana was checking that I was equipped.
Extra equipped. She said that the reason she wanted
me to have double the supplies was that if I twisted my
ankle or something that there would be no way for me
to call her and get someone to send help. Cell phone
service here is nada."

Trip nodded.

"And folks probably wouldn't go out after me in
the dark, so I might end up under a ledge somewhere,
spending the night. She wanted me to be safe."

"If she's good with navigation, she would know that
if you took the seven hours of the normal hike—"

"Plus some time to grieve and say good-bye to Lei Ming."

He nodded. "Depending on how much time you spent at Hermit's Cave you had a good chance of getting all the way back to the lodge right about the time when this storm slammed into us."

"To what end? Why would she hide that weather from me?" Dani bent with her hands on her knees as a wave of anxiety flooded her.

"Thank you for coming back for me," she panted.

Trip crouched in front of her. They were eye to eye.

Her emotions roiled. Her life wasn't worth Trip and Valor's lives. She was at once overwhelmed and humbled by Trip's courage and sacrifices. "Thank you for getting me off the ledge. Thank you for putting yourself into this position, so that I survived."

"You're welcome." His voice was nothing like hers. He was steady and calm, while she felt dizzied by the turbulence of today. Of right now. The existential threat of the moment.

They listened to the ice pellets against the window. The howl and anger of the wind. Dani just prayed that the cabin could take the onslaught, and they'd live through the night.

# *Chapter 30*

### *Trip*

They lay on the futon; their hands clasped between them.

They were silent while outside the bomb cyclone raged.

Valor panted at their feet. Even she felt the anxiety, yawning and shaking, trying to deal with the stress.

The longer he talked to Dani, the less concerned he was that Dani was a danger to herself. But, then again, she was incredibly smart. Maybe she was throwing him off the right train of thought. Maybe she had been suicidal and had changed her mind when she was under the pile of dirt—had a come-to-Jesus moment and knew that if she got back, and a mental health report was sent to the military, her career would be over.

Maybe her thoughts were self-destructive followed by self-preservationist.

Trip squeezed Dani's hand then released it. "We should eat. I'm going to heat some MREs. Do you have a preference?"

Dani waved her hand through the air. "I'm not hungry."

"Even so, Dani, I'd like you to eat. You know the rule. There's no sure next meal. Eat while the eating's good." He swung off the futon and moved toward the kitchen counter.

"Ominous." She sighed.

She sighed a lot.

When he was in therapy at the hospital, he'd noticed people who were depressed did that. Sighed.

"Fine," she said. "I'll eat. I don't care what." She turned so she was facing him, posting her hand to prop up her head.

"I'll feed Valor first. When I said eat, she perked up."

Trip wished he could shake his concern that while physically healthy, that maybe Dani's mom had been right. Maybe Dani was despondent. It would be so easy. All she needed to do was pop the beam off the door, walk straight out into the black of night until her foot went over the edge of the cliff.

The cabin wasn't big. But he was nervous about getting out of arms' reach.

And yet, nothing Dani had done, or said, would lead him to those conclusions. He was framing this situation through two lenses, that Valor had acted like a different dog around Dani, and his conversation with Bob.

Trip opened a can of dog food. "Story time?"

Valor wandered over and sat, politely waiting for her food.

"Might as well."

Trip scooped the food from the can. The smell filled the cabin as Trip clanged the spoon on the side of the metal bowl to dislodge the goo. "This is a story about me and how I'm messing up."

"I'm all ears."

"When I joined Iniquus as a member of their tactical search and rescue team, I trained with some of the teams connected to state emergency management. There was this one night, we were sitting around the campfire, and I'm listening to what was going on. It was an opportunity to hear stories, learn from them. I'm going to tell you one of them. The takeaway here is that the lens the storyteller looked through created the reality they lived. The thing that focused their thinking was the last story they heard."

"All right." She reached down and rubbed the bandage on her heel.

"Let me set the stage. These were some hardcore searchers. We were at the base camp, sitting around a campfire, sharing war stories of past searches. One of the last stories they told was the night before, only one searcher was in the area. It was a single woman who worked at the park. She was in her office. At that time of year, she was the only one who was supposed to be on park property, the park being closed to tourists. She was there doing paperwork for the next day's training. Late in the evening, she heard some men talking outside. She listened as they circled around the office cabin."

Dani pulled a foot onto the chair, wrapped her hands around her leg, and rested her chin on her knee.

"Go on," she said.

"Dani, you can't sit like that," he said. "You don't have much on, and it's damned distracting."

Dani looked down to her bare legs and shirt. Nope, not a lot on, and she'd just flashed him her crotch. So… there was that. *Shit.* She stood up and moved to the futon where she lay down and crossed her legs at the ankle, pulling her shirt as long as it would go down her thighs.

"The woman called over to the village and several men came over and did a search. Finding no one, they went on their way."

Trip picked up the chair and moved it farther into the room so they could talk face to face. He sat down on it backward.

"The strangers came back and tried the woman's door handle. She racked the slide on her semi-automatic and called out, 'Leave now, or I shoot.' They hightailed it out of there.

"It was an odd story because no one should have been testing her door's locks. It was also concerning because, like I told you, no one was supposed to be in the area, not even park staff other than her. Now, skip forward to the morning. We'd gathered around the fire at the search base. There was a husband and wife team who had camped over in the tent camping area all alone. They said that the night before, they'd listened to the lady tell her story of the men rattling her door and promptly forgot it. That is, they forgot it until they were in their tent. It was the only tent in the whole campground, and the campground was a good distance from the base where the other searchers had their RVs. No big deal, they were comfortable in the woods. As they laid in their tent, a dually truck drove around the camp twice, nice and slow."

"Yikes!"

Trip nodded. "Right?"

Valor jumped onto the bed, and settled, gently resting her head on Dani's stomach.

"Was it the same guys who were rattling the woman's door?"

"Doubtful, but let me finish the story. The wife said that these were her thoughts after the men drove through—She's in silk long johns in her sleeping bag. Her boots are a hassle to get on. No one would hear her if she screamed. Her pack was in the car. She had no gun. She didn't even bring in her knives. It was around twenty degrees outside. There was nowhere to run except deeper into the woods. Dressed the way she was, there wasn't a good chance of survival if she ran toward the woods. She said that she figured her best option, if these men came back to cause problems, was to get past them, out the small tent door, down to the bathhouse, and lock herself in the shower room. Of course, she said, she'd be barefooted and in almost no clothes, so unless they left quickly or there was a ton of hot water available, she'd probably freeze."

Dani looked toward the door with a frown.

"The lady said the story about the men—who tried to enter into the park office and had to be chased off with the threat of gunfire—was worrisome. Worrisome enough that she only slept lightly, keeping an awareness of the sounds, trying to catch footfalls coming toward the tent. As they got dressed before coming to breakfast, she was talking about it with her husband. Of course, he was in the same straits she had been, clothing and weapons wise. He'd heard the same story and the concern of folks not on the mission being in an area that was supposed to be empty. He went through almost the same thought processes as she did. Though nothing happened. They were both awake all night prepared for the worst. As it turned out, the truck they heard was one of their search party, driving in late from out of state, trying to figure out where they were supposed to be to park their RV, not a dually after all."

Dani furrowed her brow. "I'm sorry, you obviously have a morality tale going on here, I'm not following it. How is it that you're messing up?"

"My takeaway from that training mission, was that I needed to be aware of the last story or stories that I heard. They'd be my lens for the way I framed my thoughts. If I thought 'bear', I'd be listening for bears. If I thought 'intruders', I'd prime myself to take on intruders. I heard 'Dani is in danger of self-harm', and I sprinted back to Hermit's Cave faster than I've run in my life. I thought that I'd missed the signals during our interaction, which meant I'd left you out there and in danger."

"You weren't wrong." She wriggled her fingers in Valor's scruff. "I was in danger. You are *absolutely* wrong that I would do something to hurt myself."

"I had the Bob story in my ear."

"The Bob story… Something is still off about all that."

# Chapter 31

## Dani

Trip leaned his hips back into the counter. His long-sleeved compression shirt showed off hard pecs and a washer board stomach. Dani tried not to stare. She tried to remind herself that things were crazy outside. They weren't safe.

Still…those tactical pants did fine things for the man's long legs.

"I'm making food," Trip announced, picking up a box. "I got sidetracked."

A sour look passed over Dani's face. Dani's brain flashed back to the conversation in the vehicle…all the things Tiana was telling Lei Ming she would be able to eat when she got back to the US—fresh fruit, sushi…

"Agreed, MREs aren't fabulous, but that look was pretty bleak."

"No, sorry. I'm back thinking about my friend Tiana. She feels responsible for Lei Ming and Daisey's deaths. She feels responsible for my pain. I can't hide that from her. We work in the same place, sleep in the same place, drove here in the same car. She was going to see I was wrecked even if I tried to hide it from her. I did stuff my emotions to get my job done." Dani licked her lips then slid off the futon in search of a glass of water. "This journey was partly fulfilling an oath, partly a gift to myself. An opportunity to unleash the grief kraken." She stood on her toes reaching for a jelly jar that the owner stacked in the cupboard in lieu of regular glasses.

She stalled, drawing a noisy breath in through nostrils, held it, let it out as a thought dawned on her.

"You knew Daisey's name." She lowered herself until she was flat footed and rested the jar on the counter. "That meant Bob and Noah were talking this over with you in detail."

"Bob was."

"Putting myself in Bob's position..." She crossed her arms over her chest and leaned one hip against the counter. "He had to make a decision about the best use of you and Valor on the search. He was weighing the possibility of the group being at Eagle's Nest or along the path between Eagle's Nest and the lodge. That was a tactical decision. He wouldn't have sent you in my direction without gathering information from you about our encounter."

"He did." Trip sounded wary.

"Can you go through that with me?" Dani moved

back to the futon away from Trip, standing too close distracted her from her thoughts. The idea of solace in his arms was a gravitational pull. The best she could do to keep control of her hormones—and with it, keep her focus on the pile of problems stacking up—was to gain some distance.

"Bob said your mother received a text from your phone saying, 'Thank you for everything. I love you. Forgive me. I can't deal with this pain anymore.'"

She put her hand to her chest. "From *my* phone number?"

Trip nodded.

"Did they say what time? I mean, I don't have my phone. There's no cell service here."

"It had to have been within the right timeframe from the point where your mother received the text until the point where I saw you. Like you said, cell service is only in the parking lot at the lodge, so three to four hours would need to have gone by. My guess is that it went out around nine thirty, ten o'clock?" He put the box down and crossed his arms over his chest, keenly focused on her. "My team goes on too many searches looking for despondent subjects for Bob not to have plotted a timeline to make sure it all fit logically."

"Tiana had access to my phone. She could have gone out to the parking lot and sent the text. Still, why would she do that?" Dani scratched the side of her head. "Was she trying set me up for some reason?" Her hand made a wide sweep. "This makes no sense."

"Bob said your mom called you back right away. When you didn't answer, she called the lodge. Their line was busy. She called the sheriff's department, and the sheriff came to knock on your door. No answer.

He and the manager did a search of the lodge and surrounding area, only then would the manager give him access to your room."

"Did Mom tell them I was suicidal? I can't believe she would do that."

"She read them your text. The sheriff got Bob and Noah involved after they found a map on the bed and determined you were going to Hermit's Cave which, the manager explained, has a sheer drop-off." Trip's voice was tight as he said, "Drop-off that would be certain death."

"Tiana could tell them why I was there. I don't understand why she didn't step forward during all this hullabaloo."

"Bob didn't mention Tiana, he did say that the sheriff found a note on your bed."

"A note? What did it say?"

He rolled his lips in and shook his head.

"I left one of the topo maps from when I signed in back at the room. I thought I put it next to the coffee pot, but I could have left it on my bed. I circled my destination and noted departing time and when I thought I'd be back. That's just Hiking 101 stuff." Dani put her hand on her forehead, thinking back. "Okay. I can't remember exactly what I left on the bed besides the topo map. I know I had been looking through some of Lei Ming's poems. There was one that I had planned to read that I'd pulled out of her binder." She turned toward her pack sitting next to Trip's beside the door, as if they might need to grab them and race out of the cabin.

"Huh." She walked to it, wincing at a shot of pain as she crouched down to unclasp the top. "I didn't see it in my pack right away when I was up there at the cave. Before I could search through, Valor showed up."

She pulled the inner drawstring wide and rifled through. "It's not here. I bet I left it on the bed. When you said they found a note, that could be what they found."

Dani gasped. She put a hand on the floor and held for a moment. The pain radiating through her back held her hostage.

Trip was instantly beside her. "You fell off a cliff, Dani. You have to take it easy."

She nodded. Squatting there. Stuck. Feeling ridiculous that she couldn't shake this off. "Psh, what's a little cliff diving, in the scheme of today's clusterfuck?"

"Slowly." Trip had his hands under her arms, and without any assist from her, he lifted her up and leaned her back against him.

It took her a moment to trust herself to stand on her own.

She nodded, and he released her. "Better?"

"Not stuck in a frog position. I'll take what I can get. Thank you."

He tucked his chin. "What was the poem about?"

"The one about Hermit's Cave talked about how it would feel to fling oneself into the air from that point, the momentary freedom of freefalling at terminal velocity through the air. The joy of it. But without there being a parachute that freedom would end it all... There was more. It was about leaps of faith, a willingness to take risks and accept the outcomes. Without Lei Ming giving the work context, if you were looking— as you were saying a moment ago—through the lens of someone who thought there was a suicidal woman heading up the mountain to jump, then sure, it could very easily be interpreted as a suicide note."

"That sounds like what Bob read to me. When I was talking to Bob, I agreed with his concerns, because the story about what was happening at base gave me a new perspective of our exchange up at Hermit's Cave. I had been confused and concerned when I was out there. I—"

"You thought I seemed despondent when we met?"

"You? No. I was thinking about Valor. I trained Valor to find someone and come get me if she found a conscious adult. She barks when she finds children, or adults in grave danger. Valor barked. And she was sitting in your lap hugging you. I have *never* seen her do that before. It was unusual behavior to say the least. When Valor was tracking you down the east trail, I was jogging after her, thinking about that. That you had seemed fine, that it was Valor who was acting odd. I thought that maybe Valor had picked up on something that made her feel that she needed to take care of you."

Dani didn't know what to say to that. She'd thought Valor's behavior was odd for a stranger K9, too.

"I was afraid for you. We ran full out." He audibly swallowed. "When we got to Hermit's Cave and you weren't there—"

"We agreed that I'd head back right away." She stared at him wide eyed wondering how that must have felt to race back, thinking you'd pull someone off the cliff, and they were gone. She put her hands to her heart, imagining the scene. "You looked over the edge for me."

"Of course I did. When I didn't find you there, I was still scared for you." His face was a scowl of emotion.

"When Valor picked up your scent on the eastern trail it was such a relief."

"And then you saw me halfway down the cliff."

"Heard your whistle, anyway."

"Did you think I jumped and failed?"

He shook his head. "I saw how the trail dropped."

"At that point, how were you framing the picture." She sat tentatively on the futon. "That I'd changed my mind? Chickened out?"

"I was focused on the obstacle in front of me. I was alone on the ridge. I wasn't sure how hurt you were. For sure, we had no help for a while, days maybe. I needed to manage Valor. Manage the scene. Get us all to the cabin. Secure it for the storm. Stuff. I wasn't assessing anything beyond that."

Dani stared at the door with its wide safety beam securing it against the maelstrom outside. "Tiana didn't tell your TOC I was on the trails." She scooted farther up the futon, her back up against the wall. "I'm remembering a night back on base. Mom had sent me a veterinarian suicide article, admonishing me to keep an eye on my staff. She did it so often it was a kind of a running joke with my colleagues. We were sitting around a campfire." She sent a scowl toward Trip. "A bunch of women drinking and laughing, shaking off the day."

He nodded; the frown on his face matched hers.

"We went around the circle saying how we'd do it if we were going to end it. Most of us said pills and alcohol, an IV line and meds cocktail. She said what she'd do is get drunk and go sit in a cold stream by a pile of rocks. The rocks would keep her body from floating away—she wanted her husband to know what had happened to her. But she'd just be cold, and wet, and drunk. She'd fall asleep and never wake up. The beauty of hypothermia, she said, was that no one could find her and pump her stomach. And if she was far enough out in the wilderness, they couldn't get her out in time to revive her. She said it was all about making sure you accomplished the task."

"She? Tiana?"

Dani stared ahead, her eyes blinking in a rhythm, turning to Trip. "She sent me out, preparing me the best she could to take the hike and get back safely. When I got back, the bomb cyclone would be revving up, making searching for her impossible. There would be nothing I could do."

Dani could see Trip thinking hard, the cogs whirring.

"Trip, Tiana had to have sent that message to my mom, knowing my mom would freak and send in the cavalry. Even if the rescuers got going right away, it would take them all day to get to me and make sure I got down safely. Tiana wouldn't know there were already searchers on the trails. She was protecting me. And getting rid of me. She knew about the storm." Dani's heart beat so hard she thought it would jump out of her chest. She gripped at her shirt, trying to catch her breath.

Trip stepped forward to kneel beside her, his hands on her shoulder.

"If Tiana went up on Eagle's Nest to die, you missed her to save me." She slid off the futon down into Trip's arms. Emotions swamped her system. She curled her fingers into Trip's sleeves and clung there as he held her tight against him. "This is one hell of an emotional horror show." She tipped her head back to look Trip in the eye. "I have to get to Eagle's Nest. I can't... I just can't let Tiana die."

# *Chapter 32*

## *Trip*

"Dani, listen to me." Trip pushed up from the floor and moved them both back to the bed, hoping that getting her off the floorboards would help with her shivering. "I hear you revving your engines. I'm going to remind you there's a bomb cyclone raging."

She nodded.

Up here, the heat from the stove was warmer. Still, she trembled against him. He figured it was fear making Dani's teeth chatter.

"I've done this job long enough to know that, as you're suggesting, Tiana might have had every intention of dying by suicide. She might be up there at Eagle's Nest. We need to go check as soon as it's safe enough to go. And we will." He held her against him, rubbing her arm gently. "There are other possibilities. Tiana might have walked up the path and changed her mind. She could very well be in your room asleep or in the lobby talking to Bob and Noah worried that you didn't reach the cabin safely with me and Valor."

Valor lifted her head and when a command didn't follow, she laid it back down, her muzzle resting daintily on her paws.

"She's there. I know it," Dani whispered. "I just do."

"As soon as the storm abates, we'll go check. I promise." He dropped a kiss into her curls. "Noah said there are possibly three weather bands. We wait until the winds die, then we get out to the Eagle's Nest to check as the snow starts to fall. If she's there we work that scenario. If not, we can get back here to the cabin before the snows get too deep."

"Okay."

Trip's gaze traveled the length of her long, silky legs stretched out and tangled with his. Even in the dim candlelight, the bruising was visible. Trip wanted Dani in a hospital, not traipsing through the woods in the middle of this storm.

Short of tying her up, he didn't know how he could stop her.

A moment later, Dani was sliding off the bed to her pack where she retrieved her map case and crawled right back between his legs where he sat with his back up against the wall. She crisscrossed her legs and spread the map out in front of her.

Trip curved over, watching her measuring with her fingers.

"I can see why they circled you this way. Cutting here to the cabin stairs. We're only about a kilometer and a half from Eagle's Nest. That's not that far. Off trail, that's a half-hour hike."

"In good conditions, daylight, pleasant weather."

"Eagle's Nest juts out and looks west with the rocks behind it. If Tiana were here, with the wind coming in from the east, she'd be protected."

"I don't think there's anywhere someone could go outside that would be protected in this."

They fell silent as they took in the enormity of the storm raging outside.

Trip's gaze ran up the wall to the ceiling. He searched for any signs that the structure was about to fail. He had contemplated next steps if the roof were to fly off or the front wall were to collapse. The only thing they could do was hide in the bathroom behind the hollow core door and the water barrels. In this wind, that was as good as nothing at all. On this narrow apron, the wind could blow them right over the edge. They were as vulnerable as a boat on the ocean.

"At least Tiana wouldn't be endangered by trees falling here," Dani was saying. "There are none. Lei Ming's poem about Eagle's Nest said that she, 'left the line of trees, clambering rolling stone to face the sunset, the rocks amassing behind her, stretching out on either side like an armchair to curl with a book. A giant's lap with loving arms of protection.'"

She moved the map off to the side and leaned back against him, her hands resting on his thighs. "The wind isn't the thing. Possibly. I hope not. In my mind, it's the temperature. The rocks were warm from today's sun. How long would that hold in the dipping temperatures?"

Trip thought back to his time on the Appalachian

Trail. Sometimes, the rocks were hot after a long day hiking with his pack. He'd lie out on them, letting the warmth penetrate his skin and loosen his muscles like a heating pad. Other times, when he tried to find shelter from storms, they could suck the heat right out of his body and leave him in danger of hypothermia.

"Depends. In this, I count rocks as a disadvantage more than a plus." Trip reached for a pillow and stuck it behind him, scooting down a bit so Dani could lean into him and relax more comfortably. "There's a lot to unpack from what you're telling me. Was Tiana drunk like she'd decided in her 'how would I suicide' scenario? Did she go out in light clothing?"

"I have her survival gear." She turned on her side, wrapping a hand around his waist, his chest was her pillow.

"Let's think this through rationally."

Dani leaned her head back to look at him, lifting a single brow.

"That's a habitual phrase I use for myself. I'm not accusing either of us of being emotional or irrational. Though, emotional is human right now."

"I'll admit to that. This is Tiana we're talking about here. She, Lei Ming, and I were the Three Musketeers with our sidekick, Daisey." A sudden crash made her jump.

"A tree just came down. It's a reminder that racing out into this would be a tactical mistake."

Her gaze was steady on him.

"You want to race to Eagle's Nest and find Tiana. Pull on your boots, grab a flashlight, and head out there."

She said nothing.

"Am I wrong?"

"No," she admitted.

"We'll wait it out."

He tucked her under his chin, sweeping his hands through her hair.

He waited for her to nod.

"I can't handle any more grief."

"You scheduled in this time to allow your emotions to surface—which would sound crazy to someone who hasn't deployed—I know it isn't. I know what base life is like."

Dani nodded, her arms wrapping around him, which was where he'd wanted her to be since he met her at Hermit's Cave. Just not like this. Not under these circumstances. He'd imagined a cup of coffee, watching the snow fall. A long afternoon of lazy conversation. A delicious meal in the five-star dining room. Maybe a drink and a laugh. Maybe later in the night, or over the next couple of days, they might enjoy a tumble or two. Some time curled up in front of the fire.

He'd projected a whole week of working Valor in the snowy conditions mixed in with relaxation with Dani. He'd looked forward to it.

"I also know what it's like when you take the lid off that box," he said. "It's overwhelming. In the midst of this day of mourning, you've had all this shit thrown at you. I wish I could stake out a space in time and place to just let you feel."

Dani reached over and petted Valor. "At the veterinary hospital, we would get soldiers who missed home. They'd come in and sit with the dogs. I thought the injured dogs were helpful to them. I saw a lot of post traumatic healing happen."

"Yeah?" Trip could feel Dani settle in as they waited for a break in the storm, and that was good. He didn't want her fear for her friend to make her lose rational thought and have her racing out the door.

He'd stop her. But he couldn't imagine a good outcome to that scene. "I'm surprised the handlers would let someone else be with their injured dog."

"The handlers were often hospitalized themselves or didn't make it back to their team. Of course, those were dangerous dogs for us to work with. Trained as a weapon as well as a nose. We were the enemy, their handler off scene, pain and anxiety makes the dogs dangerous."

Dani lifted her arm, and even in the dim light, Trip could see the silver scars. He traced them with his finger.

"Each scar has a story. That one you're looking at was not a fun day. But we got the job done. Karma needed an amputation. She came through, retired, and now she's living the life. I get photos and stories every once in a while." Dani turned sideways and cuddled in closer, looking up so Trip could press a kiss onto her lips.

He meant for it to be light and comforting, but they paused, their lips a whisper against each other's. She made a little humming noise, then tucked in.

Trip's body liked that hum and wanted more.

"Karma had a tight bond with her handler. I'm glad they got to stay together. She was a dog of his heart."

"A dog of the heart, I know how that feels. That was me with Rory. When I first got to Iniquus, before I made the search and rescue team, I worked with a dual operations K9, drug detection/bomb sniffer named

Zorro. Great dog. We did some good things—stopped a terrorist bomb in a D.C. restaurant. The bond was okay. It wasn't like Rory. And to be honest, I was hurting and didn't want another bond like Rory."

"It's not like nursing a bruised heart, is it? It's more like—yeah, you were saying earlier—like a lost limb. I can't quite figure out how to function without it. That's what it's been like."

"I'd say that's about right. It's different for me, though. I get those weekly updates from Ty. And I have hope that I'll get to be with Rory again in a few years. To have that hope taken away from me? Whew."

Trip was by nature a private man, an introvert, the strong silent type. A dog guy. All along this misadventure, he had been surprised at how open he was with Dani. Trip could go whole days without saying much more than was strictly required of him, and yet here he was telling stories about his life and his family, sharing his feelings like he was back in therapy but without the sense that it was being pulled from him against his will. It had all been natural. He was comfortable in the discomfort of this conversation.

"My mouth wants to say how sorry I am for Daisey's loss," he said. "Inside, I know I'm not courageous enough to conjure what that would feel like so I could better empathize. I think of myself as a courageous man. But my courage has more to do with running into the building and doing the job I'm trained to do. Cuts to the skin are different than cuts to the soul."

"Yes. Thank you. Yes. That's how it feels, a thousand little paper cuts to the soul. My memories of failure are the salt that makes the sting vicious."

Valor clambered down to the end of the futon and

curled up. A few thumps of her tail told them she was content despite the storm.

"I've watched you with Valor. She's a dog of the heart. Isn't she?"

"She has been since the moment I saw her."

"Iniquus assigned her? Who did her training?"

"I did her finishing and accreditation. When she was one year old, I got her from Lackland. She left the military because she didn't have a play drive."

"Mmm." Dani sent a maternal smile to Valor. "And I was giving her her high-dollar ear rub reward at Hermit's Cave, so I'm guessing she's affection driven. That can get you in a world of hurt, Mama. You have to be careful about that."

Valor comically lifted one eyebrow and then the other.

"To be honest," Trip said, "Valor's reward is the pride of a job well done." Up on the trail, when Valor hugged Dani, that was a part of the puzzle that Trip hadn't put together yet.

# Chapter 33

*Dani*

"She's two?" Dani asked. "I wonder if I took care of her at Lackland. Who was her dam?"

"Domino."

"I remember Domino. She gave us a real scare. She'd developed a fever and had her puppies early. We had to work hard to keep them alive. Domino was too sick to care for them." She paused. "Domino fully recovered and had a successful litter since then. It was a tough go with her first litter. In our vet center, each of us took a puppy. We were trying out a technique like kangarooing for humans. We kept the puppies in a sling up on our chests, so they could hear our hearts beating, and wore them around all day. It was a successful experiment, all the puppies kept steady vitals and gained weight on schedule. They all went out to foster families for their initial training. I had the purple collar." Dani looked over to Valor and her heart squeezed. "Are you Purple Collar? Is that why you climbed in my lap and hugged me—because that's how I carried you?" Dani stared hard at Valor's markings, the little wings of black next to her eyes.

Wow. The small world of military working dogs.

Emotion built up and crashed through Dani. Tears slipped down her face to drip from her chin. "Has to be. What a crazy turn of events. I saved you, sweet girl, and then years later, you end up saving me?" She blinked hard as the emotion bubbled up and then moved off. "You grew up to be so beautiful. Such a good girl."

The ebb and flow of grief and discovery.

"That's a story for the ages," she said. "I'll also have to research how the dogs did moving through the MWD program. I wonder if they all became affection driven and had to move on to other careers. That would be interesting to know." She sent Trip a self-conscious smile.

"Military Working Dogs is a small community."

"I was just thinking that," Dani said. "Are you reading my mind?"

"We have Valor in common. Rory and Ty in common. Do you think there's more to that list?"

"There would have to be. I've probably had some interaction with almost all of your colleagues and their K9s at one point or another."

Trip tipped onto one hip and dragged his phone from his cargo pocket. Looking down at the screen on his phone, scrolling through his photo album. "Here it is!"

She could hear the smile in his voice. "This is a picture Ty sent me from when Rory was injured. This is at your base. And…" he flipped to another picture "… there's Rory hanging out with the clinic's care dog. Is that Daisey?"

She took the phone and frowned down at it until the screen timed out, and it went black.

Trip swept a finger over the phone then scrolled further. "There are more of her. Wait a second."

He reached in front of her, leaning over her shoulder as he adjusted the screen, stretching his finger wide to enlarge an aspect of the photo. "You," he said.

There, Dani crouched in scrubs, her hand out protecting Rory's foot from Daisey's tail.

"I thought I recognized you." He flipped back a few more. "You," he said, showing a picture of Dani in full surgical PPE, gloved hands in the air, protecting the operation room's sterility, looking down at Rory lying on the surgical table looking dopey.

"Man, that's kind of nuts." He stalled as they looked at the photo. "Thank you for taking such good care of Rory." He leaned in and planted a kiss on her shoulder.

He left his lips against her for a long time.

He breathed deeply.

Dani understood the sensations running through his system. The kinship this depth of emotions engendered. War and dogs. The tight-knit K9 family. Life and death. Damage and victory.

After the moment passed, Dani scrolled back to Daisey in her nurse's hat. She paused and sent Trip a smile that quivered at the corners. "She had a face only a mama could love." She rubbed her lips together as tears laced into her lashes.

Trip reached out and wrapped her hands in his. "She

had a face that was dearly loved. Nurse Daisey. Great hat."

"Nurse Daisey, yes. That's what my colleagues called her. The title was cemented when she started wearing her hat." She laughed softly then sniffed hard. "Daisey was always so proud when she wore it. Like she was putting on her uniform to go do her important job." She gazed down at the photo, wishing she could absorb it into her system. "She *was* important. Daisey was my greatest teacher. I had never loved as profoundly and purely before her. She was my heart." Her voice cracked. "Now, my heart is broken."

Dani turned out sideways so she could see Trip. She realized in this position he was cradling her like she was a baby. She felt weak and bereft. Trip offered her support. She wasn't going to act brave in front of him. She didn't have it in her.

From the depth and pain in his own eyes, Dani could see they had a shared gulf of pain.

"I loved her." She put the phone down. "I'll always love her. But I loved her physical presence in my life. She was a pest. She was needy. She made my life complicated. I mean, I got her to go to Afghanistan with me to help in the hospital. Can you imagine what I had to go through to do that? I moved Heaven and Earth to keep her with me. For my sake and the dogs I was tending."

"How did you do that?"

Dani slid her hands back through her shoulder length curls. She twisted the length, wishing she had her hair tie, but somehow it had been lost during her rescue. "I developed a study, and she was Phase I. The question was 'What were the effects on a patient K9's level of pain care, time in PT, and overall recovery and return to work with Nurse Daisey versus without Nurse Daisey.'"

"And?"

"The operators themselves seemed to have the most profound effect on the K9s' recovery." She dropped her head. "In the absence of an operator..." She stalled. She wasn't going to say out loud why the handler couldn't be with their dog. "In the absence of their handler, Daisey had a pretty profound effect. Not just on their dog, but if the handler was convalescing, we sent cute pictures and video. I'd put a nurse hat on Daisey's head. Mom sent it to me from the Halloween store. They could see that their dog was being cared for by us veterinarians and by Nurse Daisey."

"I imagine that's true." He smiled. Such a wonderful warm smile. A truthful smile not a player's smile. His smiles came from his eyes as much as his lips.

"Don't let me puff her up too much in your imagination. Daisey was a nuisance," she said. "She whined all the time when someone was hurt. She'd make these high-pitched sounds down deep in her throat. An alert that attention was needed. We were at a base where pain was a given—physical and emotional. And she wanted me to fix it. As if I had that power. Such a nuisance!" Dani shook her splayed hands in the air. "And I loved her past that. I loved her past her terrible gas that woke me up at night. I loved her past my chewed-up shower shoes. Past her insistence that I rub her belly until my fingers became so sensitive that they hurt. And she loved me back. All of my idiosyncrasies. All the ways I failed. My bad moods. Me. She just loved me. I miss being loved that way. Infallibly." She looked up at the ceiling and rubbed her hand over her eyes. "You're meeting me on my grief journey," Dani reminded him between hitches of breath. "I had designated this week to allow grief. I promised myself this. I told myself I could fall apart this week. I'm telling myself to pull it back together because of this unexpected turn of events. But no part of me is cooperating. I apologize."

"You're apologizing to me?" he asked, concern lacing his voice.

Valor came and shoved her head up under Dani's arms until she could get to Dani's face and lick her.

Dani pushed her down and rested a hand on Valor's head. "Thank you, Valor." She wiggled her fingers behind Valor's ears. "Strangers, especially cliff-jumping rescuer strangers, shouldn't be subjected to this."

"Don't try to hide this away for my sake. I don't need that. I'm comfortable being around emotions. I mean, I hate for you to be in pain, but when I was in the hospital with valley fever, and we had to do the therapy route, I learned to sit with other people's stuff."

Dani swallowed as sorrow dragged at the corners of her mouth. "I can't imagine a time when this is going to hurt less." She sniffed again and was able to look at Trip. "My mother sent me articles that were circulating around about grief. They described it as a box that was all but filled with a ball, a person's awareness being the box, and the ball being the grief. Any little jostle of the box and that ball of grief would touch the sides, and there would be a shock of pain. The therapist said that as time went by, the box got bigger, but the grief ball wouldn't get smaller. Same size ball, but it would bounce into the sides with less and less frequency. And while I hate how this feels, I'm also afraid that I'll stop feeling it. It seems like it would disrespect Daisey that I'm not... I don't know. Those emotions don't have words to go with them yet."

"And they don't need to. I get it. Grief holds our loved ones close and reminds us that their lives were significant to us. But I don't think that the memories and closeness have to show up as pain."

Dani's brows pulled together.

Trip lifted a hand. "I'm not telling you how to grieve. I'm talking about my personal experience here."

Dani exhaled, hoping some of the tension would leave her body. "Yeah. All the memories. The times when I felt like I was doing the best for her, the times she was plucking at my last nerve, the times when I felt her communicating so clearly with me. I remember this night in the States when the gate at my friend's house where I had been staying was open. She was gone. Usually, when she hears me call, 'D,' she comes running, knowing there's a treat on the other side of the door. But not that night. That night I walked down the road calling out over and over, getting frantic that someone had picked her up, or she'd been hit by a car. Then I saw her. She'd come out of the shadows just to show me she was there and okay, but she wasn't coming over to me. So weird. 'Come on, pretty girl, we need to go home.' She was clearly annoyed. I got a thought impression from her. 'I'm having fun. I like it out here now.' And I made her go home."

"Of course you did. It was dark and late, and she was in danger of getting hurt."

"Exactly. And she didn't pout about it. It always seems to me to be the thing, that when she was having the most fun, I cut it off. There was a storm when we were driving through Wyoming. The wind was so strong, it was blowing semis over. I was on the phone trying to find a motel where we could get off the road, or even a parking garage, something. I was scared. Everything was so flat. I wasn't used to that wind. I remember that there was this yellow-colored bird that must have found some respite in the draft of my car because it was flying right outside of my driver's window. Just this little yellow bird. But it was so strange and ominous. Then a buffet of wind hit us, and the bird rolled sideways and out of my view. Then it was just me and Daisey. We get to this town, I guess, I mean there were some buildings. The motel had no office. There was a sign that said to stay at the motel you had to go to the gas station."

"Wow."

"Yeah. So we got the last room. I took our stuff in and then I took Daisey to potty. I'm telling you, the wind was so strong, though, not as bad as this." She looked toward the window where the shutters struggled to stay together. "I was terrified the wind would pick Daisey up, and I'd be flying her like a kite. Daisey, on the other hand, thought all of this was just marvelous. Her ears were flapping in the wind like that old-time cartoon Wonder Dog. Flapping. Flapping. Daisey had her head into the wind, and I got one of those impression bubbles from her. 'Weeeeeee! Awesome!'"

"But you dragged her back to your room away from her fun."

Dani's face crumpled and turned red. "I did." She sniffed. "I'm an East Coast girl and that wind… I was trying to remember what I had heard about tornadoes.

I mean, the place we were staying seemed like it was as flimsy as cardboard. I wasn't sure what I'd do if a tornado came through. I decided I'd grab up the mattress and go get in the bathtub with Daisey and put the mattress over our heads. I made Daisey sleep with her leash attached, and I had the handle around my wrist."

They sat in silence for a long moment then she laughed. "One of the things that I had heard about tornadoes was that they sound like a train before they hit."

Trip tipped his head waiting for her to finish that thought.

"As it turns out, the motel I was staying in was long and thin. Basically just rooms lined up with the doors on one side and a window on the other. And it ran, oh, about twelve feet or so from a train track."

"No!"

"Yup. A very busy train track. About every hour or so, a train would come through. But there must have been a curve in the tracks before it got to the motel because I could hear it long before I could see the light. Every hour, there I was peeking through the curtains trying to decide if it was a train or if we were going to die. After the third time, Daisey stopped poking her head up to see what had frightened me. She posted her chin on her paws and rolled her eyes up at me as if to say, 'Really? You don't think I'd warn you if a tornado was heading toward us?'"

"Dog instincts." He reached out and scrubbed at Valor's fur. Valor rolled onto her back so that would turn into a belly rub.

"Exactly. After that, when I heard the train, I'd reach out to see what Daisey was doing. And if she was fine, I was fine." Dani threw her arms over her face. "She's not fine, Trip. She's not fine." She reached up and scratched her head, scrubbed her fingers against her eyes, and sniffed tiny puffs of air into her clogged nose. The pain washing over her had its own current.

Trip was quiet, letting the power of her emotions swell and flow out of her.

He waited until she was able to hear him past the cacophony of memories. "At Hermit's Cave, I was intruding on your sacred space. This was time you allocated to do this grief work. I respect that. Don't stuff anything because you think the emotions are too big. I can handle being around your pain. It needs to come out."

"It's an awfully small space for the expanse of what I'm feeling. It fit better in the forest."

# Chapter 34

*Dani*

"I have confidence that you're going to find your way through, tough as this is. I'm going to add this—advice from my dad. He and mom had me late in life. They've been married now—" he leaned his head back to look at the ceiling "—fifty-two years. He told me that marriage was like sandpaper always rubbing at you. If the person did it right, they'd rub with the grain and bring out the beauty beneath. In a relationship you had to stop and self-assess, recalibrate, shift. If you weren't growing, what was the purpose of the relationship? He never said that was unique to marriage. Personally, I like it when my friends challenge me. I'm not talking angry, finger pointing arguments, I mean thoughtful arguments where theories and philosophies can be refined. And I found that in my counseling work at the hospital. There were three things that were my life's greatest teachers—the Appalachian Trail, my work with K9s, and contracting valley fever. Those things grew me in ways that I had no idea I had to grow."

"Share something."

"One was not to expect perfection of myself. Like your mom said, so I guess we share this philosophy, I'm gonna suck sometimes. I'm a fallible being. Another was, in a relationship everyone is fallible. And that meant I needed to treat myself with grace as much as I did others. We all have our bad days. Our 'I'm so sorry I failed you' days. The days when we realize how bad we sucked and the mistakes we made."

"You know—"

There was an enormous splintering and crash.

Suddenly, the room was pitch black.

Dani flung her body over Valor, grabbing Valor's collar in one hand, wrapping the other over her head. She was lifted and dragged. She clung to Valor. Her mind battling, let go of Valor or hold her? Was this like Daisey? Was this decision life threatening? What was happening? Trip! She flailed out for him.

His voice was in her ear, hollering, "Do you have Valor?"

She nodded her head, feeling her cheek brush against Trip. He'd get the signal.

"I've pulled the futon over the two of you. Don't move. Can you hear me? Don't move!"

She nodded. But he was already gone.

Dani clutched Valor's collar with a death grip. She imagined the wind picking up Valor's body and slamming her into the cliff.

Here, under the claustrophobic weight of the futon, Dani had no idea what was happening around them. Wriggling around, she got her legs wrapped around Valor and full body clung to her. Dani prayed that Valor would understand that Dani was trying her best to keep her safe and that Valor would stay calm.

Valor was too well muscled to stay still if she didn't trust Dani or the situation. Would Valor bolt? Was the cabin still intact?

Dani used her free hand to lift the edge of the futon up.

The cabin was dark except for a bobbing light toward the front.

It took Dani a second to figure out the geometric shapes in the near darkness.

Trip was at the front of the cabin. He had lifted the dining table and tipped it flush to the window opening, using it to block the wind from blowing into the cabin.

The front shutters must have given way. Trip had his back pressed against the bottom of the table, his legs bent, using his muscles to hold it in place. Trip's headlamp swept the room, searching for a solution.

Dani thrust the futon to the side, wrangled her legs underneath her, and stumbled toward the kitchen. There she yanked open the cabinet that held a toolbox.

Digging through by feel and memory, she pulled out a box of nails and a hammer, then hustled to the front of the cabin.

Grabbing a handful of nails and putting them between her lips, she plucked them into her fingers one at a time. Using the power of her adrenaline surge, she hammered them in at cross angles so the wind couldn't slide the wood down the nail, turning the table into a projectile.

She filled the left side, then the right. She crouched at Trip's feet and nailed below. Then she put her back next to Trip's to trade places, handing over the hammer so he could put in the nails across the top, too high over her head for her to have reached properly.

He stepped away.

He signaled her to do the same.

They watched to see if it would hold.

"That was unexpected." Trip trained his headlamp on her. The light slid down her body. "Stay still for a second." He moved off. "Hey, Little Mama, are you okay under there? There's my good girl. What a day we're having, huh?"

A candle flame jumped in a glass jar.

Another. And another until they were all lit again.

Trip wrestled the futon back on the frame.

Valor jumped up and lay down with her head on a pillow. She didn't seem to be worse for wear.

Trip turned off his head lamp as he moved over to her. "Dani, would you put your arm around my shoulder? I'll lift you up."

Confused, she followed his finger as he pointed down, finding herself standing barefooted in a pool of glass shards.

He bent with one hand behind her back and one hand scooping under her knees.

She wrapped her arms around his neck to keep her weight close to his frame where it would be easier. But he hadn't even grunted, so kudos to his workout routine.

He sat her on the edge of the futon and knelt at her

feet. He switched on his headlamp and looked at her soles one at a time.

As a picture, Dani thought, this would be lovely, caring, possibly even romantic—Studly McStudMuffin gently blowing glass shards from off the bottoms of her feet onto the plastic bag he'd used from earlier first aid ministrations. But Dani was keenly aware that she'd been racing up and down the mountain in hiking boots all day. Her feet had sweat emotional perspiration. She was horrified by this whole situation.

"Not a single cut, good job."

He complimented her as if she realized she was walking on broken glass and had done it with the skill of a martial arts master.

She looked over at the tabletop nailed flush to the window opening. The four legs sticking out into the room.

"I hope that holds, I'd hate to be impaled by a kitchen table and have that go on my epitaph. The storm can't last very much longer." She frowned, looking down where Trip kneeled beside her. "Can it?"

# *Chapter 35*

*Trip*

Trip checked his watch, canted his head, and listened.

It had been fifteen minutes now of near silence.

Dani curled into his arms after the window blowout and had eventually fallen into a fitful sleep. As he'd stroked her back and combed his fingers through her hair, that sleep had grown deeper, and he thought she was finally getting some recuperative rest.

When the wind stopped, there was supposed to be a band of time before the heavy snows started.

Trip could really use a radar readout right about now.

He wanted to make the trek to Eagle's Nest alone.

Two things would stop him. He knew he couldn't convince Dani to stay even if he asked her to do it to keep Valor safe. And if Tiana were there and alive, Trip would need help. Dani was the doctor. Dog doctor, but farther up the chain of knowing what to do. Trip got training as a SEAL, but the focus was battlefield injuries.

Dani had more in her medical catastrophe survival pocket than he did.

"Dani, I need you to wake up."

She sprang up, eyes wide and staring. She looked around disoriented.

He wondered for a moment if she'd had a brain injury that was made worse by falling asleep.

She quickly shook off the confusion. "The winds died down." She scrambled off the bed, grabbing up her pants, ripped and stiff with her blood, wincing and slicking air past her teeth as she drew them on.

"I think we should take the toboggan. If we were to find Tiana up on Eagle's Nest, we can use it to drag her to the lodge." What he didn't add was that if the snow became a blizzard, and they didn't have a visual field, it might be a lifesaving shelter overhead.

In January, Iniquus's Panther Force had been part of an extraction team when an FBI agent was in a car accident and hiked out of the West Virginia mountains through a snowstorm. It took him three days to get to a road. Special Agent Finley was known in the halls of Iniquus. He let Cerberus Tactical talk to him about how he'd stayed alive and functioning, unprepared for the winter storm and with only the equipment found in his FBI pool car.

They'd gone into the woods on the Iniquus campus and tried out a couple of the techniques, including a hut made from plastic sheeting and a Mylar blanket.

Cerberus Tactical changed up the materials in their packs based on their findings during that training evolution. While those were good designs, serving their purpose in the West Virginia snowstorm, and Trip had the materials in his pack, Trip thought those designs were unlikely to hold up in blizzard conditions. He had no idea how fast the winds would be blowing when that second band hit.

Having a weather report from Noah would be golden about now.

The toboggan, and Valor's ability to dig on command, helped Trip feel more confident about heading up the stairs.

Trip watched as Dani buttoned her pants and reach for her fleece.

He had layered clothing with him that protected him with space age technology. Each layer explicitly made to top the one below. Merino wool base layer like Dani was wearing. A turtleneck made of high-tech fibers cooled or heated depending on his body temperature, plastic fleece that shed water but was lined with reflective material to bounce heat back at him. His jacket. Each layer was thin and maneuverable but when he had them in place, he was good to go down to zero degrees.

Dani's clothes weren't of the same quality.

He reached in his pack and pulled out another hand-warmer, shook it to life, and handed it over. "You're going to need this." Then he handed off a pair of gloves. "And these."

Trip zipped his coat, pulled on his pack, and clipped a lead on Valor.

"We're going to drink a big glass of water and use

the toilet, then we'll go. Once we're outside we're pushing hard. We don't know what this window of opportunity looks like."

Trip was glad to find that the steps had been carved out of the cliff's side. It meant there was no fear of the rungs rusting out or their attachments shaking loose.

He planted his foot on the cliff wall, grabbed the metal handrail and gave it a few tugs. It was in there solid.

While the wind whipped the air, with their ball caps on and their hoods up, they were mostly protected. Trip added a pair of safety goggles and handed Dani his spare. Even though they were high tech, they'd still fog up. He had to weigh which was the biggest threat, losing footing or a projectile stabbing into an eye.

Protecting their eyes won out.

Trip pulled line from his bag and quickly tied Prusik knots that he attached to the handrail. Lucky for them, it looked like a single metal pole, bottom to top. He attached the knot to a carabiner, the carabiner to the hasty that he wrapped around Dani's legs.

"Have you used these before?" he yelled.

She nodded. "About a decade ago."

"Slide it up as you go. If you were to lose your footing, it'll catch and stop you from falling. Not perfectly, the pole is too slick for a great grip. Enough that you won't tumble down. You go first."

"So you can catch me when I fall? That's not a good idea. You've got Valor."

"No, you're going first so I can watch your ass as you climb the stairs." He sent her a wink and was rewarded when she snorted. A bit of the grimness left her face.

She headed up.

The pair of winter climbing gloves he'd pulled from his pack were huge on Dani's dainty hands. He hoped that wouldn't become a safety issue.

Trip had his own Prusik in one hand. Valor's lead was clipped to Trip's pack, and dragging behind him was a rope with the toboggan, a molded plastic design that Trip hoped would stand up to the thrashing it was getting as the wind lifted and dropped it as Trip hauled it up.

He had a moment of horror as he imagined the sled becoming a parasail and jerking him off the staircase. It might not be a brilliant idea to have it along. Could be the worst idea he ever had.

Time would tell.

It wasn't a long climb, about four stories here, Trip reminded himself.

Watching Dani up ahead of him would tell Trip how bad Dani's injuries were, her back, her legs.

She'd pressed through like a champion on the trek to the cabin.

Now, just a dozen or so steps up, she bent in two. One hand slid the Prusik, the other was on the stairs.

At this point, whatever it took. They were neither up nor down. The way this wind was hitting them, he thought if or when they came back to the cabin, they'd probably end up crawling backward down the stairs like toddlers because of the sheer weight and heft of the gusts.

When he and Valor reached the point where Dani bent, Trip understood why she'd put her hand and knees down, getting herself as low as possible. Here, above the cabin's roof, there was a wind shear that stole his breath.

Valor balked, trying to lie down on the stair and curl up against the onslaught.

Trip didn't want to fight Valor all the way up. He thought it would teach her bad behaviors for future rescues in difficult environments. Trip turned and clipped Valor's tactical vest to his gear. He'd just carry her. That seventy extra pounds dragging him backward meant that he had to grab hold of the railing and hoist himself up hand over hand.

The sky was gunmetal gray. A strange color for early morning. The cold was brittle. The snow was already accumulating on the treads.

Trip rounded the top of the stairs on the mountain ridge. The first thing his eye sought out was Dani. She knelt on the ground, just to the side of him, her hands plastered on either side of her head. Her mouth agape.

Trip turned.

The trees were toppled in piles like pick-up sticks from his childhood. There wasn't a single tree standing as far as his eye could see.

Leaves and debris spread across the landscape. The path that had been right here that led to Eagle's Nest wasn't visible beneath it.

It was Armageddon.

Total destruction.

Trip crawled out onto the land and unhooked Valor from his harness and attached her lead, immediately.

"We go to Eagle's Nest. We check. We get back down." He pulled his glove down to see his watch and set a timer. "I'm giving us forty-five minutes to get there. If we can't make it through this by the time my alarm sounds, we'll go back to the cabin. Those stairs are already treacherous."

She glared over at him, and that pissed him off. He knew she meant to battle through any weather that showed up to get to her friend. It was written all over her face.

"I swear to god, Dani. If I have to subdue you, tie you to this toboggan, and drag your ass back to the cabin, I will. Forty-five minutes is as generous as I'm willing to go."

"Can you hear yourself? Are you serious, right now?" Dani asked.

"Dead serious."

Trip instantly regretted the phrase.

# *Chapter 36*

*Dani*

Dani couldn't tell how far into the forty-five-minute time limit they had traveled. She pushed herself as hard and as fast as she could. Daily PT on base was one thing. This reminded her of the obstacle courses at boot camp, too many years ago to be of any use.

Dani was definitely feeling her age.

And the fall.

And her angst.

She was beating herself up for being pissed at Trip.

He was absolutely right to set clear thoughtful objectives while she was emotional about the situation.

Her go-to was to beat herself up for any imperfection in action or character.

Dani could say that growing up around her mom's

anxiety, some of it had rubbed into Dani's emotional patina. Her mom would say that, neurobiologically, smart women were anxious by nature. Either way, calling herself emotional was gentler than the crazy that was burning through her system, thinking that she had lived, and Tiana had died, and it very easily could have been the other way around.

Yup, a lot of survival hormones just bubbling and boiling through her veins.

"So there was a woman." Dani needed a different focus.

"Is this going to be one of your weird facts?" Trip was just back to her left. He had his pack, Valor, and the toboggan. How he was keeping up with her and making it seem effortless pissed her off a bit.

Dani was determined that someday she was going to find some rust on his suit of armor, his high school anger issues aside. Right now, though, she'd be grateful for the parts that shined.

"Possibly," she said. "Probably. Though, you might have studied this as part of your search and rescue medic training."

"Shoot."

"There was a woman. Her name was Anna. She was training to become a surgeon."

"Where is this? When?"

"Norway, I believe. And it was when I was in junior high, so somewhere around the turn of the century."

"Wow, you're that old, huh?"

"Yeah, a whole two weeks older than you."

"Okay, future Dr. Anna in Norway…"

"She and her friends were up on the mountains

doing some skiing. Anna fell, her skis came off, she went right off the side of the mountain."

"This is sounding familiar, only in my story, the woman was a veterinarian not a surgeon."

"I hit a ledge. The falling was the last thing we had in common in our falling stories. She kept going, and she didn't have a special ops guy jumping after her. So, thank you for jumping after me."

"You're still welcome from the last time you thanked me."

"I would have died."

"Meh. It's not your time."

Dani planted her hands on a fallen tree and threw her leg over the trunk.

*It's not your time.* That was one of the mantras that Dani had used to help her cope—that they had died, and she had walked away. Whole in health, broken in spirit.

*They died in their time. If you're not meant to die...* She said aloud, "Something intervenes."

"What?" Trip asked.

"An aside—this isn't about Anna. I was thinking about back at my base in Afghanistan. A K9 handler with his bomb sniffer were outside the wire and all of a sudden, he bent in two. He said it was almost like getting punched in the stomach by some biker angel. Boom, he took a fist to the solar plexus. He was a scrapper. He knew what a punch to the gut felt like. When he yelled, 'oof,' and bent in two, a string of bullets whizzed right over his head. He said he could feel their heat on his scalp. He would have been dead." Dani turned to Trip. "It just wasn't his time."

Trip lifted his brow.

"Anna. Anna fell down the slope. Losing her skis, she fell all the way down the mountain, all the way out onto a frozen stream, and then through the ice and into the water. Her friends were skiing after her, trying to get down and help. The current in the stream dragged Anna under the ice. Her friends find her. They can't get her out. I'm assuming the weight of Anna and her wet clothes along with the current was too much for them. They were able to get her braced in a spot where there was a pocket of air. In those cold temperatures, she went unconscious pretty quick."

"That's a rough decision-making point. The friends had to be wet and cold and at risk of hypothermia, too. They probably couldn't tell if Anna was able to breathe in that pocket of air. She could be deceased or alive. What did they end up doing?"

"They knew help was coming. The friends stuck with Anna. Rescue arrived eighty minutes later."

"Are you bargaining for more time? That forty-five minutes is the hard mark. We *will* turn around if we haven't found Tiana by then."

Dani sighed and ducked under another trunk. "The eighty minutes, Mr. Rigid as Shit, is part of my story. The rescuers got there and got her out of the water, her body temperature was only fifty-five degrees."

"We were trained that cold and dead is different from warm and dead. Even if she were fifty-five degrees, we'd treat her as if she were alive until we got her temperature back up to normal."

"Exactly what that crew did. In modern health care, surgeons will, in some instances, put a person into hypothermia, so they can perform the surgery. Anyway, through tests, they found that Anna's brain had frozen before she went into cardiac arrest, which meant that her brain needed like zero oxygen." Dani's whole body burned from exertion. Talking helped keep her mind off the pain, kept pushing her forward. She could almost hear the clock ticking down.

She couldn't see herself willingly turning around.

She could see Trip tying her to the sled and dragging her ass back to the cabin.

"Anna was okay?" Trip asked.

"She was unconscious for close to two weeks. When she came to, she was paralyzed from the neck down. Eventually, though, she made progress, walking and even skiing again. I don't know if she had the capacity or dexterity to follow her goal of becoming a surgeon."

Trip put his hand on her back, helping her over the trunk.

His watch started beeping.

Dani spun wide eyed toward him.

Valor raced forward to the end of her line, her whole body stiff with concentration, her nose working hard. She turned to Trip and sent up three sharp barks.

"Search," Trip commanded, dropping the toboggan and unhooking her lead.

Valor took off. Trip raced right behind her.

Dani climbed off the trunk, snatched up the sled, following along as fast as her body would manage.

She climbed around the rocks and found Trip bending over a prone Tiana. Valor off to the side in a down stay, tongue lolling, looking proud.

"I'm not getting any vitals," Trip said. "The Anna story, how do we do this?"

"In the Anna story, they started CPR."

"Got it." Trip rounded over her, adjusted his hands and started the thrusts. "We need a plan."

Dani reached across to the radio on Trip's strap and pressed the button. He had been trying the radio every few minutes since they reached the top of the stairs. He had said the sat phone would be a no-go, but he had hopes for the radio. Maybe here on the outlook, they could get enough signal. "Dani Addams for TOC. Come in, TOC."

She lifted her finger from the radio button and listened to the static.

"Mayday. Mayday. Mayday. This is Dani Addams. If you can hear this call, please respond."

"Dani, I need you to help me figure this out. I can't keep up the CPR and get her out of here. Getting her down to the lodge will be one thing. Then we need to get her to a hospital. If we had radio signal, I think they could get a helo in here with a basket during the lull between weather bands. If it's you and me doing the rescue, it's hours through this mess down to the lodge, and the next band of weather is going to be dumping snow. Getting her to the cabin is faster, but we have nothing there to help her. How do we handle this?"

"Tiana," she whispered, lifting Tiana's limp hand to her lips. "I don't know. I'm a veterinarian not a people doctor."

It was an impossible situation and not like Anna's at all.

"Dani, focus on your medical knowledge now. Do we start to warm her with Mylar blankets and hand warmers? I could lay Valor on the sled with her to help warm her. Or do we try to keep her cold, so she stays in that state? There's no way to tell if she's alive right now. We have no way of telling if any decisions we make will make any difference at all."

"God, Tiana, what have you done?" Dani looked down at her friend as she tried to make that decision. Warm with no CPR or cold with no CPR?

There was a snag in the static on Trip's radio.

He reached up and pressed the button. "Tripwire for TOC. Come in."

Nothing.

He stood and looked at the rocks towering above them, leapt to his feet, and rounded out of Dani's sight.

After a moment, she heard his voice above her. "Clear the net. Clear the net. Clear the net. This is Tripwire for Iniquus TOC. TOC, do you read me?"

"Tripwire, good to hear your voice. Go for TOC."

# Chapter 37

### Dani

Trip wrapped his arms around Dani, easing her off the back of the snowmobile that had met them as far up the trail as the fallen trees had allowed.

She tugged the helmet strap, her fingers stiff with cold.

Trip lifted the helmet from her head and handed it off. He wrapped a hand around her waist and aimed them toward the front doors where, not twenty-four hours ago, she'd set off on a trail of bereavement and had faced one of the biggest challenges of her life.

As they hustled forward bent against the snow, falling fast and heavy, Dani could hardly believe they were here at the lodge, safe.

Trip had wanted her to go to the hospital with Tiana,

but when the helicopter dropped the basket out at Eagle's Nest, they were told the helicopter could only hold one patient, since they'd added a trauma specialist and nurse to support Tiana during the flight.

Dani was fine with that. She didn't want to get stuck in a hospital in this storm.

She wanted to be with Trip.

They burst through the doors to a crowd of cheers.

Thankfully, Trip managed his team. She was too exhausted to do any glad-handing. His arm wrapped around her, he said, "Let's get you to your room and cleaned up."

The manager pushed over to them, his face pink with embarrassment. "Major Addams. I'm so sorry. I've let your room go." He turned and pointed toward a closed door. "I have your things in the concierge room."

Dani scowled.

"The lodge was full to capacity, and we had travelers caught on the highway with nowhere to go. I put a family in that room. Since you...weren't here." He pointed toward the hall. "I have rollaways in the ballrooms to accommodate everyone who needed shelter. I can find one for you as well."

Trip gave her a squeeze. "That's fine, Dani. Let's get your stuff, and you can stay with Valor and me."

Her first thought was, "any port in a storm". But that was reflex cliché. Dani was glad to stay with Trip. She wasn't ready for them to be separated in different rooms.

The manager unlocked the concierge door. Dani pointed to her bags, leaving Tiana's there.

Trip pulled them over his shoulder, keeping her tightly tucked under his arm.

Valor, who had ridden all the way back lounging across Trip's lap, like the good girl that she was, paced along beside them like this was a day just like any other day.

Mission accomplished, time for a snooze.

Trip swiped the card over the lock. And pressed the door wide.

Valor pushed ahead of them, galloped through the room, and leapt onto the bed.

"My team brought in my bags," he said, tucking her luggage next to his. "I didn't realize it had only the one bed." He turned to her. "I would have told you when I invited you."

"We've already slept together," Dani said. "I slept with you, anyway. You were being vigilant. I'm fine with the arrangements—" she sent him a smile "—if you are."

He crossed his arms over his chest and leaned a shoulder into the wall. "I don't know about that. Do you snore? Steal the blankets? Kick in your sleep?"

"I don't know. I'm asleep."

"How about I go get that raw steak for Valor while you get into that hot bath you've been promising yourself?"

Dani turned and went into the bathroom. "Do you think there's hot water?" She got the tap running and wiggled her fingers underneath it. Success. This was going to feel so good.

Dani stood and crossed her hands over her fleece top and stopped cold. "Oof."

Trip filled the doorframe. "No?"

"Yes to the hot water. No to my body functioning.

That snowmobile ride did me in." She stood there, shirt halfway up her chest.

A slow smile slid across Trip's face. "I wouldn't mind helping you."

"Would you, please?"

Trip slowly lifted her arms over her head. Pulling first the fleece, then her base layer over her head. He lowered her arms.

"Can you reach your bra clasp, or do you need help?"

Dani could probably reach her bra clasp. "Help, please."

He reached behind her and like a magician, pinched the sides together and released the band. He slid the straps down her arms and put the bra on the counter. He looked down at her breasts, painted his hands over them. "Your pants?" he asked.

"Mmm hmm."

He knelt at her feet and unlaced her boots, pulling them off and setting them near the sink. Then her socks. Her hands resting on his shoulders.

He turned her, reaching around to unbutton the waistband, sliding the zipper slowly down. He tucked his fingers into the band and skidded them down her legs. His arm reached around her hips to balance her as she lifted one foot then the other as she stepped out of them.

"I think they can go in the trash. They've done their duty."

"Panties?"

"Yes."

She felt his hand slide across her bottom.

"It was unprofessional of me, but you bent over in

these when I was cleaning your cuts, all I wanted was to slide my hands across the satin."

"Really?" she asked. "That's all you wanted?"

Trip chuckled behind her. "I'll tell you what, I think that it's better to show not tell." His thumbs went into the sides of her panties and skated them down her legs. "You need a good soak. You're covered in cliff debris, and it'll do your muscles good." He stood. "I'm going to leave you for a couple minutes to go get more first aid stuff. And I'm going to stop by the bar and get you a drink and some food."

"Something tall. A dark and stormy."

"Sounds appropriate."

She stood naked in front of Trip. She was surprisingly comfortable as his gaze explored her curves.

He held her hand as she stepped into the tub and bent to shut off the water.

Dani winced as the water stung her raw skin.

He lowered her in. "You relax. I'll be back."


"I was gathering news." Trip and Valor had blown through the room door, pushing a cart. A moment later, he was back in the frame of the bathroom door. His eyes sweeping down her length, probably thinking how sexy she looked.

"You're going to turn into a prune in there. Do you need help getting out?"

Prune. *Not* sexy.

Dani held out her hand. "I could use a hoist."

Hoist, also *not* sexy.

He reached out a hand and pulled her from the tub, opened the drain and held out the big white fluffy robe with the lodge crest. He wrapped it around her, gently lifting her hair free then dropping a kiss onto her shoulder.

She was facing the mirror, watching in its reflection as Trip reached for a hand towel, then used it to gently rub the dripping water from her curls.

Their eyes caught.

A wolfish smile slid across his face.

*Definitely* sexy.

He reached for her hand and pulled her into the bedroom. "I talked to Tiana's husband. He called your phone to thank you and make sure you were okay." He waited for her to get comfortable on the bed. "I hope you don't mind that I answered your phone."

Dani squeezed his arm. And stared at him wide eyed.

"She's alive."

Dani exhaled.

He pulled a note from his pocket. "The doctors checked Tiana's potassium levels, and they were normal." He lifted his gaze to meet hers, asking Dani for an explanation.

"That means that her cells weren't significantly damaged. That's good news. What are they doing for Tiana? Did Derek say?" She pulled the note from his hand and stared down at the chicken scratch then handed it back. "Who wrote that?"

"I did."

"You scrawl like a doctor. Can you understand that?"

He read off the note. "They're trying cardiopulmonary bypass."

"That's when they pump the blood out of her body and gradually bring the temperature back to normal."

He nodded, sliding the note back in his pocket. "They said that that would take about six hours."

"Alive, though."

"She has a chance." He gestured toward the trolley. "I have drinks and food. The food can wait under these little metal hoods. The waitstaff said the plates were on warmers. So that gives me time to do some first aid." He looked at her. "How do you want to do this?"

"Toss the robe? Flip over?"

"Okay, let's do it that way."

Again, *not* sexy.

She frowned as he dug through the first aid box.

Dani slipped out of the robe, tossing it across the bed, out of the way.

Trip still had his hand in the first aid kit, but he froze.

This time it was Dani who was wearing the slow smile. She lay luxuriantly on the bed, giving him a show in his peripheral vision.

*Sexy.*

She rolled languorously over. "And everyone else from the adventures of the last day?"

He cleared his throat, his voice low and husky, he said, "Everyone from the photography crew got back before the storm." The mattress dipped as he moved onto the bed beside her. "The guy who was in the parachute accident, Pierre Roujean, is out of surgery. His status is guarded."

His hand slicked up her uninjured leg from ankle to hip.

Mmm, yes. *Very* sexy.

"You look beautiful." He laid a kiss on her low back.

He pushed up the bed and lay beside her then pulled her across him. "I want to feel you here, safe."

The fabric of his pants rasped her inner thighs as she splayed her legs and let them rest on the bed on either side of him.

"This was quite the adventure. Is this how you manage all your first dates? Leave a girl breathless by your skill and stamina?"

"Oh." He chuckled, moving a damp curl behind her ear. "I haven't even begun to show you my skill and stamina." He rolled until she was underneath him. His hands framed her face. "A miracle of a day. I'm so grateful. You're a remarkable woman, Dani Addams." His lips lowered to hers, soft and probing.

She opened her mouth to him, tipping her head back.

"Don't let me hurt you, Dani," he whispered between kisses that trailed down her neck. "I'd never want to hurt you."

She shook her head.

Hurt wasn't sexy. It was nowhere in this picture.

She curled her fingers into his shirt, pulling it free of his pants. He reached behind him and yanked the shirt over his head, tossing it to the floor. The warmth of his skin against her was delicious. She moaned and tipped her hips side to side.

*So* sexy.

His weight balanced on his forearms; his gaze sought hers. Questioning.

"Happy moans. 'Yes, please' moans."

"You have to swear you'll tell me if it's anything else."

"You'll stop, and I don't want you to."

"Ah." He kissed down her side and sent a flick of

his tongue across her belly making goose bumps appear. "How about this. You promise you'll tell me that you're uncomfortable and in return…" He kissed across to the other side, taking a little nip at her waist. Then kissing the spot to soothe the brightness. "I'll promise that I'll see that as an *opportunity* to explore ways that feel good."

So, *so* sexy.

He pressed back into his heels, kissing her hip, her thigh.

She moaned.

He looked up to catch her gaze again. "Promise?"

"I promise if you do," she exhaled.

"I do." His lips whispered against her thigh. "You need to talk to me, so I know how you're doing. Just like on the ledge. That's your job."

"K." She slid her hands into his hair, feeling the silkiness of his military tight cut. Her eyes closing as he licked.

"Good?" His breath was warm against her.

"Mmmmm."

"How about here?"

As his tongue slid across her clit, Dani squeezed her thighs tight. "Yup. That's a good place… Very good."

Sexy as *fucking* hell.

They'd slept, eaten, made love a second time, and now, they were in the shower.

Trip was rubbing soap bubbles over Dani's breasts in long gentle strokes. "Lackland then Afghanistan, huh?" he asked.

He was thinking the same thing she was. This was a moment in time, then it would be over.

"I think our moms are pretty incredible women." He moved her under the water to rinse her off. "Your mom set the world on fire trying to make sure someone was out there saving you."

Dani looked up.

He smiled. "I'm glad it was me."

"I'm glad it was you, too."

"It's kind of remarkable that my mom called and told me that I was going to marry Wednesday Addams. Just too darned coincidental that happened on the day you were flying in from overseas."

"Almost seems like the fates were conspiring and had our moms playing their roles." She swallowed hard. She was just going to say it. Just…lay it out there. "I feel… I don't have the right words. 'I like you' isn't right. I feel connected, not just by events, not just by people we have in common, but my heart feels like…" She shook her head. "Look, I'm someone who has tried and failed at long distance relationships. With you, I'd like to more than try. I'd like to see where a relationship might go."

"Now that we both have our adult brains?" He sent her a teasing grin and a pop of his brows.

"It's a plus." She shrugged. "You seem pretty levelheaded."

"Yeah, I think that with you, Dani, I've found the person I'm supposed to go on the long haul with."

"And we have Valor to help smooth the road."

"She loves both of us." Trip held Dani's hands. "And I always trust my dog."

# *Epilogue*

Dani was unprepared for the swell of people who met her as she crossed through the security doors and into the waiting area of the airport.

Overhead, she heard an announcement: "Ronald Reagan Airport proudly welcomes home Major Danielle Marie Addams. Major Addams is returning to the United States from her deployment in Afghanistan where she was a surgical veterinarian protecting our war dogs' health. She is now joining our forces at Fort Meade. We are indebted to her service abroad. And we wish her every success as she joins her new station here at home. Welcome home, Major Addams."

Dani was wide eyed and red faced as everyone turned to stare at her. Strangers with their luggage, clapping and cheering for her was overwhelming to say the least.

Her gaze sought out Trip's. He was laughing at her reaction. He stepped forward and wrapped her into a protective hug. "The announcement was your mom's idea," he whispered in her ear.

Of course it was.

She sighed. Looking over his shoulder, she saw her family, the Cerberus Search and Rescue Team, Tiana in a wheelchair with Derek behind her.

"I invited folks, though."

"I hate that. You *knew* I would hate that."

"I did. But I wanted them here. I knew the second I had you back in my arms, that I couldn't wait a second longer." He bent down on one knee.

"Here?" she squeaked. They had agreed to marry over a video chat, and she had made him promise that he'd make things low key. He'd just slide the ring on her finger when she got home. "You swore," she whispered. "Low key."

"Valor talked me into this stunt."

When Trip whistled, Valor trotted out from behind Ridge, carrying a white box by a pink ribbon. She dropped it into Trip's hand then sat in front of Dani, a paw lifted to wave at her.

Dani choked on her tears.

Trip popped the box open. "Will you do me the honor of joining me on the long haul?"

Valor barked her share of the question.

The crowd laughed.

Dani swiped tears from her face. And nodded.

"Dani," he said under his breath, "it's my job to kneel down here with the ring. It's your job to answer me."

"Yes. You know this. Yes."

She held out her left hand, and Trip slid the ring into place.

Valor grabbed Dani's sleeve in her teeth and dragged her down to join her and Trip.

With one hand Dani rubbed Valor's ears. Her other arm wrapped around the man who was her everything. Their heads pressed together in a mind meld that meant they were the same pack.

The crowd around them faded from her awareness.

This was the next step on their journey through this crazy life.

Dani couldn't have been happier.

* * * * *

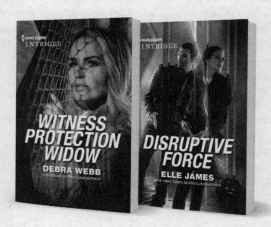

"CHELSEA, WHAT'S GOING ON?" Johnny clutched his cell
phone to his ear and at the same time he sat up and turned
on the lamp on his nightstand.

"That man…that man is here. He tried to b-break in."
The words came amid sobs. "He…he was at my back
d-door and breaking the gl-glass to get in."

"Hang up and call Lane," he instructed as he got out
of bed.

"I…already called, but n-nobody is here yet."

Johnny could hear the abject terror in her voice, and an
icy fear shot through him. "Where are you now?"

"I'm in the kitchen."

"Get to the bathroom and lock yourself in. Do you hear me? Lock yourself in the bathroom, and I'll be there as quickly as I can," he instructed.

"Please hurry. I don't know where he is now, and I'm so scared."

"Just get to the bathroom. Lock the door and don't open it for anyone but me or the police." He hung up and quickly dressed. He then strapped on his gun and left his cabin. Any residual sleepiness he might have felt was instantly gone, replaced by a sharp edge of tension that tightened his chest.

*Don't miss*
Closing in on the Cowboy *by Carla Cassidy,*
*available July 2022 wherever*
*Harlequin Intrigue books and ebooks are sold.*

Harlequin.com

# Get 4 FREE REWARDS!

**We'll send you 2 FREE Books plus 2 FREE Mystery Gifts.**

Both the **Harlequin Intrigue®** and **Harlequin® Romantic Suspense** series
feature compelling novels filled with heart-racing action-packed romance
that will keep you on the edge of your seat.

---

**YES!** Please send me 2 FREE novels from the Harlequin Intrigue or Harlequin
Romantic Suspense series and my 2 FREE gifts (gifts are worth about $10
retail). After receiving them, if I don't wish to receive any more books, I can
return the shipping statement marked "cancel." If I don't cancel, I will receive
6 brand-new Harlequin Intrigue Larger-Print books every month and be billed
just $5.99 each in the U.S. or $6.49 each in Canada, a savings of at least 14%
off the cover price or 4 brand-new Harlequin Romantic Suspense books every
month and be billed just $4.99 each in the U.S. or $5.74 each in Canada, a
savings of at least 13% off the cover price. It's quite a bargain! Shipping and
handling is just 50¢ per book in the U.S. and $1.25 per book in Canada.* 
I understand that accepting the 2 free books and gifts places me under no
obligation to buy anything. I can always return a shipment and cancel at any
time. The free books and gifts are mine to keep no matter what I decide.

Choose one: ☐ **Harlequin Intrigue**          ☐ **Harlequin Romantic Suspense**
                  **Larger-Print**                        (240/340 HDN GNMZ)
                  (199/399 HDN GNXC)

Name (please print)

Address                                                                          Apt. #

City                                      State/Province                    Zip/Postal Code

Email: Please check this box ☐ if you would like to receive newsletters and promotional emails from Harlequin Enterprises ULC and
its affiliates. You can unsubscribe anytime.

### Mail to the **Harlequin Reader Service:**
**IN U.S.A.:** P.O. Box 1341, Buffalo, NY 14240-8531
**IN CANADA:** P.O. Box 603, Fort Erie, Ontario L2A 5X3

Want to try 2 free books from another series! Call 1-800-873-8635 or visit www.ReaderService.com.

*Terms and prices subject to change without notice. Prices do not include sales taxes, which will be charged (if applicable) based
on your state or country of residence. Canadian residents will be charged applicable taxes. Offer not valid in Quebec. This offer is
limited to one order per household. Books received may not be as shown. Not valid for current subscribers to the Harlequin Intrigue
or Harlequin Romantic Suspense series. All orders subject to approval. Credit or debit balances in a customer's account(s) may be
offset by any other outstanding balance owed by or to the customer. Please allow 4 to 6 weeks for delivery. Offer available while
quantities last.

**Your Privacy**—Your information is being collected by Harlequin Enterprises ULC, operating as Harlequin Reader Service. For a
complete summary of the information we collect, how we use this information and to whom it is disclosed, please visit our privacy notice
located at corporate.harlequin.com/privacy-notice. From time to time we may also exchange your personal information with reputable
third parties. If you wish to opt out of this sharing of your personal information, please visit readerservice.com/consumerchoice or
call 1-800-873-8635. **Notice to California Residents**—Under California law, you have specific rights to control and access your data.
For more information on these rights and how to exercise them, visit corporate.harlequin.com/california-privacy.

HIHRS22

# IF YOU ENJOYED THIS BOOK
## WE THINK YOU WILL ALSO LOVE

*Danger. Passion. Drama.*

These heart-racing page-turners will keep you guessing to the very end. Experience the thrill of unexpected plot twists and irresistible chemistry.

**4 NEW BOOKS AVAILABLE EVERY MONTH!**

HRSXSERIES2020

SPECIAL EXCERPT FROM

**◑ HARLEQUIN**
# ROMANTIC SUSPENSE

*One night of passion with Marcus Jones led to a
pregnancy Chloe Ryder didn't expect. And when a
serial killer they captured launches a plan for revenge,
Chloe wonders if she'll survive long enough to tell
Marcus about their child...*

*Read on for a sneak preview of*
The Agent's Deadly Liaison,
*the latest book in Jennifer D. Bokal's
sweeping Wyoming Nights miniseries!*

"You think this is a joke? I wonder how many pieces of
you I can cut away before you stop laughing."

On the counter lay a scalpel. Darcy picked it up. The
handle was still stained with Gretchen's lifeblood. Chloe
went cold as she realized that she'd pushed too hard for
information.

Knife in hand, Darcy slowly, slowly approached the
bed. Chloe pressed her back into the pillow, trying in
vain to get distance from the killer and the knife. It did
no good. Darcy pressed Chloe's shackled hand onto the
railing and drew the blade across her palm. The metal
was cold against her skin. She tried to jerk her hand away,
but it was no use.

Darcy drove the blade into Chloe's flesh.

The cut burned, and for a moment, her vision filled with red. Then a seam opened in her hand. Blood began to weep from the wound. She balled her hand into a fist as her palm throbbed, and anger flooded her veins.

Chloe might've been handcuffed to a bed, but that didn't mean that she couldn't fight back.

"Damn you straight to hell," she growled.

With her free hand, Chloe pushed Darcy's chin back. At the same moment, she lifted her feet, kicking the killer in the chest. Darcy stumbled back before tumbling to the ground. Had Chloe been free, she would have had the advantage.

But shackled to the bed? Chloe had done nothing more than enrage a dangerous person.

Standing, Darcy brushed a loose strand of hair from her face. She smiled, then scoffed before echoing Chloe's words. "Damn me to hell? Hell doesn't frighten me, Chloe. Nothing does—especially not you."

*Don't miss*
The Agent's Deadly Liaison *by Jennifer D. Bokal,*
*available July 2022 wherever*
*Harlequin Romantic Suspense books and*
*ebooks are sold.*

Harlequin.com

HRSEXP0522

# *Love Harlequin romance?*

## DISCOVER.

Be the first to find out about promotions,
news and exclusive content!

Facebook.com/HarlequinBooks

Twitter.com/HarlequinBooks

Instagram.com/HarlequinBooks

Pinterest.com/HarlequinBooks

YouTube.com/HarlequinBooks

ReaderService.com

## EXPLORE.

Sign up for the Harlequin e-newsletter and
download a free book from any series at
**TryHarlequin.com**

## CONNECT.

Join our Harlequin community to
share your thoughts and connect
with other romance readers!
**Facebook.com/groups/HarlequinConnection**